Suppression

Craig S. Maltby

Crosswater Media —Elgin, IL
ISBN: 979-8-218-20723-6
Library of Congress Control Number: 2023909793
Title: *Suppression*
Author: Craig S. Maltby
Digital distribution | 2023
Paperback | 2023

This is a work of fiction. The characters, names, incidents, places, and dialogue are products of the author's imagination, and are not to be construed as real.

Acknowledgements

The author wishes to express his gratitude to his friends and family for their encouragement in writing this book. To J.D. Maltby for his support; Erin Maltby-Addelia for her critique of characters and story elements; Don Rudy, Ph.D., for telling me more than a year ago he would be highly interested in reading what I was thinking about writing; and Sara Opie for telling me to go with the damn story and not have it analyzed to death.

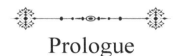

Prologue

IMPULSE

Dr. Larry Eckoff was free. His summer was wide open. No classes to teach. No papers to grade. No students to mentor.

Except for his ongoing research, which he could schedule at his convenience, he was able to fully enjoy a long weekend in which he attended the annual Pride Parade in Des Moines, a festive affair that proceeded on this warm, sunny afternoon from the Iowa State Capitol down Court Avenue and ended at the Polk County Courthouse.

Larry had often envied those who marched in the parade. It looked fun, and, of course, affirmed the joy and security they could experience in being openly gay and accepted in their Midwest community. Iowa, after all, had been the second state in the country to declare gay marriage legal by virtue of a magnificently written Iowa Supreme Court decision several years earlier.

But Larry was still not ready to publicly participate in this event. His assistant professorship at a local private college was something he didn't want to jeopardize. Maybe he was being overly paranoid and frightened, but living in a small town adjacent to Des Moines, with four evangelical churches alone (let alone the Lutheran, Baptist and Catholic congregations), he would take no chances with any public display of his gayness.

But, this was Pride Week. Summer. No work obligations. The array of floats, marchers festooned in every costume conceivable, horn players and drummers, drag queen bar champions and many other assortments of Pride participants, made for a memorable afternoon.

After the parade, he ventured to The Lucky Q, a long established bar in the city's downtown east side where straight and LGBTQ patrons all mingled cheerfully and enjoyed the semi-controlled party atmosphere. Things never got out of hand here. No cops were ever called. Good times and respect. That was the MO at The Lucky Q.

Tonight was classic rock night at the "Q." A dance floor resembling a disco of years gone by, complete with mirror balls, pivoting colored lights and strobes, was full of revelers dancing to Grand Funk Railroad, AC/DC and Led Zeppelin. Later in the night, drag singers would grab a mic from the DJ and belt out their best Ann Wilson "Crazy on You" rendition. Then slow it down with a Carole King or Barry Manilow ballad.

It was all mad fun for Larry. By the time last call rolled around, he wasn't ready to call it a night. And as luck would have it, one of the guys he had been eyeing throughout the evening approached him.

"Lare Bare? You're Lare Bare?" the stranger asked.

"Yes," said Larry Eckoff, trying not to seem as excited as he was. "And you're Hud?"

"Live and in living color, my man. Great to finally meet you. Can I get us a couple drinks? What are you having?"

"I'd love to, but I think last call has ended."

"Well that's perfect because we've got a party starting in one of the First Street Lofts. You want to head over there with me? We can walk. It's just a few blocks from here."

Larry was stunned. And it showed. He had a pretty uneventful love life; a brief relationship or two in grad school, but that was it. Nothing lasting. Nothing intense.

"Um, I guess I can, but I can't stay too long. It's really late for me," he said. Larry was mildly shaking by now, nerves stimulated by endless Moscow Mules and a couple cigarettes consumed in the alley outside.

"Hey, no worries. This is just a spur of the moment thing and no one will notice who's coming and going, so to say," quipped Hud, aka Chet Hunter. "I haven't seen you here before, but you looked like you were having a blast. I like that. Let's keep the party going!"

Larry's nervousness was now transitioning to excitement. The rest of the night would be a far cry from a normal weekend of binging Netflix or hitting the Saturday farmer's market with a couple faculty colleagues. He was eager for this adventure.

The two exited the Q through the rickety side door and briskly headed down the street toward a large converted textiles and furniture warehouse, First Street Lofts. Dim yellow lights glowed from several windows in the hulking brown brick structure nearly one block long and five stories high. But on the fifth floor, a throwback purple glow of black lights and a pulsing rhythm from a stereo turned up a bit too loud served as a raucous beacon for their destination.

Chet pressed an intercom button outside the main entry. A voice asked for a verbal ID code, after which the building entry door was unlocked. Larry and Chet opted to skip the elevator and climb the back stairway to the fifth floor. By now, Chet was holding Larry's hand, giving Larry at once a sense of comfort and slight arousal. Down the hallway, they arrived at the loft and knocked on the door. Amid the music, no one heard the knock, so they opened the door.

Larry gasped slightly. Torrid sex was taking place right in front of him, bodies writhing on the hardwood floor, rugs, couches and chairs. Two guys appearing to be in their 30s approached Larry and Chet, one shirtless and in jeans, the other in a tight AC/DC t-shirt and cargo shorts. The four of them gingerly crept to one corner of the purple-lit living room. For the next 90 minutes, Larry existed in a surreal world, one that he could have only fantasized about. He was dizzy and at the same time supercharged to take full advantage of this dream. Tonight, he would live his life with complete fearlessness.

As the carnal cluster morphed, writhed and constantly repositioned in total bliss, Chet slipped away and quickly, gingerly walked among the masses of flesh to a hallway leading to a guest bedroom. In the room's guest bath, he pulled out his phone and Bluetoothed it to his sophisticated smart watch, one with 120 minutes of video recording capacity. He had only needed a few minutes, though. The biggest challenge was to position himself over Eckoff, arms crossed, while Eckoff was in action, folding his arms so that his watch could capture the full visual field and clearly identify Eckoff's face, not to mention his body.

The imagery of the moaning contortions going on down the hall wasn't pristine but clear enough, especially with the watch camera's night filter activated. He captured and stored the video on his phone. He now had two devices with the video saved on each of them. Great operational redundancy that people in the art of highly priced subterfuge, such as Chet "Hud" Hunter, valued.

Chet returned to the party, grooved a little to The Bee Gees, grabbed a beer from a cooler on the kitchen island, and continued watching. Arms crossed. Just in case some extraordinary new scene involving the professor took place.

Chapter 1

A loser. Or maybe a late bloomer. Or even a pioneer. That's what Lawrence Eckoff, Ph.D., would occasionally think to himself. Forty-one years old. Doctorates in plant science and microbiology. Part of the research team that mapped and edited the genome of drought-resistant, nutrient-dense wheat, saving countless sub-Saharan lives from starvation.

And here he was at Iowa's Norwalk College. Enrollment 1,877. Coaching the women's cross-country team. No athletic scholarships were awarded at Norwalk. If you were lucky, you might get a lower-cost student loan or a few thousand in financial aid to offset an annual tuition of $37,000.

The student-athletes of Norwalk ran and jumped and dribbled and passed (but no football; too costly for this school) because they loved their sports. Nothing more. And where did all that tuition money go? Certainly not to him. An assistant professor barely making $43,000, Larry had lately been wondering what the future holds at a school that often imposed budget cuts, staff layoffs and offered no faculty tenure.

"Push that last half mile hard! You can do it!" Larry yelled to his top runner, Destiny Diggs, who rounded the final turn on a 4-mile country club course, firmly in 9th place.

Professor Eckoff had been offered his faculty position eight years ago with the condition that he would coach the women's cross-country team for an extra $885 per season. He jumped at the opportunity. He was not a runner himself, but he had helped out with record keeping and managing the track team equipment during his undergraduate years at Purdue. So, that qualified him to take on cross-country at Norwalk.

The horn sounded at the finish line as the runners came in, some 800 yards separating the winner and the last-place finisher. Eckoff proceeded to walk the course to gather marker flags and signs. Another race, another lower finish in the final results. Oh well, what would Norwalk do? Fire him? He was a bargain. They knew it and he knew it.

The autumn air on this sunny Friday afternoon in rural Iowa was crisp, clean, with a slight fragrance of a rural bonfire burning nearby. It was one of the benefits of this job. No urban congestion, cheap gas and really cheap steaks and chops. And one of the few places where $75,000 could buy a modest, older two-bedroom house. Gravel driveway, no garage of course, serviceable washer and dryer in the basement and a roof that had never been replaced. The high school football stadium lights and marching band horns were all vividly present a mile away during many Friday nights. And he liked that. It was a perfect accompaniment to a cool dusk filled with applewood brat smoke, a bottle of light beer and infinite rural starlight.

A $13 green fee could get you 18 holes at the local golf course, a country club with a knotty pine dining room that sold memberships but was always open to the public. If the athletic department had a few extra bucks at the end of the season, he could take his team to the club for a buffet dinner; fried chicken, spaghetti and meat sauce, green bean casserole, potato salad, and lemon chiffon pie. His nubile athletes ran miles and miles every day, so the carbs and calories didn't add an extra ounce to their physiques; in fact they were necessary to keep the energy levels high enough to fuel their athletic feats. Even though his runners could not harbor Olympic aspirations or even compete for small college championships, they were able to perform distance running throughout their youth and eventually their adult years, something that 99.99 percent of the population could never achieve. While Larry might struggle running a slow mile, that he was involved in their lives gave him a point of pride.

When he saved enough money, he could grab a direct flight at the nearby Des Moines Airport and be in Orlando, New York, Dallas or Denver in quick order. Most of the time, he traveled for pleasure. A weekend in Vegas helped break up the routine of Friday nights grilling brats or butterfly chops (ribeyes were way too expensive) over coals on his back stoop, even though the view of bucolic pastures hosting grazing cattle was like a Grant Wood painting.

In a rare instance, he could fly to a scientific conference. Norwalk College would pay for his plane ticket and meals, but he had to pay for the registration fee and hotel. His last trip was to Charlotte, NC, for the annual conference of the Association for Experimental Biology. He loved the poster sessions, the presentations of new research and the networking cocktail hours. Many drank martinis and old fashions. Dr. Eckoff had to limit his budget to Bud Light. But he was doing research no one knew about, and would not know about for a long time, if he stuck to his plan.

This autumn weekend in Norwalk would be a bit special; he had another new test subject, driving from hundreds of miles away, visiting him tonight.

…..

"Dr. Eckoff, can I ask you a question? Why here? Why Norwalk?" The question came from Destiny Diggs, Norwalk College's best distance runner and lab/project assistant for Larry Eckoff.

Destiny, a senior biology major, helped Eckoff with his ongoing research; research that, unbeknownst to Ms. Diggs, was not sanctioned by the college. Tonight, five hours after finishing ninth at the Iowa Collegiate Conference cross-country championship, she was helping prepare the materials for the next participant in Eckoff's research.

"I like it here," said the professor. "There's no pressure to find research funding or publish something every three years. That fits me well."

But Eckoff had asked himself that question a thousand times. He had often surmised that he likely had a reputation for not playing well with others. In his honest view of himself, he did great work in graduate school, but probably didn't interview too well for fellowships. He was listed as junior or adjunct investigator on published research, or not listed at all. People took complete credit for his data, and that, as one might guess, severely pissed him off. So much so, that Eckoff started some major confrontations with colleagues. That does not play well in the academic community. He failed at several grant requests for research funding, had a hard time getting peers to sign on with projects, and not many others wanted Eckoff on their team. A scientist today has to be a team player, not just a solitary nerd behind a computer or a lab bench. That wasn't Eckoff, and he knew it.

At some point, Eckoff needed to start earning a living. Big research opportunities were drying up, and he was hard up for cash. He almost had to sell his shitty old VW Rabbit. Thank god, this little college in Iowa badly needed a biochemistry professor, even if he wasn't the best interviewee around. It was a match made of desperation.

"Well we really like you as a professor. And a coach. I hope you're wanting to stay here for a while because you're good for this college," said Destiny, suspecting she probably wasn't getting the full story.

Eckoff appreciated her words. Norwalk College, est. 1898, was a series of older but well-kept buildings nestled among the newer neighborhoods and houses (just not Eckoff's). The developments were sited on former farmland sold to builders when farmers decided getting $40 million for their acres was a better deal than planting corn seed at $600 a bag with harvesters costing $500,000 for a crop that brought in $3.75 a bushel. The faculty was dedicated to teaching, not research, and while there were several Ph.D.'d professors and department heads employed there, many instructors had master's degrees and worked in other jobs in Des Moines 30 miles away.

The college had an easy, close-knit feel, with faculty serving as school board members and local church elders. Students did their student teaching in nearby school districts and got internships at the many insurance companies in the city. Larry's students usually ended up getting jobs in ag biotech, teaching high school biology or chemistry, or opting for a general business career. One or two students each year would apply for medical school or enroll in a graduate program somewhere. But generally, these were kids who wanted to work right out of college and start paying down their student debt.

Eckoff's students liked him. He was a tough but fair grader, and he made sure his students understood advanced chemistry constructs they would need to get a decent job or pass a GRE admissions test. He didn't put up with late assignment excuses. But he also had plenty of time to mentor students one-on-one. His mop of long blonde/gray hair, jeans and suspenders, and Birkenstocks (worn with socks to at least comply with the lenient Norwalk dress code), ingratiated him to his students. As long as he was consistently getting favorable reviews from students on Norwalk's annual instructor evaluation form, that's all that mattered. Happy students– not scholarly publication–meant reliable tuition flow and job security.

When coaching time rolled around, he had to don his green, gray and white Norwalk College polo. A typical afternoon team workout might include a slow paced 3-mile run around the streets or walking trails of Norwalk, a 10-minute rest, then 2 miles at a moderate pace, rest, then a mile at competition pace. Wednesdays were "Hill Days," where the team would run eight uphill sprints on the winter sledding hill at a local park, with each sprint followed by a slow downhill jog. The runners hated Wednesdays. But the running courses on the college meet schedule did not do the athletes the courtesy of avoiding hills…or 90-degree temps or rain or even sleet. They didn't call it an endurance sport for nothing.

His girls would, of course, have to endure whistles and catcalls of local teenagers, even some of their male cohorts at Norwalk College. It was unavoidable in a small town, even in this so-called age of wokeness. But nothing got too out of hand. Last year, the star wide receiver of Norwalk's high school football team peeled off his shirt, donning nothing but his skimpy spandex-like shorts and training shoes, and started running with Destiny on mile two of the practice route. His teammates howled with delight as the male stud set out to show that running with the women, especially this black girl who was out of place in his town, was easy and even a bit farcical.

"C'mon you big, bad girl. Is this all you got? I thought you folks were supposed to be fast! I know you're fast at something. Just not running!"

After keeping pace with Destiny for three quarters of a mile and laughing and taunting with every stride while his teammates looked on laughing hysterically, the soon-dehydrated football hero seized up with a pulled quadricep and fell to the pavement in front of Ed's Hardware, writhing in pain. Destiny ran two small victory circles around the injured jokester, saying nothing, then continued on her way. But that didn't stop the young jerk's embarrassment from turning to rage.

"You black bitch! You think you're tough? I'll whip your black ass next time and it won't close!" His teammates were now aghast at their comrade and ran over to him to shut him up. Destiny continued on, ignoring him.

The high school principal, school board president and district superintendent issued a formal apology to Destiny and Larry Eckoff the next day. Mr. Football Hero missed the next three games and was almost kicked off the team.

Thursday's workouts were lighter, so as to not wear out the team before a Friday or Saturday meet. Eckoff would mount an electric stand-up scooter and drive to various spots on the training route to make sure no one was dogging it. Many cross country coaches run with their teams during practices for at least for part of the regimen. Not Eckoff. After making the rounds on his scooter he might stop into the convenience store off Main Street, take a leak in the grungy bathroom, and get a soda or an Eskimo Pie. He'd then head to the end of the practice course and applaud his runners for completing an exhaustive workout. Such was the life of a microbiology Ph.D.

Eckoff's science building was one of the newer ones on campus, built with funds donated by regional ag businesses who liked the caliber of students Norwalk was turning out. And Destiny Diggs was one of those students. She enrolled at Norwalk four years ago, the recipient of a full-tuition grant from Landmark Nutra Science, a global animal nutrition company focused on making cows and pigs fatter quicker so they can be turned into steaks and chops as efficiently as possible.

Destiny was not the typical student who might fancy a career in agricultural science. The only child of working-class parents in Waterloo, Iowa, she was a good track athlete in high school, but an even better student.

She had avoided the traps of a tough urban life in Waterloo, if you could call that city urban. Waterloo was home to Iowa's largest black community and with that came the racial disparities in healthcare, education and income so common in bigger cities. Waterloo was at least a bit more hopeful for black folks wanting to prosper. Good students had a good chance of getting into one of the three state universities. The city had several major industrial and financial companies that depended, to some degree, on minorities for their workforce.

Destiny had her sights set on the University of Iowa. But when Norwalk came calling with an offer of full tuition endowed by Landmark, she couldn't refuse. Her cornrows and dreads stood out when she was on campus, as did her deep dark, flawless skin and sleek athletic build. But she liked the atmosphere, the faculty and her teammates. For the most part, they were welcoming and encouraging.

She had met Professor Eckoff during her freshman orientation four years ago, and had impressed him. He was in the early stages of a research project, and he welcomed the chance to hire her as a part-time assistant. At least Norwalk had the budget for that. If she attained her degree, she would have an inside angle at a job with Landmark after graduation if she chose.

As Destiny and Professor Eckoff prepared the space, Eckoff cranked some of his favorite tunes over his Bluetooth speaker; George Michael, Madonna, Cher, Gaga, even some Nitty Gritty Dirt Band. He was feeling confident, almost a bit giddy.

It wasn't easy being a 41-year-old gay man at a small college in red-state Iowa, but a little musical escapism helped.

And with his newest research trial participant scheduled to arrive in a couple hours, Eckoff eagerly anticipated that this could launch the final step in his small but audacious effort to change the world.

Chapter 2

The executive office was just short of dazzling. Though small by U.S. CEO standards, it boasted two walls of tinted windows bordered by custom polished steel frames etched with platinum contoured inlays. The wide glass and blond wood desk appeared Spartan, but contained obscured control panels for a ceiling mounted AV screen, web-powered temperature and light settings, smart TV screens covering the side interior wall, a glass data display completely voice driven, and a switch that rolled out an 8-person conference table from the long side of the L-shaped bamboo desk.

Hans Mogen slightly respected his US and UK counterparts in the global pharma industry, but he prided himself as a different kind of cat. His office, for example, would not replicate the largesse and hubris of other CEOs. His reflected Swiss efficiency and modernity, yet was richly distinctive and highly advanced in function and comfort. His office and those of his global executive teams served the company, not the ego of their inhabitants. And he had achieved the results that proved it.

Microneutics, of which Mogen had been CEO and chairman for the past 14 years, had grown to be the largest, most diversified drug and bioscience company in the world, surpassing such giants as Pfizer, Roche, GSK and Novartis. The 58-building campus in the company's headquarters city of Zurich, Switzerland, was but one of many campuses throughout the world. Microneutics had built a campus in Secaucus, New Jersey, just to dish out a little market intimidation to the US pharmaceutical giants and startups whose home offices populated that corner of the country.

The company's stock price had been rising for years, having split three times in the past eight years when the shares reached meteoric heights. One of Mogen's greatest business wins was fending off a hostile bid for controlling interest in the company from Warren Buffet's Berkshire Hathaway. Buffet settled for a large noncontrolling equity stake in Microneutics, which made all parties happy and, of course, ratcheted up the stock price to dizzying levels.

Mogen's life could not have been better: A financial estate that would fund generations of his offspring; a private fleet of jets to take him and his family anywhere at any time; too many honorary doctorates to count, though he did have his own legitimate research doctorate in economics and game theory from the University of Paris; and one of the world's largest charities focused on cancer research. Hans Mogen spread billions of dollars and Euros throughout the hundreds of cancer research centers around the globe. Oncology drugs were Microneutics' biggest business, accounting for nearly 70% of the company's $400 billion in annual revenue.

The war on cancer played beautifully into Mogen's core business. The company that his great grandfather founded in 1910, selling cleaning fluids–mostly vinegar derivatives–to industrial factories in Bavaria was now a worldwide behemoth.

…..

"Let's start off with market share updates," said Hans Mogen to his team of divisional presidents, 5 in his office and 13 Zoomed in on the massive glass monitor. "Who wants to go first?"

Suzi Park Ae-Cha from the Seoul office chimed in first. "We're steady at 61% in our region," she said. Market share reports were called in every quarter. In the pharma business, one fiscal quarter of market-share data did not mean much. Based on product lifecycle, marketing investment, competitor activity, lengthy timelines for science and research developments, a two- or three-year number was more meaningful. But Hans Mogen would not have it.

"We've been stalled at 61% for 3 quarters now. What's happening? Or not happening?" said Mogen.

"Our blood therapeutics are doing quite well and we have made great strides with the new pancreatic treatments," said Suzi Park.

"But we're still at 61%," said Mogen with a distinct tone of irritation. "Tell me again, what's not happening?"

"We are having some minor difficulty getting our sales force up and running for our stage 4 non-small cell lung cancer treatment," said Suzi Park. Two general sales managers left 6 months ago and that put us in a bind. I'm hoping to hear tomorrow that we have at least one manager hired and that will start moving us to where we need to be. Revenue and gross margin are still good."

"I do not want good. After three quarters, I want great. And I want share, said Hans, quietly and intensely, his eyes shooting darts at Suzi Park. "Grabbing share injures competitors. That's how we grow."

"I totally understand, Dr. Mogen. And I will bring you a better share number soon."

Mogen moved on to the next president's report without a final response to Suzi Park. She turned off her audio and exhaled heavily while trying to maintain a motionless, static face.

.....

Marypat Hammond pulled her rusty Ford Fiesta into the empty parking lot outside McLandry Science Hall on the very edge of the Norwalk College campus. The building was named for Harold McLandry, chairman emeritus of Landmark Nutra Science, who had donated $6 million of his own money plus $10 million of Landmark funding to build the facility eight years ago. The building was small by university standards, but clean, modern and perfect for a small college setting.

Marypat parked under one of the two parking lot lights on this crisp, cold December night. The holiday lights of Norwalk Iowa, glimmering from the streets lined with modest but newer ranch and split-level homes enveloping the grounds of the college helped brighten up the Spartan grass and walkways surrounding the science building. Obviously, all the money had gone into the building with very little remaining for landscaping.

She walked up the short brick path to the main door and pressed a 3-digit code on the security entry panel. A buzzer connected her to Eckoff's small lab.

"Yes, Dr. Eckoff here. Are you Marypat?"

"Yes."

"Great. Please go ahead and step inside when you hear the door click and my assistant Destiny will be there soon to meet you."

McLandry Hall did not have a security guard at night, nor during the day for that matter. Any faculty member in the building after hours could program the entry intercom to connect with their office or lab.

In less than a minute, the athletic silhouette of Destiny Diggs appeared in the dimly lit hallway. Marypat waited while Destiny approached and greeted her. She was not what Marypat expected. Instead of a nerdy, pale lab geek in a white coat, Marypat encountered a tall, slim, striking black girl who could easily be seen in the dance clubs of Marypat's home city of Chicago. The sight of such a lab assistant made her uncomfortable. Was this college and this science lab legitimate? Or was it a third-rate snake-oil kitchen that preyed on desperate people such as herself, whose car had barely made it to Iowa on a shaky transmission.

Marypat had envisioned coming to a grand facility where denizens of lab-coated scientists were bustling to their next project or classroom, lights blazing on all floors and computer displays with complex dashboards glowing in every room.

"Am I in the right place," she asked.

Destiny had seen this many times during the past four years. Folks were a little bewildered when they first arrived.

"Yes, Marypat. You're in the right place and you'll be in very good hands with Dr. Eckoff. I know this seems a little weird, but please don't worry. This won't take long and we'll answer every question you could ever want to ask."

They headed down to the end of the hall, took a stairway to the basement level, then navigated another long narrow hallway until they rounded a corner into a dead end with one door, which stood slightly ajar.

The dimly lit room looked more like a graduate faculty lounge, with green leafy plants everywhere, a giant Persian rug covering the bland linoleum floor, a small dorm fridge and a couple computer monitors. On a white Formica rectangular table sat a small, one-ounce glass vial with a plastic cap. A light-green label wrapped around the upper third of the vial displayed the digits IH-3314.

"Marypat, please have a seat here," said Destiny, guiding her to a low-back metal chair that could have come from a military surplus store. The chair was adjacent to the white table. Marypat nervously and quickly sat down, looking around the room and wondering still what she had gotten herself into.

Soon, Dr. Larry Eckoff emerged from a small anteroom holding a relatively new 4G digital camera. Dressed in a respectable white collared shirt and decent navy slacks, he had tried to look as professional as he possibly could. A tie might have been overkill, but he had ditched the suspenders and instead wore a shiny black belt he had bought at Wal-Mart a couple days ago.

"Hello Marypat. I'm Larry Eckoff. I can't tell you how grateful I am that you are here. I hope your travel went smoothly. Did you have any trouble finding our lovely campus?"

"I suppose it was easy enough as long as my car held out. I just hope I can make it back home."

"Can I get you a soda or water to drink?" asked Destiny.

"No, I'm fine, thanks. I just want to get on with this if we could."

Marypat Hammond was born and raised in Chicago. A daughter of a neighborhood meat cutter and elementary teacher in the Bronzeville section of south Chicago, she had a decent middle-class upbringing. Her parents had both passed away early in life, her father from alcoholism, her mother from congestive heart failure. Both might have lived longer, but insurance coverage had always been limited for their family; they were determined to never accumulate large out-of-pocket deductibles for addiction treatment or even regular cardiovascular checkups.

Marypat was 45 years old and had never married, but had learned data entry skills at a local technical college. She built a modest career with those skills, working in banks and call centers and earning enough to pay rent for a one-bedroom apartment in a decent, safe neighborhood.

"Sure, I understand. Let's get right to it," said Eckoff. "So I would like you to take off your jacket and scarf and pull down your blouse top just over the top of your shoulder."

Marypat did as directed. And there, instantly, was the disturbing evidence of why she had traveled to Norwalk. The tumor was large, maybe two inches in diameter. Destiny found herself short of breath as she absorbed what she was seeing. She had never seen a tumor this size protruding from the side of the neck. Squamous cell neck cancer that had metastasized and grown such that it was starting to infringe on the carotid artery and impact Marypat's speech clarity.

Larry Eckoff did not flinch as he closely observed the mass.

"Marypat, I would like to photograph you if you don't mind so we can get a baseline image before we proceed. I'd also like to get an ultrasound image as well. Can you let me do this?"

"Why do you need to do that? I thought I was just coming here to get the treatment and leave."

"We just need to make sure that as the treatment proceeds, we have imaging records every step of the way so we can measure and see what takes place, to know if we are succeeding. It's part of my methodology. No one will see your photo. If I show it to any other researcher, your face will be digitally obscured. Your name will not be part of any records outside of this lab. We'll assign your case a numeric code. Your name will never be made public."

"Ok. Yes, please do whatever you need to."

While Eckoff held the camera close to Marypat's neck and took multiple photographs from numerous angles, Destiny rolled over a sonogram, or ultrasound, machine. Larry had bought it used from a closed Planned Parenthood clinic in northern Missouri. Got it for a great price with some small grant money he had secured a couple years before. And it still worked great. There weren't any medical device companies in the region that still serviced the outdated model. But he was hoping he'd never need to have it fixed. Just a few more months and his research would be complete.

Destiny put on a pair of latex surgical gloves and squeezed a small blob of conductive ultrasound gel onto the transducer wand. She then very lightly rubbed the gelled wand over Marypat's neck and tumor area. Monochrome images of the tumor clearly appeared on the screen, with the machine recording the image onto a flash drive as the wand moved over and around the area. It looked like a large black hole in space, blocking and obscuring almost everything around it.

After several minutes of imaging work, it was time to wrap up.

"Right now, Marypat, I want to administer this small dose of liquid for you. It is a tincture, or alcohol extract, of several varieties of fungal spores that I have hybridized over the years. It won't have much of a taste, maybe just a little pungent or smoky, but I'll just squirt some under your tongue while you let it sit there for a few seconds and absorb in your soft membrane under your tongue. Think you can do that?"

"Please, let's do it."

"OK, here we go."

Marypat opened her mouth as best she could with her impaired neck; Dr. Eckoff placed a full dropper of the tincture fluid under her tongue and squeezed the rubber top. The fluid massed in the bottom of her mouth and sat there for several seconds, eventually dissipating. Larry repeated the same procedure one more time.

And that was it.

"I am going to give you one additional vial of this liquid," said Eckoff. "I think you can administer it yourself, since this went so well. Please wait 2 weeks from today before you do this second dose. But before you do, I want to have a Zoom chat with you so I can see your neck."

Eckoff added a final directive, "I need to remind you, also, of the nondisclosure agreement you signed in the preliminary paperwork we sent to you before you traveled here. Confidentiality is imperative for many reasons, including the requirement that we protect your personal health information. You cannot tell anyone about this trial or about any results you might observe before the trial is complete. If you do so, we have to stop your participation and remove all data from our trial records. Do you understand?"

"Yes, I do."

"Whew! Thanks. Glad I got that out of the way. I hate being the heavy and giving these warnings, but it's such an important part of this research. I'm glad you're participating and I hope this doesn't put a bad taste in your mouth, no pun intended! Destiny will show you out. And please, please, please, drive home safely."

Marypat got in her car and pulled out of the dimly lit parking lot, onto a residential street that after one mile merged onto a gravel road that would take her past several Iowa farmsteads to a frontage road that put her on Interstate 80, eastbound for Chicago. She would try to get to Iowa City by 11 p.m., find a cheap hotel there, then get back to Chicago in the morning. She was nervous and excited, wondering what the substance she had just ingested would do to her body….and her tumor.

By the time she reached Iowa City, her hands and arms started tingling mildly, and she noticed a slight fever had come on. Dr. Eckoff had warned her of possible side effects. Now they were not just possible, but real.

Chapter 3

Brandon Abrams was living his dream. A smart, short 24-year-old MBA graduate from New York University, he was on the cusp of igniting a career he had worked years to prepare for. Born and raised in Hoboken, New Jersey, he excelled in his high school academics, earning a partial scholarship to Rutgers where he got his bachelor's degree in biochemistry. But he was not set on medical school or a graduate school research track.

While Brandon's parents were both accomplished physicians with sterling credentials in family practice and cardiology, Brandon was intensely interested in the business side of healthcare. He enrolled in NYU's MBA program, with mom and dad gladly footing the bill, so he could build a career in the pharmaceutical or medical equipment fields. Perhaps both. Strategic marketing or finance in a large corporate environment sounded very appealing to him. Or perhaps he could be a part of a biotech startup and gain equity early that could mushroom into dazzling wealth down the road. He might even launch a dot com that digitizes any number of medical or manufacturing processes.

The sky was the limit with his NYU degree, he thought, and he was ready to get rolling. So naturally he was thrilled when he landed his first job with the Healthcare Business and Innovation Society of the U.S.; H-BIS as it was known in the industry.

Brandon was determined to learn the business, and this position would be the ticket to doing so. He had moved from his studio apartment in lower Manhattan to the H-BIS headquarters city of Washington D.C. He missed the energy and crowded closeness of New York. And the bagels and slices. He traded the friendly confines of Jones St. at 4th in the Village for the clean, sterile sprawl of McClean, Virginia, where he took the Metro from his high-rise apartment to his headquarters office every day. There, he would toil for a year to become a highly qualified business professional with both an MBA and invaluable early-career experience with the largest health-care industry organization in the world.

H-BIS was headquartered in D.C. but had government relations–aka lobbying–offices in every state, where H-BIS could monitor and influence any policy development in every state capital that might harm–or benefit–the healthcare companies that were dues-paying members of H-BIS. H-BIS members were drug companies, large and small; medical equipment manufacturers large and small that made everything from pacemakers to next-generation MRI machines to artificial joints and connective tissue; hospital holding companies, university bioengineering departments, surgical instrument and telemetry companies, software developers, even law firms with 2,000 attorneys that represented mostly medical industry clients.

H-BIS was a commercial colossus that generated membership dues income from the leading and not-so-leading companies of the largest single industry in the United States; the $4.4 trillion healthcare industry. The "Society" owned, not rented, a private jet. Its Washington office probably fueled the success of more high-end restaurants in the capitol area than any single entity. More than the defense, insurance, firearms, food or energy industries.

And Brandon's role in this world of big healthcare? Industry analysis and policy. Brandon reported to Ron Holtzman, Senior Vice President for Member Services. Holtzman, age 49, was a dapper, tailored-suit-sporting, athletic-looking man, tall with longer, slicked-back hair and a dark complexion. He looked like he should be coaching an NBA team or possibly be a drug lord. Holtzman was not the President and CEO, but was actually paid more, having been with H-BIS for more years than he would want to remember, his job was extremely important in the growth and enormous cash flow of H-BIS. With his staff of 47, Holtzman kept members happy and willing to fork over hundreds of thousands of dollars–each–in yearly corporate membership dues. Small companies and startups were charged less, but would hopefully grow into large companies and hence, larger cash contributors.

Brandon had made it through three rounds of interviews before he made it to the final session with Holtzman. Ron had been impressed with Brandon's technical and financial aptitude, but he also saw in him a young guy who would work his tail off and not think of himself as any kind of young gun prima donna. He wanted to build a career. Holtzman sensed Brandon wasn't the kind of kid who would run back to mom and dad if he found a job too demanding or couldn't go to happy hour at 4:00 every afternoon.

16

Brandon would soon receive his first real assignment as a newly minted employee for H-BIS, and it would be nothing like he had anticipated.

…..

December in Washington D.C. was a bit warmer than normal this year. Sure there was frost every morning, occasional fender-benders on the streets circling the Capitol, perpetrated by drivers who were not well practiced in the art of driving and braking cautiously on newly slick pavement. But the grass still had some remaining green color, the sun still shone brightly, casting dramatic, early-winter shadows on the city's innumerable majestic brick and concrete facades, and birds were still chirping happily, enjoying a cool reprieve from D.C.'s sweltering summer…and fall.

The H-BIS headquarters building was a rather modest but stately, large structure on K Street, a multi-story red brick colonial style with a few white-framed arched windows on the ground level and ample underground parking, a valuable perk for the 200 staff who occupied the office.

A small brass plaque sign flanked the main entrance door, with the black-tinted words of Healthcare Business And Innovation Society etched on it. Inside, the office layout resembled the newsroom of a cable network or major newspaper more than any garden-variety business office. Cubicles dominated each floor, with very few private offices on the periphery. Cubicles were organized by client service areas such as hospitals, manufacturing, start-up and digital enterprises, pharma and research, retail health, and on and on.

The top floor of the H-BIS building was, of course, reserved for four people: The chairman of H-BIS, Turner Mansfield, his assistant, Ronald Javier Holtzman, and his assistant. Mansfield, the longtime leader of the organization, was reclusive and occupied a modest office of dark wood and tartan carpet.

Holtzman, who had grown in his role to be the public face of H-BIS and the lead strategist, had an office three times the size of Mansfield's, with Italian leather and chrome furnishings, a bar the Four Seasons might envy, and Persian rugs too numerous to count that supported the lavish furnishings over a polished white marble floor. Many industry policies and laws had been negotiated in this room with senators, CEO's and even, once, the President of the United States.

Brandon was in Holtzman's palatial office today to get briefed on a new assignment. Together with Shawni Phillips, H-BIS's director of government relations, they had settled in on Holtzman's tan leather couch, facing the boss directly across a glass coffee table on which three glasses of rare, small-batch bourbon were sitting.

"Alright, if everyone is happily supplied with their beverage, let's talk about a project in Wisconsin I would like you two to take on," said Holtzman.

Brandon and Shawni nodded and took a sip of their bourbon.

"There's a bill proposal introduced in the Wisconsin senate that looks to be gaining steam. It's SB-57, and it's crucial that this bill never see the light of day in the Badger State. Shawni, why don't you tell Brandon what the bill's about."

Shawni shifted herself toward Brandon. She was in her late 30s, a fourteen-year employee of H-BIS. As government relations manager, she wasn't your typical buttoned-down, high-collared business executive. She had long flowing platinum blonde hair, a beautiful face that needed minimal makeup, a leather suit jacket and wide leather belt that cinched up her dress chino slacks covering slender long legs and eventually intersecting with obscenely expensive ostrich skin cowboy boots. Shawni had grown up in rural northern California and had taken pride in never converting to the Gucci clique of the Washington lobbyist community.

Ron Holtzman liked this about her. She didn't have the appearance of a high-powered lobbyist representing the most powerful influence group in the capital of the most powerful country in the world. Shawni projected an image of approachability and empathy packaged in striking yet honest beauty. She could talk shop with the best of them, yet lawmakers and government power brokers would confide nearly anything in her because, well, at the end of the day, she was a beautiful yet down-to-earth woman.

She hadn't studied political science or public policy or even life sciences in college. She had been a music major at UC Santa Cruz, studying cello while learning acoustic guitar in her spare time so she could make a few extra bucks playing in coffee houses. Her career sights had been set on being a public-school music teacher. How she ended up in D.C. working for Ron Holtzman was a classic career success story. She had joined a regional touring band in northern

Virginia after college, deciding she could put off the teaching track for a year or two. She got a part-time job in the H-BIS mailroom during the week to supplement her meager, tip-based band income. As she would see Holtzman in the elevator from time to time, he noticed her ability to discuss anything and everything during their small chat sessions. That turned into longer chats in the corporate cafeteria. Holtzman eventually decided the mailroom was too confining for her cerebral talents and communicative skills, and he mentored her into a government relations career path at H-BIS. She was eager to take advantage of the opportunity as her band was going nowhere and paying the rent was getting harder every month. No cheating sex, not even flirtation. She was single, Holtzman was married with three teenagers at home. They respected each other and their own lives too much to ruin things. Not that there hadn't been a temptation or two along the way. And when both of them entered a room at any given business conference, they instantly turned every head in the room.

For Ron Holtzman, she had grown into his weapon of choice in shaping government policy and rules to his clients' advantage.

"Brandon, this project has to do with state tax policy in Wisconsin. Senate Finance Committee may soon mark up a bill that will then go before the full chamber for a vote. If it passes the closely divided senate, it's almost certain to pass the house and would then get signed by the governor. We have to stop it cold in the senate. Nothing more, nothing less.'

"Understand," said Brandon. "And what does the bill do?"

"It closes a research and development tax credit healthcare companies get from the state. Wisconsin is home to huge medical software companies, big research hospitals, and lots of small biotech startups launched from research at UW-Madison. This tax credit is worth millions to the big players. And for the small players, in a given year, it could mean the difference between staying in business or closing up shop."

"So why does the state want to get rid of this tax incentive?" asked Brandon.

"It's always about revenue," Holtzman chimed in. Many state lawmakers will tell you there's never enough tax revenue to fund schools and universities, Head Start programs, public parks and all that stuff. They think the extra revenue from closing this loophole will be a huge windfall for state revenues. And they're right. It could add $200 million to $400 million to the coffers. Many lawmakers think these healthcare companies are fat and happy and wouldn't miss this tax credit. But there is a price. And that's where you come in."

"Huh? Ummm. I mean okay," Brandon stumbled. "But you guys have access to tons of biotech experts, lawyers, state lobbyists who know Wisconsin inside and out. What am I going to do that they can't do a whole lot better than me?"

"Two things," said Holtzman. Number one, we're going to communicate to lawmakers a cogent, intelligent story about this tax threat that the local folks simply can't. You ever hear a research scientist or software guru try to articulate fiscal policy or complexities of modern tax law? Especially to a bunch of rural, stump-humping, hayseed state legislators? They would be disastrous. You and Shawni will work with our members in Wisconsin, have them standing by your side when you appear at the statehouse or on TV, and make a clear, understandable case on why the legislation must be defeated.

"Number two, we have to project a national presence in that state; one that tells the legislature and their constituents this bill is important enough that the entire US healthcare industry will descend upon Wisconsin and make some serious trouble for the state if SB-57 passes. And this message will also get clearly communicated to all of the other 23 states that have such research tax credits in place. 'Don't mess with the healthcare business, or we'll get nasty with your ass.' That's the message any lawmaker should understand, quickly and clearly."

"I'll be the public face and messenger of our campaign in Wisconsin," said Shawni." Your role will be to put together for me a convincing set of facts and figures that someone with your dual interest and studies in healthcare and business can do so adeptly. How the bill will injure the many startups in Wisconsin. How it will affect employment and research funding at large companies. How it will kill jobs because companies will move to other states that offer similar research tax credits. Talk to our members there. Get their input. Maybe put together some calculations of your own. You get the idea."

"So, how often do we need to fly there for this project?" asked Brandon.

"Only once," said Holtzman. "Because once you land in Madison, you will live there for the duration of the legislative session. Mid-January through April, maybe longer if the session runs long. And if, god forbid, the bill passes, you may have to stay through June to ensure the governor never signs that bill into law."

"Welcome to brass knuckle politics," quipped Shawni. "Get used to a lot of brats, cheese and local beer. These are the fights we live for."

Chapter 4

Marypat Hammond woke up in her small apartment on a tree-lined street in Bronzeville, a south Chicago neighborhood. The drive home from Norwalk two nights ago had been uneventful, even with the tingling she experienced, which had subsided within three hours.

She would be free today, having taken paid time off to make sure any potential after-effects of the tincture mixture she had consumed could be dealt with. Dr. Eckoff had given her some basic guidance for such effects, should they occur. He was confident they could be handled with a visit to any pharmacy (all within easy walking distance in Bronzeville). Hopefully, a couple days' worth of ibuprofen, over-the-counter allergy treatments or just a good regimen of water and sleep could overcome anything she encountered.

So far, so good. No side effects. She slept well, had no fever. No dizziness. In fact, she had some thoughts that if no side effects emerged, maybe the substance she ingested was snake oil, a complete sham.

Such thoughts got her past her hazy early awakeness and compelled her to sit up with her legs dangling over the side of her highly-perched bed.

She hesitated to feel or even look at the lump on the side of her neck, a lump that had been there for many months. She thought it was benign, something that could eventually dissipate. She had minimal health coverage and panicked at the thought of how full-blown cancer treatments could wipe her out financially. She was able to get a physician at a local Chicago free clinic, Dr. Luis Hernandez, a friend of a friend whose parents had been friends of her late parents, to order a biopsy that would require a co-pay she could afford. For now.

The biopsy came back positive. Squamous cell carcinoma. Marypat clearly remembers the feeling after getting the diagnosis.

Total mental numbness. A surreal feeling as if she was in a different universe. A slight feeling of being unable to breathe.

Dr. Hernandez had printed out the exact lab report from her biopsy along with a standard treatment plan. She had taken those printouts home.

"When are you starting treatment?" Luis asked. "We should get this going."

"I'm still thinking about it," said Marypat.

"What do you mean 'thinking about it'? What else can you do?"

"I don't know. But I do know my out-of-pocket deductibles and co-pays for oncology drugs will wipe me out. I mean really wipe me out. Not to mention the measly pay I would get for short-term disability. I might as well check into a homeless shelter."

"You've got to get this treatment going. Otherwise, barring some miracle–which, by the way, I have yet to witness in my medical career–you are not long for this world. Which is not how you want to play this."

"I understand. I'm just...I'm just confused and not thinking real straight right now. I need time to get my head together and sort things out."

"Well don't take too much time, please. This is nothing to toy around with."

The good news was that the tumor was lodged in the rear-side of her neck, so it wasn't obstructing the throat or larynx and the ability to swallow or breathe. The bad news is that surgery carried significant risk of cancer spreading to lymph nodes and risk of damaging the carotid artery, requiring further major surgery to repair the artery. Depending on the size and growth trajectory of the tumor, metastasis to the brain was a real possibility.

So Marypat began scouring the Web for alternative cancer treatments, knowing there was a world of scams and false hope being peddled every hour of every day. High Google search rankings were awarded to holistic cancer "spas" in the Caribbean and Asia, cancer diets, exercise regimens, mineral springs, herbal teas. Taken together, they were too numerous and globally distributed for the FDA to regulate or shut down. But people desperate for solutions will look at many options, even the outrageous.

Marypat considered herself sensible enough to spot the quackery. And at the end of a long workday, at home surfing through another hour's worth of bogus promotions for cures, a link caught her attention.

She clicked it and a simple page appeared.

There was no menu. No page after page of nebulous treatment descriptions, wild claims, fake testimonials, easy payment terms. Just one landing page with some simple text:

TRIAL PARTICIPANTS WANTED

Cancer patients presenting with visible symptoms.

This is an experimental therapy with no claims or guarantees of outcomes.

We believe outcomes can be positive, but may also have no effect or efficacy.

There is risk of side effects, minor and major.

Participants will pay a reasonable monetary cost plus travel expenses.

Please contact me at the email address below.

Marypat then sent an email message. Dr. Eckoff responded the next morning. He asked Marypat to attach images of her neck and PDFs of her biopsy and clinical diagnosis. After a week he scheduled her for observation and dose administration at his office.

The cost was not exorbitant, but Marypat would need to trade her car in for an older model to assemble the cash for a 50-percent upfront deposit, and withdraw a small part of a modest annuity her parents had left for her to complete payment upon her nighttime visit to Norwalk College.

Marypat got out of bed and briskly walked to her small bathroom. Upon seeing her reflection in the mirror, she held her breath for a few seconds then let out a small gasp.

The tumor in her neck was a fraction of the size it had been just 24 hours earlier. She rubbed her fingers against it, amazed at how small the mass felt compared to what she had been accustomed to for many months. She had been hoping Dr. Eckoff's tincture could maybe start making a small difference over the course of weeks or months. But this was beyond any possible expectation.

Eckoff had sent an extra dose home with her to ingest two weeks from now. Marypat was tempted to take it this morning and see what the next result would look like. But she tempered her excitement and was glad to just marvel at what she was seeing and feeling. She wanted to call Dr. Eckoff right now and joyfully shout the news to him. But it was 6:30 in the morning. That wouldn't be fair to her new hero.

Chapter 5

The meeting had been scheduled just two hours ago. Normally, any Microneutics executive needing to meet with chairman and CEO should plan on a two-day lead time, minimum. A week was typically the norm.

But Ursula Halgren, vice president and corporate brand manager, had special access to Hans Mogen. Her title was a bit misleading, implying that Ursula had marketing management responsibilities for all Microneutics pharmaceutical and over-the-counter products worldwide. And she did, sort of. In reality, the real marketing work was done by individual project managers, reporting up through business groups and geographic senior managers, who reported up to corporate marketing executive vice presidents, who reported to the chief marketing officer. Ursula was positioned in a side-dotted-line role to the CMO, with another dotted line to Hans Mogen. Her position was unique as was her access to Mogen, and many in the company had never understood why.

Microneutics did not do much advertising. They might cut a television ad or two for the US television market, running on the Sunday morning news shows in order to maintain a positive corporate image in the eyes of congressmen, senators and regulators who watched those shows and impacted Microneutics business fortunes. YouTube videos and Twitter updates seemed to work well for patients and future patients who would be using their drugs to help them cope with mild or serious diseases and symptoms.

But all in all, Microneutics investment in marketing was concentrated on its vast global sales force, calling on doctors, researchers, and health system executives large and small, all to ensure Microneutics' drugs were top-of-mind when prescriptions were written, pharmacy formularies were stocked, and research clinical trials were conducted. Large cash sums were dedicated to industry trade conventions, dinners, golf outings, concert tickets and retirement parties for longtime physician and health executive "customers."

It was a system that had worked well for decades and would continue to render profitable results as global drug therapies continued to evolve and large population centers–and their doctors–demanded new research and new treatments. Mogen had always admired, surprisingly, the Obama campaign of 2008. The then candidate had invested huge sums into field offices and organizing canvassing staff, as opposed to heavy rotations of TV ads. And it worked brilliantly. In Mogen's view, getting face-to-face with clients and prospects, even in the digital age, was the most efficacious way to grow a vast, global client base. And profits. And efficacy was what the drug business was all about.

"We've got some intriguing chatter going on in Centrifuge," Halgren told Mogen. Centrifuge was a digital social site, similar to Reddit, only entirely encrypted, where members could discuss topics privately with no public views. New members were invited to join, purely through invitations from other members. It wasn't quite the dark web, where servers and participants were extremely difficult for even the most skilled hacks to trace. Centrifuge was a private community populated by scientists, physicians and patients, where free-flowing discussions about new treatments, experiments, data and patient experiences were encouraged. These were smart, caring people who were disenchanted, even fed up, with what in their eyes was an overpriced, corrupt, healthcare industrial complex. All were anonymous, well outside the crosshairs of regulators. Ursula Halgren, a digital architecture wizard, started Centrifuge, with generous, undetectable, laundered financial support from Microneutics. Mogen saw such an underground digital community as a great way to observe possible developments in the healthcare world…before others even knew what time it was.

Sometimes early, unpublished data from important drug trials were divulged. "Fugees," as participants liked to call themselves, might give early warnings on medical innovations that were showing failing results. Even possible mergers or acquisitions of major healthcare companies were tipped off. Anything was fair game. And members seemed to trust each other that their "news" was fairly accurate. Most stock analysts and investment bankers did not know about Centrifuge. The few who did try desperately to join, but always failed. Thorough vetting of new members was a staple of the Centrifuge terms of service. New member applicants had to be endorsed by a minimum of three existing members.

"Tell me what you're seeing," said Hans Mogen.

"Some intriguing narratives from consumer members are appearing. They are going into great detail about a cancer therapy they claim is working wonders for them. Tumor shrinkage, remission, minimal if any side effects, etcetera. We see these kinds of claims from time to time; usually they fade away, the scientists don't pay much attention to them. The health world is full of quacks, usually medical spas in Mexico or China, trying to get people to pay 40 grand to spend a week getting infused with coconut water. They're a dime a dozen, with lots of desperate takers."

"So why is this now getting your attention?"

"The stories started about a year ago. In recent months, more of them have cropped up. And they seem to all contain some similarities; a unique 'tincture' as they call it, quick acting within a matter of days or weeks, intense emotional descriptions of their experiences, dosing that seems to be very consistent and precise. I haven't seen any string of messages and personal stories like these for this kind of topic before."

"How many posts are we talking about?"

"A year ago it was one or two every couple of months. Now I'm seeing one or two a week. Still a very small number when you consider the hundreds of millions of patients in this world. But if you consider the 13,000 members active on Centrifuge, it's not a small number, and may be a bit more than a coincidence. Hard to tell."

"Do they say where they are getting this tincture?"

"That is the thing. It's like they are sworn to secrecy. They say they are desperately wanting to say more about where they are getting this substance and how and from whom, but are forbidden to do so without jeopardizing their entire treatment 'success' and even the entire trial. It's like this is happening purely through word of mouth, and I mean flesh and blood word of mouth, not social media, not texting, not email, not even ink-on-paper snail mail. It's a bit perplexing."

"Well, keep an eye on it. I appreciate your early warning on this. I can't help but think this is just another snake oil scam that's having a big placebo effect. I don't think one or two testimonials a week will change the world."

"That's also an unknown," said Ursula, who flipped her long jet-black hair back behind the thin shoulder strap of her sheer, flowing, frontier hippie dress. With minimal makeup, a hippie's wardrobe and jet black, hi-heeled construction boots on her narrow feet, she did not project the appearance of a modern-day cyber punk. She certainly was an aberration from the Swiss Microneutics corporate office attire of crisp haircuts and sleek, Euro-chic suits. But Mogen knew talent when he saw it, and her work product was leading edge and extraordinary.

"How so?" asked Mogen.

"These Centrifuge posts are only the ones we know about. And it's a very small community. How many others are taking part in this tincture trial? How many have completed the trial? What are their results? How wide and how long does this go?"

"Good points," said Mogen as he leaned back in his ergonomically-tailored chair and steepled his hands under his nose and over his mouth. "But, cancer is our business and I can't believe someone out there, anonymously mind you, has suddenly gained a leg up on the mystery of this ghastly disease. We've been studying all types of cancer for nearly a century, as have our respected competitors. The trillions our industry has poured into research and treatment therapies, I just can't fathom how someone else has come across some revolutionary compound. I don't want to be cavalier or hubristic, but I've got to think this will be a flash in the pan that goes away soon. And a small flash at that."

"Understand," said Ursula. "I'll keep tracking it."

Chapter 6

Brandon Abrams and his supervisor colleague Shawni Phillips pulled up to the extended-stay hotel three blocks away from the state government office campus surrounding the grand, domed capitol in Madison. They had rented an all-electric Chevy Bolt in case any of the politically progressive lawmakers they were targeting saw them driving around the capital city.

Brandon preferred a traditional gasoline engine so he would not need to mess with finding charging stations, but Shawni had overruled him. Image was crucial in the government relations game. Shawni had even altered her wardrobe. Cowboy boots were too "Texas," replaced by several pair of patent leather pumps, which she hated. She kept a couple leather coats–necessary in the Wisconsin winter–but traded out chinos and denim for dress wool slacks and thinner belts. This was war, and sacrifices were necessary.

"Let's go get a beer and go over the strategy and players again, then start planning who we're going to contact and what our pitch will be," said Shawni.

This was all new and somewhat bizarre to Brandon. He thought he'd be planted in Washington for a year or two, working on spreadsheets, financial metrics, maybe a bit of web design and supporting drug commercialization issues before moving on to his next job. Instead, he was encamped in Madison, Wisconsin for who knows how long, heading to a college bar with a cowgirl and researching rural Midwestern citizen lawmakers who spend most of their year farming, running hardware stores on main street or operating a chain of funeral homes.

They found a table at a bar on Johnson Street between the capitol and the college bar district. The few students playing pool or watching college hockey on the big screen made for a semi-peaceful environment where they could easily talk without shouting. After ordering two Spotted Cows on tap, the planning commenced.

"We've got to start with the chair of the senate finance committee, Scott Woodson," said Shawni. "He had his own accounting firm for several years and now owns a regional chain of organic food stores, plus a few higher-end tattoo shops. How he got appointed to chair that committee I have no idea. But I guess his businesses must be good money-makers and he knows state tax law inside and out. He's our last chance before the bill is marked up and makes it to the full senate."

"When do we talk to him and what do we say?" asked Brandon.

"I'll call his office on Monday morning to schedule a meeting. He lives about a half hour from here, and since the legislature doesn't start its session for a couple weeks, we can see if he'll meet us at some local watering hole. Meantime, you should put together a presentation deck that shows the economic impact of removing this tax credit. R&D, product development, employment, equipment sales, and, most important, disadvantages created for Wisconsin when compared to other states that have this tax advantage."

"I actually have most of these numbers already."

"You do?"

"Yeah. Grabbed them earlier this week before we left. Have to fill in a couple holes in the research employment and income tax through-line."

"Holy shit, you're an all-star already. Think you can get those numbers by next week?"

"Monday, no problem. I'll check in with McKenzie at the office on Monday. She's been working on those metrics for me. I'm sure she'll have them for us."

"You got McKenzie, the world's most work-resistant worker, to actually do something productive?"

"Yeah, we got to talking about indy rock music and the best live music venues in the district, and she was all over me. I think she may be my work buddy now."

"Amazing! I've got to get out more. Keep that connection going. We'll need it."

"No problem. And let me know when you want a primer on Porridge Radio or Hippo Campus."

"Huh?"

"Never mind."

…..

31

The Eckoff lab at Norwalk College, which was really an office and not much of a lab, was not where Destiny Diggs wanted to be on an unseasonably warm December Saturday morning. Especially with her 5-year-old daughter, Shay. She could be doing crafts at home with her baby doll, making a leisurely breakfast of pancakes in her daughter's favorite Mickey Mouse-shaped griddle, or even playing at the city park playground in such warm temps.

Instead, she had data to input, supplies to organize and label, and reading lists to start on for the upcoming second semester. With any luck, Dr. Eckoff would give her a few days off so she could go home to Waterloo and spend some holiday time with her family. But today, Shay would be immersed in Dr. Seuss books, crayons and coloring books, and maybe a short nap.

She had sacrificed much to have the chance to get her degree from Norwalk. Living in a one-bedroom duplex just off the town square. No budget for cable or sat TV. And a young daughter to raise. With an internship awaiting her at Landmark Nutra Science during her upcoming final semester, the pay would be a huge benefit for her and her daughter's daily life. But the extra work, time away from home, lab assistant duties and continuing academic demands would challenge her like never before. She had contemplated asking Dr. Eckoff if she might end her work for him. But the small stipend she earned from her 10 hours a week was too valuable to just walk away from. That paid for clothes bought from Goodwill, and an occasional indulgence like Friday night pizza with her daughter and a few track teammates.

Shay was born five years ago, the result of a high school relationship that seemed so promising. Destiny and her boyfriend vowed to parent the baby and build a life together. But as delivery day drew near, the father-to-be suddenly decided life in the military was much more preferable. He had secretly held an appointment at the U.S. Marine recruiting station at the mall on the edge of Waterloo, and was gone four weeks later. A phone call from a bus station was all she got as he was heading to boot camp at Parris Island, South Carolina.

Through smarts, a brilliant ability to organize, sheer determination, support from her parents and unceasing love for her baby daughter, Destiny had conquered the last five years, and nothing was going to knock her off her path now.

The phone rang. Destiny knew that anyone calling this unpublished lab land-line number had something important to talk about.

"This is the Eckoff Lab. Can I help you?"

"Destiny?" said a whispering voice.

"Yes, this is Destiny."

"Destiny, this is Marypat Hammond."

"Yes. Hi Marypat. How are you doing?"

"That's what I wanted to talk about. I didn't know if anyone would be at your lab on a Saturday so I was going to leave a message. I've completed the follow-up dosing and waited 10 days after that to check in with you. I know I was supposed to schedule a Zoom meeting with Dr. Eckoff after the first dose, but I couldn't wait. I had to take the second dose."

"Well let's not worry about all that right now. Please talk to me. I've got access to your patient file and can do any updates we need to. What's going on with you?"

"The tumor. My lump. It's completely gone! I mean, it just went away!" Marypat's voice was intense but still raspy and shaky; what she was verbalizing was emotionally overwhelming. She had never said anything to anyone about any aspect of this "project." Today was the first time she could listen to herself talk about it out loud.

Destiny was slightly taken aback. She had indirectly heard of testimonials from other trial patients, very carefully and vaguely described by Dr. Eckoff, but had never heard directly from them. The magnitude and emotion of the moment stunned her briefly. After a few seconds of silence she took some deep breaths.

"Marypat, this is amazing news. I have to ask you a few basic questions that we ask all participants. Can I do that now?" Destiny was now assuming the follow-up role that Eckoff would normally perform. But after four years, she thought she deserved to take some extra initiative.

"Oh yes! Please! I've got all morning!" exclaimed Marypat.

"OK. Have you pressed deep beyond outer skin layers to see if you can feel anything that might be in the muscle tissue of your neck? I mean really press hard."

"I'm doing that as we speak and can feel nothing. In fact, my neck and shoulder movement is really a lot better. I'm sleeping better. It's just crazy."

"Great. Can you check for any other small, even really small, lumps or surface abnormalities throughout your head and neck and upper torso? And take your time with this. You don't have to do it now."

"I will. But I'm really, really confident nothing else has formed."

"Great. Final instruction. We want you to keep checking that tumor site every day. Just a few seconds for a feel test. And in six months, we want you to come back for a CT scan. We want to make sure nothing else is happening with you. Dr. Eckoff can explain how this all will work better than I can. But I will get your report to him ASAP and update your case with this great news."

"Thanks so much, Destiny. And thank Dr. Eckoff for letting me be a part of his research. By the way, can I tell anyone about this yet? My social circle is pretty small, so I don't think there's much risk."

"I know Dr. Eckoff would ask that you don't. I know that's hard to resist. But what we're doing will be at great risk if the scientific and medical community becomes widely aware of it. I can't control your life and your conversations. So I leave it up to you. But please don't go online with any discussion, no matter how anonymous and general you think you're being. That could shut us down."

"I understand. But this is just too amazing to keep quiet."

"I know. It truly is amazing. Be strong. Stick to the plan. And I'll have Dr. Eckoff schedule that CT scan with you. He'll be really, really happy to hear your news."

After hanging up, Destiny was still in a startled state of mind, having heard directly from a patient detailing such a miraculous development. What exactly had Eckoff been keeping from her these past four years?

Chapter 7

The Landmark Nutra Science headquarters campus looked regal in the late-afternoon gray light of a Midwestern winter. The vast parking lot was mostly empty as employees were accustomed to leaving their offices and labs by 4:30 or 5. That is, those employees who worked on site at the headquarters. Many were allowed to work remotely if they chose. In all, the work culture of Landmark was a generally happy place with low employee turnover. The company founder and chairman emeritus had made sure that valuing employees and their life away from work was a priority as he built the agriscience giant. This priority held firm at all of Landmark's branch locations–manufacturing facilities, applied research labs, sales offices–across North America and around the world.

Dr. Larry Eckoff pulled his 2009 Chrysler 300 sedan into the parking lot. He parked near the only car in the front row of the lot, closest to the main entry. And that vehicle would be the chairman emeritus' 2023 Jaguar SUV. The chairman wasn't a pretentious guy, not into vanity possessions or grand exhibits of wealth. His home was fairly modest by multi-millionaire standards: a beautifully landscaped and restored early 20th century farmhouse in rural Polk County. But he did let himself have one indulgence: a cool imported SUV.

He didn't really run anything at the company. As founder and chairman emeritus, he was given an office to work from whenever he wanted. It wasn't located in the C-suites on the top floor of the four-story sprawling, louvered stone and glass building, flanked by similar looking buildings housing R&D labs, manufacturing, large conference and entertainment halls and testing facilities. His office was actually on the first floor, just a short walk from the reception desk in the large, plant-festooned lobby, right next to the facilities management department.

Larry walked in as the receptionist was packing up her large, baggy purse and turning off her computer monitor, getting ready to leave. She cheerfully greeted him and contacted the founder on her telecom console, who told her to direct Larry to his office.

Larry walked 50 feet down the hall then turned into a small hallway and knocked on the one forgettable, windowless door. The modest metal-etched office sign next to the door frame said "Harold McLandry." No title, no middle initial. It could have been the custodian for all anyone would know.

"Come in Larry! Great to see you!" said McLandry, a tall, silver-haired man clad in a navy blazer, khakis and bright purple Nike running shoes. His looks belied his 79-year-old body. Straight posture, lean physique and a hairline most 50-year-olds would kill for. Still, he walked gingerly, his gait exhibiting caution needed for an elderly man wanting to avoid a fall at all costs.

Harold McLandry was raised in rural Minnesota. He studied music in college at The U in the Twin Cities, and taught band in Minnesota and Iowa public schools for a decade. In his 30s, he was tiring of lessons, weekend band commitments and endless solo and ensemble competitions.

A college friend suggested he try a career change in sales. Specifically, ag seed sales. McLandry, with his teaching skills and penchant for making difficult concepts easy to talk about and understand, excelled at the small corn and soybean producer that hired him from his friend's endorsement. And when genetics and advanced hybridization of seed and other feed ingredients started taking off in the 1980s, McLandry became obsessed with the idea of creating a company that could explain these world-changing advances to farmers big and small, helping them create greater wealth with fewer acres and fewer head of livestock.

He borrowed heavily from friends and family to start Landmark Ag Products. He and his skeleton sales force traveled from farm to farm selling a couple basic but highly productive hybrid seed strains that a small team of seed geneticists developed for him on contract. In time, he paid back his original investors in double-digit multiples, and eventually became a coveted lending target for large banks across the Midwest. As Landmark revenue from its biotech patents zoomed into the stratosphere, he changed the name to Landmark Nutra Science. And through recessions, economic contractions, inflation, competitor upstarts and buyout offers, Landmark never stopped growing.

McLandry led the company for 38 years and managed this dizzying growth while keeping private control of the company. Endless streams of money-center stock analysts and investors sought audiences with him to persuade him to take the company public and increase his wealth to levels unimagined. Never before had so many private planes of investment bankers traveled to Central Iowa over a 20-year span. But he resisted and continued to own 95% of Landmark equity, with the remainder split among family members. They became wealthy. McLandry became enormously wealthy.

But in the twilight of his life, he wanted to explore new possibilities with a planet full of new ideas and new science. He had grown bored with agriculture. For him, what else was there to conquer? He proceeded to turn the management of the company over to a small group of executives he had recruited, led and trusted for years. He even distributed a 10% tranche of equity among them with hopes of them staying with Landmark for the rest of their careers. That was the first time anyone outside the McLandry family had an ownership stake in the company.

When he met Dr. Larry Eckoff at a reception for Norwalk College benefactors eight years ago, that "new possibility" for his remaining time on Earth suddenly hit Harold McLandry between the eyes.

"How did the cross country season go?" the founder asked.

"We're had a ton of fun, that's for sure," said Coach Eckoff.

"I understand. Is Destiny making a mark in her senior season?"

"Well, she finished in the middle of the pack at the conference meet this fall. With all she has going on in her life, that's pretty damn good."

"I'd say so, too. I'm so glad Norwalk was able to snag her. She has many talents and we certainly have our sights set on her after she graduates. But don't tell her that directly. Don't want her to get too confident too early!"

"Believe me, she keeps everything in great balance and perspective. If she ends up at Landmark, it will be well deserved and she'll be more than prepared to start contributing quickly."

"Well, thanks for all the work you do with her and how you've mentored her so adeptly. And speaking of her work–and yours of course–I hear you have some intriguing news."

"I'd call it the capstone of my research trial. We have a very promising result from a trial participant in Chicago. It's been a month since her last dose. Initially she was presenting with a very large mass in the side of her neck. Diagnosed by her Chicago doctor as squamous cell carcinoma. Neck cancer. She has been in contact with Destiny. The tumor appears to have completely regressed. Dissipated entirely. I have to view it myself, not just on Zoom, which I already have, and will do so again in several months when we do a follow up CT scan. And of course, we'll track her for several more years."

"That is unbelievable. Well, of course, I believe it. But such an amazing outcome, repeated across so many malignancy platforms, is almost incomprehensible, even to an old biology nut like me."

"I know. It's hard for me to fathom as well. But after 1,400 trial outcomes, and a 95% efficacy rate with this final spore formulation, I think we may be ready to move to a scaling plan and a business plan."

"What do you need from me?"

"I need to find someone who can work in complete confidence and help us map out manufacturing and distribution in a way that will stick to our original vision: an interventional compound that can be provided to cancer sufferers at a greatly affordable cost that will help them beat the disease, adhere to FDA compliance requirements, and keep our business sustainable for the long term. And, of course, this will take a significant new infusion of capital to accomplish this. I can't even calculate what that amount is. That's why we need a new team member who can create and validate those plans and calibrate the financing they'll require.

"Larry, you make it sound so practical and workman-like. Which is great, because we need to be focused and realistic. But I tell you, this will set the world on fire! It's exciting beyond imagination. And I'm here to help create that excitement. I'm willing to put up the next round of capital, no doubt about it. But I'm confident we'll have wannabe investors beating down our door once we've reached the place where we can share this publicly."

"I share your excitement, Hal, but let's not get too far ahead of ourselves. We've got a ton of work to do just to turn this into a viable small enterprise, let alone a world-beating colossus. And I'm not sure we want to go there anyway and still retain control of the business, let alone our vision."

"Yes, you're right. Thanks for bringing me back to reality."

"Well, being a killjoy is kind of my specialty lately, but don't lose your excitement. Though we've got to be disciplined and focused, this will save lives and change lives."

In ways they had not yet anticipated.

Chapter 8

The crisp, sunny winter afternoon at the Chicago Public Health free clinic was calm for a change. Luis Hernandez, MD, sitting in his small cubicle in the back of the single-story Bronzeville brick and timber medical building, was not hearing nearly as many bell-ringing entries from the front door as patients stomped the slush of their boots from the snowy, unshoveled Chicago sidewalks.

This afternoon, for whatever reason, he had the luxury of some serious office time, where he could catch up on administrative tasks, maybe take a quick online CEU, and, if he was extra lucky, get out by 5:30 to meet his wife, a nurse at Provident Hospital a few blocks away, and grab a happy hour cocktail.

As he was looking over patient files for follow up, he came upon a patient who had been documented as refusing a treatment plan for a malignant neck tumor. "Patient states she will think about it," was the entry in her last consult record.

Normally, north side and suburban clinics have nurses and assistants do follow up calls with patients. Not at this clinic. The docs do their own, and hopefully they can find time to return calls within a few days. Since this patient had opted to not move forward with a treatment regimen, she was moved to low priority. But Luis was at least interested if there was anything new happening with her.

"Hello, is this Marypat?" Luis asked, a bit surprised she answered the phone on his first call.

"Yes," came the voice, firm but with a bit of hesitance in her tone.

"Hi Marypat. This is Doctor Hernandez from the Bronzeville clinic. I was just going over your patient file this afternoon and noticed we hadn't connected for a while. Just wanted to ask if anything is new with your health, specifically the mass on your neck. Have you started any chemo or radiation treatments?"

Silence.

"Let me ask, have you seen an oncologist since your last visit here?"

More silence.

Hernandez started silently berating himself for possibly being too direct too fast. He liked to get to the point and talk honestly about medical issues and patient experiences. Now he figured he'd intimidated Marypat Hammond by asking these questions right off the bat and skipping any small talk. If she was clamming up, he was to blame, he thought.

"Marypat, I'm sorry. I didn't mean to be abrupt. I know I can be a bit quick and pointed with people, and I apologize. But I'm just so interested in what you've been experiencing these past couple of months. You came to us with a serious health condition. I just want to do anything I can to understand where you are right now. Does that make any sense?"

Now, Luis thought, he gave her complete control of the conversation and she could have the upper hand and respond in full confidence. He was kind of proud of himself. He was getting better at this.

"Doctor Hernandez, I appreciate your checking up on me. I do. You were so important in helping me understand what I'm dealing with and achieving a diagnosis. I can't thank you enough for that."

Now we're getting somewhere, thought Luis.

"Well I appreciate that, Marypat. I'd like to see if you…."

"...The tumor is gone!" Marypat interrupted.

"What?!!"

"It's gone. I'm on top of the world about this. Feeling better than I ever have, to be honest."

Now there was silence on Hernandez's end.

"Dr. Hernandez, are you there?"

"Marypat, let me see if I understand what I think I'm hearing from you. You're telling me your tumor has dissipated? Totally regressed? Is that what I'm hearing?"

"Yes. That is exactly what I'm telling you."

"Marypat, my jaw is on the floor right now. I don't doubt you, but this is something I cannot comprehend. And you've had no chemo?"

"No."

"No radiation?"

"No."

"No treatment of any kind?"

Again, silence.

"Marypat, you still there?"

41

"Dr. Hernandez, I can't talk about what I've been through. It's not allowed. But it's been miraculous. I'll bet you agree."

"This makes no sense. Why can't you talk about it? Yes, it is miraculous, especially if you stay cancer free. But why can't you tell me what's happening?"

"I'll get in trouble and not get any follow up that I might need."

"Marypat, this isn't right. You've got to tell me how this happened. If you don't want to talk to me directly, fine. Send me a text. An email. Send my nurse a text. Send my dog a letter. We've got to understand more about this."

"I can't say anything to anyone through any means. Just know I'm doing great. I thank you again, and please don't contact me anymore."

And from there on, Luis Hernandez, MD, would live in a fog of bewilderment.

Chapter 9

Worley's Coffee and Wine Bar was the perfect place to hold a quiet, productive discussion. A couple miles east of the Wisconsin state capitol campus even farther from the UW, most patrons went there to enjoy the menu offerings and see friends, not to talk business. Instead of being surrounded by government offices and power dining spots, Worley's was surrounded by new townhouses, high-end "family" apartments and a shiny new middle school. Small sapling trees were everywhere amid the new construction. Worley's was kind of an outlier: a bit of old campus town in the suburbs. And people loved it. There was a miniscule chance anyone would overhear a serious discussion, or even try to.

The interior was covered in macramé plant hangers, bright, colorful painted walls and posters of some of the great concerts that came to Madison in the 60s.... The Doors, Jefferson Airplane, The Byrds.

Scott Woodson loved this place. Someday, with the profits of his local organic food store empire and tattoo shops, he might even try to buy it. Or build something like it. But today, this was business. Woodson actually wore a blazer today, something he only did during the legislative session. He was meeting two people from the largest, most powerful healthcare organization in the country, maybe the world. A sport coat might offset his graying ponytail and sleeve of arm tattoos, and present him as a worthy counterpart to the high-powered lobbyists.

Many regulars of Worley's knew who he was, but no one cared. This was a chill place where the great public affairs debates of the day had nary an audience. He was more likely to be asked about volunteering to sell beer at the upcoming indy rock fest than he would tax policy or education funding.

He already had his coffee, so he would be in fine shape if his guests wanted to buy him another, since state law prohibited public officials from accepting more than five dollars' worth of meals or beverages from any constituent or interest group.

Shawni Phillips and Brandon Abrams entered Worley's with a slight rush of winter air following behind them. They instantly saw Sen. Woodson at his table and headed toward him.

Woodson saw them, too.

They approached his table and introduced themselves. Woodson politely introduced himself and they shook hands. They all ordered coffee at the counter, then sat down to start their quiet confab.

Woodson knew why they wanted to travel from D.C. to meet with him. That was no mystery. He had certainly toyed with the option of refusing to meet, telling them to write his office a letter stating their concerns with SB-57. But when H-BIS wants to talk, it's probably a good idea to humor them a bit and make sure you don't become a total adversary. Who knows, they may be a needed ally in future legislative battles. If they want to start building a bridge with you, at least show up to the construction site.

"So how was the flight from D.C.? Obviously you were able to rent a couple snowmobiles and make your way around Madison!" Woodson joked.

"We also have snow in Washington, senator," Shawni chimed in. "We know how to rough it. Two inches on a 30-degree day builds us Washingtonians into hardy, tough souls!" A little laughter broke the ice, along with some banter about Badger football and Brandon's beloved Rutgers team, setting the stage for the topic at hand.

Shawni began, "Senator, we're obviously here to talk about a very important bill proposal that your committee will soon mark up for a full vote in the Senate soon after the legislature convenes. We know your committee's view of this bill is very favorable because of the new revenue the legislation will produce and we appreciate that. State governments seemed to be constantly strapped and unable to fully fund anything these days. Wisconsin certainly is not alone in this struggle. But as Brandon will summarize, this bill will produce much more financial and economic hardship in the long run. And we hope you'll hear us out for a couple minutes on this."

"Sure," Woodson replied. "Please keep going." He was proud of his patience and the 'camp counselor' role he was playing.

Brandon started in, "Senator, Madison alone currently has 79 health-tech startup companies, all doing important work in drug and medical device development, along with new digital platforms for diagnoses, telemedicine, even insurance operations. Multiply that by 10 and you have nearly 1,000 startups throughout your entire state. And that does not include established companies that are doing large research initiatives for new products and improved, next-generation products. The R&D tax credits for these companies are a huge part of their ongoing resource platforms that fund their work. And when they score a commercial win, the revenue–AND TAXABLE EARNINGS–from those new business revenues more than offset the tax credits, in some cases by five-fold in the first three years. So we would like you and your Senate committee to rethink the benefits of this bill. We truly can demonstrate that this bill would generate some short-term cash at the expense of long-term economic growth."

"So are you saying R&D would just stop at these companies?" asked Woodson. "Regardless of tax credits or no tax credits, our health industry still has to develop new products, continue with applied research and the like."

"Yes they do," replied Shawni. "It's just a matter of where they will choose to do it."

"What does that mean?" Woodson asked, slightly irritated.

"We think many of the companies and start-ups we've mentioned will want to carry out their research and product development strategies in states with more favorable tax policies," said Shawni. "Many of these companies, if not nearly all of them, are members of our H-BIS association."

"Are you telling me you'll encourage them to move out of Wisconsin?"

"We are simply pointing out facts to them; that moving R&D to Michigan, Minnesota, Illinois, for example, would be an efficient way to continue receiving the state R&D support they've become accustomed to."

"That sounds a bit like blackmail to me."

"It's simple business decision making, Senator. We can't make our member companies do anything. They make their own judgments. But it's pretty easy to see the impact that such a migration would have on local economic activity, employment, income and property tax, you name it."

Brandon jumped in: "I have all the financial analysis of this on a shared presentation link that I'd be glad to send to you, Senator, for you to share with your committee colleagues."

Woodson had his own point to make. "OK fine, send it to me. But while you're at it, how about you develop some additional analysis on how this R&D tax credit is reducing our schools' ability to add new teachers and upgrade curricula, reducing our ability to fund our portion of Medicare for poor residents, robbing our funding for basic social services for people in dire need of housing and food security. Those budgets have been flat or ever cut since this R&D tax credit took effect. In fact, I have those metrics on a PowerPoint, and will be glad to share it with you to show your members."

"We appreciate the quandary you're in, Senator, we truly do," said Shawni. "But we strongly believe a strong healthcare industry in Wisconsin, not a weakened one, can do more good in the long run to help those constituencies you mentioned."

"Well, you guys can recite all the lofty platitudes you want, but I deal with people on the ground here, every day, facing big problems in their daily lives. These people don't have the luxury to worry about tax perks for fancy, already-profitable companies. As you can guess, I'm not hearing anything that would dissuade me from moving this bill through committee and onto the floor."

"It's called taking the long view, Senator, and we hope you can at least appreciate that. We understand where you sit on this, and we thank you for at least hearing us out."

And with that, after a few forced pleasantries, an experienced professional and a rookie functionary representing the most influential business group in the country, got up from their table, ready to leave the small coffee shop in Wisconsin. Woodson was glad he stood his ground. But he couldn't help respecting the sharp woman and young man he had just talked with. Especially–with her stunning looks and quick brain–that sharp woman.

"Oh by the way senator," said Shawni, "my brother's niece just started here at UW this semester. She's looking for a local bank for her small checking account. Any suggestions?

"Madison State Bank. Been with them for years. Great service. Great people. Tell them I sent her."

"Wonderful. I'll do that. Thanks again for the meeting."

"Well, looks like we're out of luck with this guy," said Brandon as they made their way across the parking lot.

"Are you kidding? We've just begun," said Shawni. "One thing you learn in business and government, there's always something else that can be tried. And when that something else changes the game, it's a beautiful thing. But, make no mistake, we're gonna be here a few more days…or weeks."

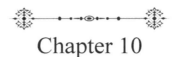

Chapter 10

T he cold night air in Norwalk was peaceful and pleasant. Not bitterly frozen, just a nice crisp chill. If cross country season was still going, Destiny could still get in a comfortable three- or four-mile run tonight. She thought she still might after she gets Shay to sleep.

She and Larry Eckoff were walking to their cars outside of McLandry Hall and as usual, they were the only ones in the dimly lit parking lot.

Destiny was nearing the end of her time at Norwalk. Her work for Eckoff had been highly productive, consistent and something Eckoff had greatly relied upon. In fact he had grown to mostly take her valuable assistance for granted.

Destiny also greatly valued the opportunity Eckoff and Norwalk College had given her. A job that helped with her household expenses, a schedule that gave her flexibility. And a boss who was kind, committed...and extremely frustrating.

She had documented the data from Eckoff's research for most of the past four years. She had dutifully worked within the confines of a very strict NDA. And the data that Eckoff wanted recorded and archived was coded, obscured with numerical keys, complex charts and graphs and scientific jargon so that no one but Eckoff actually knew the real-world progress and outcomes his patients were experiencing.

And Destiny, whose lifelong value of obeying parents, respecting teachers and toeing the line for coaches and teammates was deeply ingrained, never really thought about asking many questions that would delve deeper into Eckoff's research. But that was changing. Especially after Marypat had contacted her and passed along the astonishing news about her health status. This was really the first time that Destiny had talked directly with a trial patient. And the first time she had been a first-hand witness to such a miraculous outcome. What was really going on with Eckoff's research? What was he really creating? And what was he really planning to do with his creation?

To say she was curious about this thing called IH-3314 was an understatement. Now that she was close to graduation, she felt compelled to go beyond the role of the quiet, loyal assistant and get real with Eckoff.

"Dr. Eckoff, I have to ask you something," Destiny said.

"Shoot."

"We've now got trial data on nearly 1400 participants: 400 alone since I've been working for you. If I'm reading the data right, these results are looking amazing, just from what I've been seeing. I mean, what's going on? Where's this research heading? Where are these tincture samples coming from? I'm graduating in a few months and it'd be great if I could get a better understanding of what I've been working on before I leave here. Does that make sense?"

"It makes total sense Destiny, and I'm sorry that the NDA you signed is so restrictive. I've known you long enough that I think I can trust you and move beyond the NDA. But I would beg you to please still keep this confidential. It's so important at this phase. Can I count on you doing that?"

"Yes. Absolutely."

"Can I drive you somewhere and show you something? Should take about an hour. Maybe less."

"Let me call my daycare and see if they can keep Shay a while longer."

"Great. And I'll pay any overtime they charge you. In fact, I'll pay the whole week's bill. You deserve it for being so patient."

Destiny was excited and a bit leery. She'd never seen Larry Eckoff like this, suddenly loosening the rules a bit and demonstrating such gratitude and generosity. He was obviously excited about something. She was witnessing a new dimension in him.

.....

Destiny and Eckoff got in his car and pulled out of the parking lot. They drove south down First Street, past a few campus buildings spewing vapor from their rooftop heat vents, toward the town square. Going straight through the square, past Franco's Pizza, the local hardware store, a few bars where college kids still drank and smoked on Wednesday nights, the county administration building, a barbershop and an Asian fast-food restaurant, they headed down a tree-lined residential road. Yellow and orange lights glowed from inside the houses as fireplaces burned and the ever-present aroma of hickory and maple logs wafted from fireplaces.

After another mile, they turned west on State Street through more neighborhoods until they reached the city limits. Another two miles on the county highway that State Street merged into and they headed south again on a gravel road, past farmhouses, barns and grain silos that populated the Iowa countryside. The road intersected with another gravel road that was more a path than a road, unmarked and seemingly in the middle of nowhere. Destiny had lived her life in Iowa but had never been this deep into the countryside. With the dark of night obscuring any sense of direction she had, she did not know where she was, or even which way would lead back to Norwalk.

The rural path was only a couple hundred yards long, with no streetlight. Larry Eckoff used his car's headlights to see where he was. But he knew exactly his location, as he'd been here hundreds of times before.

He pulled in front of a rusted gate, got out of his running car, unlocked the padlock, and opened it. Once past the gate, he got out again and locked it. A worn grass path led to a wide yard area where they parked, vacant pastureland surrounding them, separated by a highly charged electric fence.

Destiny got out of the car after Eckoff and looked around. Directly in front of them, not visible from the nearest road or path in the nighttime, was what looked to be an abandoned grain storage elevator. Illuminated only by cloudless moonlight was a worn logo 100 feet high on the old hulking structure that said "Landmark Ag." The old elevator had been a facility owned by Landmark Ag Products 75 years ago, when the company produced and sold basic seed corn directly to farmers, and also stored and dried their crop in the elevator. Decades before agriculture became a diversified genetics and multi nutritional industry, Landmark Ag was a reliable partner to farmers in a 10-county region, a nice swath of Iowa's 99 counties. Farmers would visit the elevator to place their orders for the coming planting season, grab a Pepsi or 7-Up from the machine inside the small office, and sit around and talk about weather, weed problems, pest problems, flooding problems and local high school football. Eventually they'd get a paper receipt for their order, turn it in to their local farm lender for validation, and await delivery of their seed in March for their spring planting.

Destiny followed Dr. Eckoff around the perimeter of the towering edifice to a triple-width garage-type entry, with a newer concrete driveway slanting down to a huge 20-foot-wide metal door. Eckoff approached a small black panel on the side wall of the door and entered a 7-digit code. He then pressed his thumb against a glass biometric panel below the keypad. After an electronic beep sounded, the door, a thick, single sheet of aluminum alloy, opened inward in one continuous, slow movement until the entry was fully exposed.

Destiny at once felt uneasy as a wave of red light washed over her.

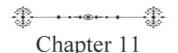

Chapter 11

The outer ring of Zurich, Switzerland was a contrast to the central core of the city. Historic central Zurich was a collection of beautiful centuries-old buildings housing a vibrant retail community of clothing shops, restaurants, bakeries and chocolatiers, quaint apartments, university buildings, government offices and tourist shops, all connected by a tram system and spaghetti-shaped streets that curved and wound endlessly.

The outer stretches of the city were more industrial, housing factories, machine tooling shops that served those factories, metal fabricators, fuel depots and meat processing plants.

This area of the city was also home to Microneutics S.A., a pharmaceutical behemoth with 58 buildings spread out over hundreds of acres. The 11-story executive and corporate administration building overlooked the far-flung campus. Here, the operations, purchasing, finance, tax, marketing, HR and facilities departments oversaw the same functions contained in the profit center businesses that inhabited the rest of the campus. Which in turn oversaw those same departments located in regional facilities around the globe.

At any minute, on any day, Chairman and CEO Hans Mogen could punch up an executive dashboard app on his phone and know exactly how much cash on hand the company had. He could also see daily operating and net profits, comparisons with the prior month, prior quarter and prior fiscal year. And if the year-end totals he received from his finance senior vice president contained anything different than what was on his phone, there would be hell to pay, save for a rounding discrepancy.

Microneutics was tightly controlled, all in an effort to keep its constantly growing business coordinated and operating with precision.

On this late winter afternoon, Mogen headed to the private elevator in his 11th floor office. He took it down to his private underground parking space, unplugged a charging cord and climbed into his Lucid electric stretch sedan.

He pulled the noiseless vehicle onto one of the many frontage roads that surrounded his campus and headed for a nearby highway. He called his wife using the voice-controlled interface on the car's pop-up glass panel, telling her he would be late getting home, but that he would pick her up at the front door and go get a late dinner at a nearby seafood place.

…..

The Lucid pulled up to a small beer joint tucked into a village hillside just off the shore of the narrow but lengthy Lake Zurich. He'd been to the Bierzimmer only once, years ago, and was glad to know it was still in business. It was a solitary place with no other retail establishments close by. Today it was not crowded. He took off his coat and tie, rolled up his shirt sleeves and tried to fit in as he entered through a side door off the outdoor biergarten. His slender six-foot frame and perfectly sculpted silver hair would not look out of place if he was dressed down a bit.

At a table in a corner over by a dart board, Ursula Halgren was waiting for him. Her flannel shirt, baggy jeans, alabaster skin and flowing black hair depicted her as someone in the bar band taking a break, rather than a corporate vice president and brand manager.

They both ordered a local wheat pilsner and looked around the room before they started in on the topic of the moment.

"So, why here? What's going on?" asked Hans.

"I'm starting to think that people may be seeing me in your office too frequently. I don't want to feed their suspicions. I wanted to get off campus."

"Understand, but if anyone from the company comes in here and sees us, that's bad too, isn't it?"

"Trust me, no one will show up here. If they did, they would be the type of employees who've never seen me and don't know who I am."

"But they'd know who I am. At least I hope they would."

"Yes, maybe. Pretend I'm your niece. Just start talking about family stuff if that happens. And leave before I do. Let me do the worrying. And speaking of worrying, the thing we need to talk about is getting too problematic to be chatting about in your office."

53

"That's what I gathered. Thank you. Now talk to me, please."

"The chatter on Centrifuge is getting more frequent and contains more detail. Detail that seems very scientific and sourced from people who know what they're talking about. Perhaps scientists, physicians. I don't know. But this tincture thing is starting to go beyond just some random or coincidental discussions."

"What makes you think so?"

"I'm seeing a knowledgeable contributor talk about his witnessing of a patient's cancer history and his or her astonishment of the dilution and complete regression of a tumor. He is talking about specific tumor size and characteristics, patient history, direct dialogue with the patient."

"Well that's one conversation. And maybe another placebo effect."

"Placebo effect can reduce fever, clear up gut irritation, reduce cold symptoms, joint pain, etc. Placebo effect does not quickly shrink malignant tumors!" Ursula found her voice reaching a crescendo and had to quiet herself, nervously looking around the room.

"You said quickly?"

"Yes. I told you earlier. This compound is fast acting."

"Still, a single episode"

"Yes. Centrifuge does not give us a picture of quantity. It only shows discussion; sentiment, depth, descriptions. All anonymous. And this latest post is getting a ton of reaction. People giving their account of patients, friends, family, with similar experience. Again, we don't know how far back this goes. Centrifuge is only three years old. For all we know, these cancer remediation experiences may go back much farther than that. In fact, I would bet they do, because it seems we're reaching critical mass, a point where years of patient experience and dialog is starting to reach a percolating phase. Things are simmering, and may soon reach a boil."

"Fuck!" said Hans Mogen quietly but intensely. "We've got to get more information on how this is happening, who's creating this snake oil, who's running these trials and where."

"If I were you, I'd stop calling this snake oil. If it were snake oil, we would not be seeing this online discussion gaining real steam, especially with such vivid descriptions and amazement. If it were snake oil, eventually it wouldn't work, and the Centrifuge chatter would dry up."

"So how do we describe this? From a competitive business intelligence standpoint?"

"I would call this an unconventional, even underground, oncological solution in the development stage that is producing startling efficacy results; it may have the potential to disrupt and completely upend the conventional world of cancer treatment as we know it."

"God, you make it sound so dramatic and earthshaking."

"Until we see these discussions start fading and going in an unfavorable direction, for the trial participants that is, I think you have to assume this very well could be earthshaking. You don't want to get caught completely flat footed in the marketplace. And remember, competitor pharma companies are also likely seeing these Centrifuge posts, either directly or through proxy participants. What do you think they are thinking?"

"I don't think I'm going to sleep too well tonight."

"Good. That shows I'm getting through to you."

And with that, Hans Mogen got up, stared straight ahead and slowly, calmly walked across the creaky wooden floor, past the warmer full of soft pretzels for happy hour, and out the door. The quiet ride home in the Swiss dusk would not be so quiet in his mind, the cacophony of a thousand questions rattling the brain of the ultra-controlling CEO.

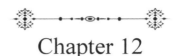

Chapter 12

The glow of the massive underground cavern was overwhelming. Low intensity red lights as far as one could see. The room was cool and damp, with several misting machines hissing their vaporous output every few minutes.

Dr. Eckoff gave her a few moments to gather herself. This was all new to her, of course, yet he also was slightly amazed every time he came here.

Below every set of lights was a circular bed of soil, each about 20 feet in diameter. Destiny walked up to one, careful not to touch anything like a dutiful, experienced lab assistant would be. In the soil were some sort of sprouting plants, only with no leaves and dark in color. She walked up to another bed where the sprout-like material was white. At least they looked white in the red light, but it was nearly impossible to tell.

"What is this?" she asked slowly while still scanning the huge, dark room.

"This is IH-3314. Or I should say, the active ingredient in IH-3314. In its raw, original form."

"What are these dirt beds all about? What's growing in them?"

"Mushrooms. Mushrooms that are the result of years of hybridization, combining certain strains of the fungus–and we know that's what mushrooms are; fungus–until I arrived at a combination of several strains of mushroom spores that appeared to tackle the cellular hyperproliferation that is the fundamental mechanism of cancer."

"But…how? How did you guess that this could treat cancer?"

"I had a working theory, a concept, based on everything I'd read and knew about plant-based bioactive materials. Of course, with my 'stellar' reputation in the research field, I had no luck getting research partners and funders to back me. So I set out on my own."

"And now you've got a solution to make tumors disappear?"

"Not just tumors. I've recorded results that appear to vanquish leukemia, bone cancer, multiple myeloma, any place in the body where cells are hyper-dividing and growing."

"How? How does it work?"

At that point, the red lights went out. Eckoff and Destiny were alone in total darkness.

Eckoff then loudly said, "NATO." And the lights came back on.

"Sorry about that," Eckoff said. "The lights are timed to turn off after a few minutes. These fungus strains need cool, damp darkness to grow. A few minutes of low-energy red light at a time are all they're allowed when people are here, just so we can see. These lights change to blue when the fungus is fruiting. Before we leave, let's record your voice print into the system so you can turn the lights back on when you're here next time."

"Thanks. But, NATO?"

"It's easy to remember. And a reminder we've got a full-on military offensive under way!"

"I've got to get back and pick up Shay. I want to talk more in the car."

"Yes, of course."

And with that, the two exited the abandoned grain elevator and got in the car. The small bright Midwest winter moon illuminated the path and surrounding fields as they headed for the obscure gravel road. The colored holiday lights of Norwalk loomed in the distance.

…..

The rare call came from just 50 feet across a large reception space on the top floor of the stately H-BIS building in Washington D.C.

Ron Holtzman picked up his receiver. The speaker phone was not to be used when a call came from the CEO's office. Holtzman for years had wished his boss, whom he saw maybe three or four times a year, would ditch the land lines and just call or text or Slack on the office's wifi network. But Turner Mansfield was as old school as they came."

"Hi Turner. How are you?"

"I'm doing well Ronald, but we have a constituent who is not, and we need to talk about how we might help him. Can you pop over here in 5 minutes?"

Mansfield could have just said "get over here now," as his polite questions were never answered with a "no" or even with an "I'm not sure." One always answered with a "yes!" If any qualification for that yes was needed, that could come later, delicately contextualized, of course.

Mansfield was winding down his long career as a titan in the global healthcare business. His decades of influencing and directing legislative and political strategy for the Society's member companies had built H-BIS and his own professional profile into a venerable, Rushmore-esque edifice of admiration and even awe among the many people and organizations that were affected to large and small degrees by his vast connections and savvy maneuvering among the halls of government and boardrooms across the country.

Holtzman quickly walked over to Mansfield's office, which looked more like a cozy Irish pub than an office. Plaid carpet buttressed mahogany woodwork, along with a worthy collection of whiskeys, even a faint smell of cavendish tobacco from back in the day when he could smoke his pipe in his office. Mansfield always looked at home in his office, a small-framed, slightly frail man of 85 with deep brown dyed hair that had maintained a healthy thickness and hairline, belying the man's pale, thin skin and bony, arthritic hands.

Holtzman, along with everyone in the industry, knew he would succeed Mansfield when the time came for him to step down. And that time was drawing nearer every day. But until then, Holtzman, who was operationally responsible for everything that got accomplished at H-BIS, had to play the loyal lieutenant to stay in good stead. And he had done so for years.

Meetings with Mansfield tended to not last long, unless Mansfield's wealth planner was meeting with him to map out his latest estate plan and asset allocations. So Holtzman leaned on the credenza on a side wall with hands in his pockets, striking a casual pose to keep Mansfield at ease.

"I just had a call from Hans Mogen at Microneutics," said Mansfield.

"Oh, is he in town this week?"

"No. He was calling from Zurich. Seems his staff have picked up on an intriguing development they've stumbled across on some social media chat site."

"I'm listening," said Holtzman. When Hans Mogen calls from his corporate office halfway around the world, one should pay especially close attention. Though Microneutics was not a US company, it had many operations in the states, and that qualified the company as a dues-paying member of H-BIS. And with $500,000 in dues remunerated every year, a meeting of the patriarchs, anytime, anywhere, was never turned down.

"I don't know much of anything about all this social media shit, the Twitter, The Facepage and all that, but Hans does. And so does your staff, I assume."

"Yes," said Holtzman. "We're pretty capable with those things."

"Well, I hope you can help Hans. He's concerned that some rogue outfit is making a splash on one of these chat rooms or whatever they're called."

As usual, Holtzman had to coax the crux of the story out of Turner Mansfield. He talked in short bursts and didn't like to ramble on about anything. But he was fine with answering a bundle of questions if that was needed to get his point across and get an assignment clearly understood.

"Well, lots of people and organizations make lots of splashes on social media."

"Yes, well this is different, apparently."

"Can you tell me how so?"

"Someone is out there peddling some miracle crap that is making tumors disappear. Malignant tumors."

"Say again?"

"Hans doesn't know who or where or how many. And he knows it can't be a conventional oncology company, because everyone would know the stages and timing and publications of clinical trials, right from the first rat or pig they inject. Mogen knows every drug that is out there in development. He has a knack for that, you know."

"Oh, I don't doubt that for a second. How does he know this is legit? And, since he came to you, does he think this is happening in the United States?"

"He doesn't know. He says everything he's reading is consistently touting some amazing patient experiences. And it's been going on for several years. And it's now picking up steam. He tells me the conversations are generally in English; US English, not UK English. With US slang and style."

"OK, but why not wait it out, see what bubbles up in public, and see if anything comes of this? He can connect us with his monitoring program and we can add some extra eyes and ears."

With all the real, tangible projects Holtzman's staff was working on at any given time – big tax issues, FDA regulation headaches, government oversight of research, elections and candidates favorable to the healthcare industry – he did not relish the idea of wasting time and staff on a wild goose chase.

"He doesn't want to wait," said Mansfield. "He wants our help tracking down who this might be. With the money he's paid us over the years, it's the least we can do."

"You know, Turner, there are a thousand so-called 'holistic' cancer treatments on the market at any time. Herbs, pot, crystals, leeches. They all have their suckers for customers and as long as they don't try to invade our space, we all leave each other alone. They laugh at us, we laugh at them. Except, we have FDA enforcement on our side if someone starts getting out of hand. We can pretty much shut down anybody."

"That's right. So let's go help Hans find these bastards and shut them down. Before they get out of hand. I wouldn't be so intent on doing this if Hans didn't think this was really important. If it's what we think it is, a small-time, shoe-string operation, it shouldn't be that difficult. We just have to find the sons of bitches."

"I'll start a project file on this. Do you have a contact at Han's office we can start with?"

"He's got some girl working on it. And please, be very discreet on this. Minimal staff involvement. And the threat of death by firing squad if anyone talks about this outside of my office or your office. We've got to keep this under tight wraps until we're ready to take the wrecking ball to this outfit."

"I just can't help but think this tumor shrinker is a fly-by-nighter who'll come and go like they all do," said Holtzman.

"That's what they thought about two Australian doctors who discovered that a simple antibiotic could cure stomach ulcers and even one type of stomach cancer," said Mansfield. "That ended up eliminating countless surgeries, long-term therapies, even psychological practice specialties worldwide."

"But that's good, right?"

"Yes, it's good, but if that same scenario is played out here–and it won't be–well, I don't even want to think about the global

60

consequences. Suffice it to say, they would be infinitely beyond the simple ulcer story."

Ron Holtzman returned to his office, looking more closely at the note Turner Mansfield handed him; someone named Ursula and a phone number with a Switzerland country code.

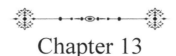

Chapter 13

S hawni kicked off her boots as she settled into her extended stay hotel "suite" near the campus. She had picked up some top-shelf bourbon on the way back, navigating the snowy landscape with Brandon as they drove past the bars, restaurants, campus buildings and lake front greenspace–now covered in white– to their base camp.

She opened her laptop. Poured herself a neat whiskey while she waited for her computer to boot up. She had been struggling a bit thinking about how closely she should involve Brandon, a newbie but a very capable one, in the next phase of the Wisconsin R&D tax project.

Scott Woodson was a likable guy, someone to be admired for his entrepreneurial achievements in building a small business success story in Madison. Shawni liked the entrepreneurial class, guys and gals who take risks to start up small businesses and eventually, with many struggles, soul searching, financial pain and sheer blood and sweat, see them grow and thrive. All of H-BIS' member companies were either small start-ups or bigger enterprises that long ago started as a small business. Shawni admired them all.

Organic food and tattoos may not sound like a business empire, but the way Woodson marketed and managed them, they produced significant earnings–and income. Woodson had said he was even toying with the idea of expanding his business into other markets like Minneapolis or Chicago. Shawni had no doubt that if he did that, he would be successful.

That's why what was to come next felt troubling to her. But she had orchestrated these kinds of scenarios many times. It came with the job. A job she was very good at, and for which she was paid extremely well. Compared to where she would have been by now as a public-school music instructor, well, there was no comparison. Her income would set her up for life, even two lifetimes, at a relatively early age.

Shawni knocked on Brandon Abram's door next to her room.

"Hey. You there?"

"Yeah, just a minute," he answered as he was trying to find the remote to the TV to get some sports highlights from ESPN.

He opened the door. Shawni stood in the hallway.

"Come on over to my room after you get settled. I want to have you start in on something with me."

It was time to get down to business.

.....

The ride back to the Norwalk city limits was anything but a serene evening drive. Destiny Diggs had a thousand questions, and only a few minutes to ask them before arriving at her daughter's daycare center.

"What the heck did I just see back there?" she asked, still a bit stunned.

"Well, like I tried to explain, it is the core facility for producing hybrid spores that, when processed further with certain applications you have yet to see, can mitigate or even cease cell proliferation that is the crux of cancer."

"But...how did you build that place? And why there, in the middle of nowhere?"

"Well, reason number one; it's close to where I live and work, so I can go there almost anytime I want. Reason number two; the land and location cost me nothing. Can't beat that, eh? And reason three, and probably the most pivotal: it's a great place to do research and pilot-stage production that can be kept secret. No one is going to mosey around an abandoned grain storage silo. Especially one that requires driving on miles of dirt and gravel to get to."

"So you built it at no cost? Tell me how that works."

"I am an entrepreneur who is very fortunate to have a very generous business partner. He is an investor who is funding this entire operation. Therefore, he owns a majority of any future earnings this whole project may produce. Emphasis on the word 'may.' There are a thousand things that could happen to make this venture go sideways or even put us out of business."

"So may I ask who this investor is?"

"Yes you may, and I'll have to decline giving you the answer. At least for now. Secrecy is so vital here; I want to protect you and him.

63

I've sworn to keep this completely confidential. I have to uphold that trust."

"Then why did you bring me here tonight?"

"Because we're reaching a critical threshold here. You've been involved in one part of this project: connecting with the patients in our trial and tracking their progress. Obviously you've known something incredible is taking shape with these people. And it is. And you deserve to know more. And you'll know even more in the weeks and months ahead. But I would again beg you to keep this confidential, the biggest secret you've ever kept in your life."

"I think I can do that, but...."

"Destiny, you have to pledge to me you *will* do that, not *think* you can."

"OK, yes. I will keep it completely confidential. But why? Doesn't the world need to know the breakthrough you're making? I mean, we are talking a cure for cancer, aren't we?"

"That may be, but I try not to use that term. We need to see how long-term health plays out among our trial patients. Can cancer return in 3 years? 10 years? 20 years? Beyond any side effects we may not yet know about, that is the biggest test. But morally and ethically, I cannot wait that long before scaling up our production and making this compound widely available. If this can alleviate cancer, even in the short term, I have to do this."

"Yes, I understand. Of course. But again, why the secrecy?"

"Because, for one, I have no patent. If my formula and process get into the hands of a large drug company, they can reverse engineer it overnight and start producing this in short order. Which would be fine except my investor partner needs to get his money back. And that won't happen if someone swipes our invention away from us. When we're ready to scale up and take off the restraints, I'll let the world see how IH-3314 is made after I gain a patent, which will be in force for 20 years. After that, if someone else wants to produce and brand IH-3314 completely on their own, they can do so."

"I guess that makes sense."

"Another reason is that I want IH-3314 to be affordable. I know we can produce it and sell it at a price nearly all people and insurance companies can easily pay for. That is hugely important to me. Yes, I want to generate a good income on this and be able to pay back my investor several times over. But I don't need or want to get filthy rich on this. If a conventional drug company gets a hold of this, you know they will price this out of the stratosphere. Heck they're doing that now with insulin and other basic drugs that have been around for years. I've got to maintain economic control of IH-3314 so as many people as possible get it."

And after that short chat about the plan to change the world, they pulled up at Jack Sprat childcare center, right next to Norwalk First Baptist Church, on the perimeter of the leafy Norwalk City Park, where Shay had been playing with Legos, waiting for her mom to pick her up.

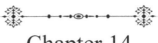

Chapter 14

Brandon and Shawni sat at Shawni's laptop. They had both drank a small glass of bourbon and talked about Scott Woodson. Brandon was being forced to get used to a regular bourbon or scotch; his college regimen of cheap beer and an occasional hard iced tea or premixed margarita was not appropriate in the world of high-stakes Washington-centered health finance and policy.

He watched her power up the laptop then log in with her fingerprint on the touch screen. All the conventional icons appeared on the screen: her MS Office suite, podcasts, social media accounts, i-Tunes, Netflix, even her own Neiman Marcus shortcut.

Shawni sat there for two minutes, not clicking anything on the screen. In fact, Brandon noticed she did not have a mouse connected to the laptop. She just sat there in her stocking feet, extremely skinny jeans and T-shirt, waiting.

Then, the screen went dark. Ten seconds later, a virtual private network icon appeared on the center of the still-dark screen. The icon was a wavy lavender and gray spherical shape, no text, and had a moving animation and slight, low humming audio signal to it, something Brandon had never seen even though his college life was controlled by a laptop.

Shawni gave a voice command. "Crosby Stills Nash," she said clearly and a bit slowly.

The icon turned from lavender to green and produced an audible ping. Command accepted.

"What just happened?" asked Brandon.

"This is my virtual private network. Absolutely untraceable. I am the only person at H-BIS that can access this," said Shawni. "Now shut up for a couple minutes," she said, smiling and winking, to her young apprentice.

A male voice spoke from the laptop. It sounded like a younger male but was obviously distorted to provide extra secrecy.

"Greta?" the voice inquired.

"Yes, I'm here," answered Shawni, now using her digital alias. "How are you Lonnie?"

"Fine. What have you got for me?" asked 'Lonnie' in a slight British accent. He always got to the point quickly, trying to minimize any exposure to any potential outside digital observers. Although hacking into the CIA's covert files was likely more feasible than doing so with Shawni's VPN.

"Name is Scott. P as in principal. Woodson. Residence and businesses in Madison, Wisconsin, USA. Businesses include Woodson Organic Foods in the Madison area and Northern Tattoo and Piercing. Both businesses have multiple locations. Banking is at Madison State Bank."

"Got it."

"How long to queue everything up?"

"48 hours. Maybe sooner."

"That'll work. I'll get the crypto to you within the hour."

"Works for me. I'll await your trigger."

And with that, the chat ended.

"Hey, now you really have to tell me. What the actual fuck just happened?" asked Brandon.

"I can tell you more after I get into my Ethereum account. Gotta get this done now. Lonnie is a stickler for fast pre-payment. All I can tell you right now is Senator Scott Woodson will be our good friend in a few days, I'm confident. I don't want to freeze my ass off in this Wisconsin winter any longer than I have to."

…..

Destiny unlocked her upstairs apartment door and headed to the kitchen with Shay. Tonight would be mac and cheese with some peas and broccoli mixed in. Shay was on a tight budget, but that didn't mean she had to bypass decent nutrition, both for her young daughter and for her own athletic health profile. She could probably eat anything she wanted, as her training regimen could efficiently metabolize any diet with room to spare.

And now her head was spinning, still processing what she had seen just an hour ago. Was Dr. Eckoff truly on the cusp of a health revolution in fighting the most vexing disease known to humankind?

Destiny grabbed a cold bottle of herbal tea from her refrigerator and looked out her living room window and gazed at the Christmas lights of Norwalk. She lived in a comfortable but small unit a block off the town square. She was contrasting the facts, as an able data analyst would: The fact that right here, where she lived one floor above the office of a local CPA firm, 100 yards from a small-town bar where a few college rowdies were always whooping it up coming out from last call; where farmers came to the local Farm Credit office across the street to line up their loans for seed, feed and fuel for the upcoming planting season; where women bought and sold consignment dresses, jackets and slacks–and where Destiny was an occasional customer if anything her size ever came in–just across the square; and where, just a block behind her, a thriving style salon served middle class women wanting a color treatment or a frizzy perm; where a microcosm of small-town life everywhere was carried out every day, a medical breakthrough that would change the world and save lives by the hundreds of millions was taking shape, maybe even nearing completion.

She was trying to process the enormity of it all.

How could Dr. Larry Eckoff have possibly kept this under wraps for so long? How could 1400 trial participants have kept their miraculous news from exploding around the world? It boggled the mind.

When she was studying high school biology and math in Waterloo, Destiny had never dreamed she might be involved in such a global health revolution. She was just proud to have survived the pressure of maintaining public high school grades that would be good enough to get accepted to college and even qualify for a scholarship.

Her family had not gone wanting while she was growing up. She lived in a warm, loving home, had all the support she needed to pursue her education, had a fun life outside of school with friends of all ethnic and social stripes. But there had always been the dim but ever-present specter of racial inequities: the promotions that her father either never got or had to struggle to get at the farm machinery factory while his white colleagues moved steadily up the ladder; the looks she alone would get from store employees while shopping at the mall with her white friends; the ignorant whispers she would hear after winning her event at track meets, owing her victories to being Kenyan or Nigerian, even though she was an 8th generation American.

Just going to college and preparing for a solid middle-class career had been her constant dream and that dream was taking shape now, even with a young daughter who suddenly entered her life. But with a mentor like Larry Eckoff, knowing what he was embarking upon, what would her career and life hold in store? Whether she liked it or not, she was along for the ride. The biggest question now for the budding science data analyst: Where would it take her? The lights of pastoral Norwalk shined brightly.

Chapter 15

The outer industrial ring of Zurich was brimming with manufacturing plants, machine tool shops, metal and plastic fabricators, chemical companies, transport depots, rail hubs, every variety of commercial production and distribution one could imagine.

One this unusually warm, misty late winter night, a new BMW EV sport sedan pulled up to a corner parking space of a vast warehouse that stored countless eight-level-high racks of chemicals used in all manner of manufactured goods, from packaging to textiles to kitchen and bath fixtures to drugs.

A slightly built young woman exited the car, her pale skin starkly contrasting her long black hair and the liquid black body of the BMW. Ursula Halgren pressed her small key card against the reader on the door and entered the cavernous structure. Down a long corridor past the myriad rows of racks, she entered a small private office at the opposite corner of the warehouse, one of only two offices, and the only one that had a window.

Ursula Halgren took a small, thin laptop out of her backpack and placed it on her desk. The computer quickly powered up, and instantly linked into her private Wi-Fi router no one else in the warehouse, with its digitally-powered inventory control system, could access.

She began scanning the posts on Centrifuge, where she had created a digital sidebar folder for all posts discussing this astounding tumor-reducing compound. Several more posts had appeared since she last checked it two days ago.

She was especially intrigued by a post from someone who seemed to be a medical professional talking about his patient's experience. *Neck tumor reduction. Complete eradication. Patient refuses to discuss substance and treatment program.*

The post originator seemed to be located in the States. Halgren was quite certain of this, but needed proof. Ursula had created Centrifuge as a way to monitor global health discussion in an unfiltered but controlled way. She insisted on anonymity and confidentiality in managing the content of the site. But she also had controls for who could participate. Her screening protocols would let only respectful, literate contributors participate. No quacks, trolls, hucksters, promoters or flame-throwers. Any contributor who broke those terms would be removed from the platform immediately and permanently. Trying to re-enter under a new identity would not work, as Ursula had assembled proprietary tools that could detect user device codes and keep them off.

But now, she was mulling the need to break her own terms of anonymity. This would be a breach of a highly valued ethical standard she had always adhered to.

Yet she knew the cost of inaction. If this rogue player who was gaining momentum in the world of cancer treatment was not identified and confronted, the worldwide healthcare industry was in peril. The normative global order of severe disease, which operated smoothly albeit at extraordinary economic price tags, would implode.

Ursula got up from her desk and headed toward a compact marble counter, unsealed a plastic package of ramen noodles, added a little of her bottled water to it, and popped it in the microwave under the counter.

As the ramen was heating up she went back to her laptop, gazing out the window at the murky, damp night in a fog of deep contemplation. She slowly called up a special dashboard on her laptop, one she had created but never used before, and typed the user's device code in the upper corner of the screen.

The shrill microwave timer alarm sounded. And she hit ENTER.

.....

The marimba-sounding ringtone of Scott Woodson's phone rang. He was deep into the business of the Wisconsin senate finance committee, with his legislative colleagues gathered round an oak conference table in a thick-carpeted committee room in the vast chambers of the state capitol building. They were just finishing their luncheon of chicken and turkey wraps, baby carrots, chips, brownies and iced tea. And, of course, cubes of Wisconsin's finest white cheddar.

Woodson looked at his phone. The caller was from H-BIS. The senator knew he should take this call, and with the committee taking a short break after lunch, this was a good time to do so.

"Hi, this is Scott," he answered as he walked out of the committee room and went toward a small cove in the hallway.

"Hi senator. Shawni Phillips here from H-BIS."

"Yes, Shawni. How are you?"

"I'm fine, senator, and I again want to thank you for meeting with us last week."

"Was glad to do so, Shawni."

"Senator, I just wanted to check in with you as I understand your committee is meeting sometime today to hopefully discuss the R&D tax bill, and I hope you…"

Woodson interjected, "Yes, Shawni, we're meeting at this hour, actually. Yes, we are discussing the bill. I brought up your discussion with me from last week and highlighted the points you made. While the committee is sympathetic to some extent with your industry's views, the clear majority of members, including several from the minority party, agree that the revenue potential and the important needs that would be funded from passage of this bill take priority. And I agree."

Woodson was fibbing just a tad. The committee was actually closely divided on the bill, and no minority members favored it. If the bill received a committee vote today, it might pass, but just barely. And if it went to the full senate, the vote would also be close, but would likely pass.

"Well, I'm sorry to hear this Senator," said Shawni, fully expecting such an answer. "I guess I'm not surprised, but just wanted to hear it from you that you are firm on your position."

"Yes I am Shawni. I am recommending we mark up the bill and take it to the full senate for a floor vote early in the session."

"I've got it, senator. I appreciate your honesty and directness. Anything else we might be able to do to change your thinking on this? Again, just gotta ask."

"Certainly, I'd let you know if there were, but I think this is a pretty straightforward issue with clear positions from our members."

Shawni paused for a few seconds.

"Well senator, you have my number if anything changes. I'll be in Madison for a few more days and am glad to talk more if need be."

"I appreciate that, Shawni. Take care and all my best to you."

And with that, the call ended. Shawni now moved on to the next step, firmly planted in her mind. She had done this a dozen times, all with necessary, effective and traceless results. This was not her preferred way of doing business. But the world was too complex, too politically charged, too rife with quick-hitting disruption and uncertainty to continue with the genteel, diplomatic ways of a bygone era. Besides, her soaring financial livelihood depended on results. Results needed to happen fast, and therefore, expediently. Lonnie, with his brilliance, his cloaked tools and unending reliability, expensive as they were, would be ready.

…..

Scott Woodson pulled into the driveway of his modern Wisconsin log cabin home. They weren't real logs, just wood veneer siding sculpted to look like rustic, rich golden logs, with all the chemical treatments to keep the termites away. His homestead wasn't considered an acreage, since his nearest neighbor was just 30 yards away. But he lived in a bucolic, forested setting that gave the feeling of a woodsy, rural getaway while being a half a mile away from the nearest Applebee's.

The senator was a bit weary from a long day on the hill, and eagerly grabbed a bottle of organic craft beer from the fridge and slowly poured the contents into a tall pilsner glass.

He settled into his favorite faux leather chair and turned on Sports Center to see the latest scores and highlights, knowing that the Badger basketball game against Purdue would start in 20 minutes. He was a big college sports fan, and cherished the fact that his businesses thrived, in part, from his advertising on the digital display ribbons at UW's Kohl Center and at Camp Randall Stadium. His business patrons, bankers, employees and legislative constituents loved that he was so closely aligned with Wisconsin athletics.

He was taking a long sip from his foamy brew when his phone rang.

"Hello. Mr. Woodson?"

"Yes, is this Jay?" Jay was the afternoon and evening manager at Woodson Organic Foods' east Madison store. The store closes at 8 p.m., about a half hour from now. Jay was one of two managers for the location, a 28-year-old who also ran the social media platforms for all of the Woodson stores, except the tattoo stores. That required a passionate specialist who could talk body piercing and tattoos and the culture surrounding them.

Scott Woodson found it strange that Jay would be calling him at home at night. That might have happened one other time in the past 5 years, when freezers and coolers went out from a blown fuse during an electrical overload in a nasty 35-below cold snap in Wisconsin.

"Yes, Mr. Woodson, it's Jay. Sorry to bother you at home, but I thought I should contact you right away. We've got a huge surge in negative posts and reviews happening right now across Facebook, Google My Business, Instagram, Yelp. We're talking tens of dozens of posts just in the last half hour. I was checking our accounts and started seeing a few appear. Then it started snowballing. Really freaking me out."

"Well, it's just a spam attack, right? Anyone could spot a spam flurry right off the bat."

"I don't know. This is really bizarre. The original posters are all discrete individuals, not the same poster trying to troll us. The time stamps of the posts are spread out, like they started this morning, even though they didn't because I check the sites throughout the day."

"Well what are they saying?"

"Everything. Complaints about spoiled, out-of-date lettuce, dirty bathrooms, rude treatment of customers, you name it. And they are not repeating complaints, copied and pasted across platforms. They all appear to be genuine, with genuine user profiles. It's just crazy."

Woodson started rubbing his temples. Wisconsin was on a 13-0 run against Purdue, with Woodson Organic Foods advertising zipping around the digital ribbon in the arena, clearly visible on his 4K TV. But Woodson was oblivious to it. He was locked into his phone with Jay, pulse rising, face reddening, respirations quickening.

"What do we do about this?" asked Woodson, his voice slightly quaking.

"I don't know. We could post a message on our pages stating that we're being trolled and to not pay attention to the sudden swarm of negative messages you're seeing. Except this is more than trolling. This is something else. Like an attack or something."

"Well let's do that. Say that this is a coordinated campaign against our stores with no known origin, and that we're committed to the customer service and product quality we've always delivered to Madison shoppers."

"Ok, give me a few minutes to post this on all our pages. Then I'll see what I can do to contact those social platforms and ask them to intervene and block these flamers."

Woodson hung up and put his phone down so he could rub his temples while staring at his faux-log ceiling. Who the hell would start an attack on his company? Why, and why now?

He downed the rest of his beer, then went to the kitchen and pulled out a bottle of Jack Daniels. He treated himself to a hefty pour over some ice, then went back to his TV chair and his phone.

After a few minutes of watching the end of the first half of Wisconsin/Purdue, he got on his phone and went to the Woodson Organic Foods Facebook page to see the comments for himself.

Before he could even begin searching the comments, he was thrown back in his chair, the result of a sudden mental jolt; a post on his Facebook page, in large white font with a dark gray background appeared:

WOODSON ORGANIC FOODS WILL BE CLOSED INDEFINITELY DUE TO STAFF AND SUPPLY SHORTAGES. WE LOOK FORWARD TO SERVING OUR CUSTOMERS AGAIN IN THE NEAR FUTURE.

The senator, now feeling helpless and desperate, checked Instagram. Same message. "Closed indefinitely." In fact, the Yelp algorithm had changed the status of his business to "Closed."

He went to the Northern Tattoo pages. Same thing. Marked as closed. Terrible attack comments on all the pages. One Facebook posting, identified as originating from the business, showed a dick pic, with a caption touting the idea that a lot of sex apparently happens in the back rooms of Northern Tattoo and Piercing. Of course, he knew the Facebook police would soon be on his case with warnings of suspending his account, if they gave warnings at all for lewd images.

Woodson was now frantic. Though he rarely got involved in social media or posted anything on his pages, he had admin status for the rare instance when he might want to post something. And this, most certainly, was that rare instance.

He fumbled his way to the new message tab and wrote, "Northern Tattoo and Piercing is open for business as usual, with our regular hours. Our page has been severely hacked. Please ignore the bizarre and disturbing comments and posts that are appearing on this page. Thank you. Scott Woodson, owner."

He posted the message. In ten seconds it disappeared.

He tried deleting the dick pic post. Success. But then it reappeared in 10 seconds.

He called his friend, Elliott James, at home. Elliott owned several Quik Signs stores throughout the area. He had a long business relationship with Elliott.

"Elliott, can I ask you for a massive favor? My stores have been hacked throughout all of social media. This is more than just pranks or mischief. I mean, someone is trying to take me down. Can you help me please?"

"What? What do you mean? Who would be doing that?" asked Elliott.

"That's it. I don't fucking know. Not a fucking clue. But I've got to act fast. I've got to jump on this shit, and I mean do it now!"

"OK, OK. What do you need from me?"

"I need 8 large banner signs by tomorrow morning. Nothing fancy. Just big and bold. Signs I can hang outside each store that say 'Open For Business. Today And Every Day.'"

"Sure. Let me look at something real fast." Elliott paused for several moments. "Holy shit!"

"What?!! What are you doing? What's going on?"

"I'm seeing Google ads on my browser. Facebook ads, too. They're saying...let me see...'Woodson Organic Foods proudly refers you to Whole Foods for your online and retail shopping. We have enjoyed serving you!'"

"Oh my fucking god!" cried Woodson. "That's what I'm talking about. You have to help me!"

"Fine, fine. I'm with ya. I'm gonna call a couple guys into the shop right now and we'll start cranking on this. We'll make them big and bold and have them ready to go before sunrise. You want to see the layout when we get the design?"

"Shit no! Just do them! I don't want to hold anything up. I trust you."

"Right-O. Full speed ahead. Man, I'm sorry this is happening. I can't even imagine who or what is doing this. I've never...."

"I know, I know. It's insane. But it's real and getting worse. I've gotta figure out how to stop it."

Chapter 16

Ed's Electronics, in the Adams Morgan district of Washington D.C., was a nice two-mile walk from Ron Holtzman's stylish Georgetown brownstone. This Saturday morning in late January, he would take the walk to Ed's while stopping at a pastry shop on the way and enjoying a leisurely coffee and croissant while he read the Washington Post on his phone.

Only this time he left his phone back at his townhouse. Deliberately. Today, he would have to buy the print version of The Post, messy and weird-looking as it was in this hip patisserie. But Ron did not care. He was one of the most powerful healthcare executives on the planet. If the hipsters thought it quaint that a fit, trim, nearly middle-aged handsome male was reading an actual newspaper, well, he was glad to entertain them.

He finished his pastry and coffee and continued his walk to Ed's. He could take his time and walk at a moderate pace. His wife and son were on a day-long mission of shopping for clothes and supplies for his son's entry into the winter semester at the University of Virginia. Jake Holtzman had completed high school in two and a half years, and was eager to start his pre-med studies at UVA.

Holtzman arrived at the store on this brisk sunny day and went straight to the cell phone displays. He was scanning the wall for burner phones. A young male employee offered assistance and Holtzman had only two questions he was glad to ask: "What is the least expensive model that will allow me to call Europe with as little fussing around as possible, and how will my burner number get generated?"

"Easy. Here's the phone you want." He pointed to a plain, black flip phone with a monochrome digital display for phone numbers and limited texting only.

"This has all the European country codes and international calling pre-loaded. You'll get 30 minutes of combined phone and text time. Your calling number will be automatically generated by the phone in a menu before your first call. Or you can enter a desired number to see if it's available. Your choice. Price is $49.95."

"That'll work," said Holtzman.

They proceeded to the checkout station. Holtzman gave him $60 cash with no change needed and declined the receipt.

The walk back to Georgetown would include a quick stop in Rose Park.

…..

The Saturday morning foot traffic at Woodson's Organic Foods in east Madison was a bit lighter than usual, but still good. The coffee and light breakfasts being served in the back quarter of the store attracted their usual customers. Employees were stocking shelves with newly-arrived inventory. The produce aisle looked healthy and colorful as always.

Scott Woodson stood outside the entrance under the big bold "Open For Business" banner, greeting customers as they came in. Some were asking him about the weird Facebook posts and ads they had been seeing. These were mostly customers who looked to the Woodson Facebook and Instagram pages for the weekly specials. Woodson explained how the business had been hacked, but that they were working on it. And he would run radio ads, maybe even some local TV spots, to fight back. This would cost him some serious money that had not been budgeted in his financials. He'd probably take on some additional short-term debt to cover it. But what else could one do?

Scott Woodson would make the rounds of all of his stores, today and tomorrow, to do the same thing. Greet customers and talk with them. Get the real facts out so they could see and hear for themselves that Woodson's food and tattoo stores were open and thriving, just as always.

As business was flowing relatively smoothly for this Saturday morning, Nel, who was running one of three web-powered payment stations in the front of the store, came outside, walking quickly toward Woodson. She looked distressed.

"What's wrong?" asked Woodson, who could see some urgency in her eyes.

"Our payment system is frozen," she said, her voice slightly elevated.

"What do you mean frozen?"

"I mean the screen is stuck, right in the middle of a customer's checked order. It simply won't proceed with the transaction any further. All of the screens are doing the same thing."

"Have you tried a system reset from the checkout screen?"

"Yes! Multiple times. Nothing happens!"

"Let me reboot the wi-fi."

Woodson walked briskly into the store, where lines of customers had now formed in front of the checkout machines. He jogged to the small office in the back room of the stores, behind the walk-in cooler and adjacent to the pallets of organic wine and beer.

He reached up to the wireless router, whose array of indicator lights seemed to signal the router was working fine with full internet connectivity.

He hit the power switch on the router and watched the LED lights go dark, waited 30 seconds, then hit the power switch again. After two minutes, all of the lights were back on in full function mode. He jogged back to the stockroom door, swung it open and yelled to the front of the store, "Is it working now, Nel?"

"Noooo!" she shouted.

Woodson's heart was now beating hard and fast. What the fucking hell was going on? It was bad enough that his good customers had to witness him shouting back and forth to his staff across the entire store. Obviously, everyone knew that something was very wrong, and the buzzing throughout the store grew louder. But to have his businesses suddenly in total paralysis. It was surreal. A nightmare that won't be over in a couple minutes.

He walked quickly to the front of the store and began making an announcement in a loud, commanding voice:

"People, people. I'm truly sorry but we have a problem with our computer system that looks like it's going to take some time to fix. I am going to have to close the store while we work on it. But please, any items you currently have, please feel free to take them with you."

Several customers did just that, walked right out the front door with their free stash of organic onions, milk, cake mix, artisan bread and ground beef. But many were sympathetic and put their shopped items back on their shelves and in their coolers.

Woodson continued, "I would also like to mention that we welcome your shopping at any of our three other stores that are all…."

Then his phone rang. He grabbed it out of his corduroy pants pocket.

"Mr. Woodson, it's Sam over at the campus store. Our checkout screens are all frozen. We can't process any payments…."

Woodson's legs grew wobbly. He grabbed the ledge of the meat cooler and steadied himself before sitting down on the floor in the middle of the aisle, cross-legged. Nel and the staff showed the remaining customers out of the store and locked the front door.

…..

Spending several winter weeks in Madison, Wisconsin was not as bad as Brandon Abrams had imagined. There were great bars and restaurants that appealed to a young man starting his new career. Arts and entertainment offerings were plentiful, even in the winter, especially when you could put it on the employer's expense account. The university community was large and active. In other words, there were plenty of ways to pass the time while waiting for the legislative process to creep along. And, working on a project or two back at headquarters was not a problem with the great broadband connectivity in a Big 10 town.

But Brandon Abrams, outstanding student, hardworking staffer, never cheating on any test or assignment throughout his academic career, was trying to understand what he had witnessed in the hotel room of his mentor for this project. Despite his considerable skill in digital marketing, research and finance, he had never seen a cyber transaction, if you could call it that, like he had seen several nights ago. Who was Lonnie? Why the disguised voice? Why no basic details of what was being arranged? It was like the whole thing was in code, but not binary code. It was abbreviated English language code, in which both parties knew exactly what they were agreeing upon, yet no outsider could begin to decipher the conservation.

Brandon was a single young guy with no steady girlfriend, no casual partner, certainly no spouse or fiancé. He couldn't call anyone to talk through what he was seeing and feeling. Except maybe his mom and dad. But that would never happen as Brandon was proving himself to his parents, making them proud. He wanted to be conquering the world in their eyes, not questioning what the hell he was getting himself into. Not after they had so strongly supported his very costly education.

Today was another meeting with Senator Scott Woodson. This time the venue would be a table in the cafe section of his Woodson Organic Foods campus location. He had told Shawni he could not break away from his store, as things were in chaos at the moment. He would give them five minutes. Ten at the most. Shawni had only been able to get this meeting because she had told him she had a compromise his committee, and the full senate, might be interested in.

The H-BIS team opted to walk to Woodson's store this morning, only a half mile away. And the winter temps this week were mild for Madison in the winter. Snow was actually starting to melt.

They passed students on their way to class, at least the classes that were not online or Zoomed this semester. The sun and the favorable temp seemed to make everyone a bit more energized and jovial, not suffering the normal gray midwinter doldrums.

They entered the store, a quaint, folksy place where a bell jingled as they walked in the door. Past the shelves of organic peanut butter, gluten-free chips and sampling trays of jams and cheeses, they spotted the senator at a small table at the coffee and pastry bar in the back corner. Customer traffic in the store was minimal; no one was at the cash register. Store employees were stationed up front with mobile, card-only payment handsets, running off the store's cell phone data account at great expense, since wi-fi was now very shaky. Woodson and an IT services firm had set up this system over the weekend to keep the businesses open while the web-powered checkout stations were out of order. Such emergency measures were driving up Woodson's debt load, tapping out one line of credit and creating the need for an emergency line of credit from Madison State Bank.

Shawni and Brandon knew his time was short. They seated themselves and were prepared to get right to the point. But that would never happen. A simple hello and greeting triggered an anguished outpouring from the senator.

"Hi senator. Good to see you again. How are things?" Shawni chirped cheerily.

"How are things? I will tell you how things are. My entire business has been hacked. And I don't mean simple mischief. I mean there is someone or something out there trying to put me out of business. Permanently. My social media is being hammered with trolls. Day and night. I'll probably just have to shut down all of my accounts. There's an online advertising campaign basically announcing that all of my stores, foods and tattoos, are out of business, directing people to Whole Foods. Can you believe that shit? My checkout system and cash register have all been knocked out. I've got teams of IT people charging $150 an hour–per person– trying to get workarounds on my payment systems so we can stay open. Or at least try to stay open."

Woodson was nearly in tears, shaking his head, looking stunned, not understanding how or why this was happening. Days of fighting this crisis were taking its toll.

"Who would do this to me? What have I done? Who did I wrong? I'm just….just….so fucking confused. But life goes on and I'm continuing my senate business. At least I have that. So anyway, I've taken up three minutes of the five minutes I told you I had."

"Well, senator, I'm so sorry to hear this. I had no idea this had been happening. I can only imagine how terrible this is for you and your staff," said Shawni, slightly dramatic and not all that empathetic.

"Thank you," said a now slightly confused Woodson.

"I hope you can get things back to normal, and if there's anything I can do to help, I'm glad to do so. Your business is a big asset in this community, I'm sure."

"Well how do you think you might be able to help," said a now suspicious Woodson, "because I'm all ears."

"I'm not really sure, but in my job, I know many people in the technology community who might be willing to get involved and do a favor for you. If you want them to. I'm sure they've seen it all when it comes to cyber security and systems disruptions."

"Wait, wait, wait. You're talking as though you're somehow familiar with this whole catastrophe," said Woodson, who was now alarmed and a bit more distressed.

"What?" said Shawni, feigning slight surprise. "Oh no. I'm just offering some assistance. I had no idea what all has happened or what a solution might be."

Brandon maintained a stoic expression on his face, not looking at anyone, but staring at the barista getting coffee for the only customer who had placed an order in the past 30 minutes. His face was getting slightly flush, but he stayed motionless and distant.

"What might the price be for your 'friends' in the technology community to come to my aid?" asked Woodson sternly but softly.

Shawni leaned a little closer to Woodson and also spoke in a hushed tone. "Well I can't speak for them, but I'm sure they would be willing to offer their help for a minimal cost, if any at all."

Woodson's anger started stirring in his voice and his breathing. "How would you even know that?"

"My business peers have always been very supportive of me and my pursuits. I'm confident I could count on them to help you. Of course, they would know of your important role in the Wisconsin legislature and how your work impacts millions of people. That would be impressive to them, and probably make them all the more eager to be of service."

"It can't be...You can't be...behind all this? Because of that fucking R&D tax bill? Did you do all this??!!" Woodson's voice was getting louder. The few customers in the store were now taking notice of the battle brewing at the coffee bar. Woodson could see Shawni was not vigorously defending herself against such an outrageous claim.

"Do all what? Please, senator. I know you're upset and going through a rough time, but..."

"...Rough time?" Woodson screamed "My company is on life support! If you think you can extort me to pass your goddamn bill, you're out of your mind!! Who are you people??"

Woodson sprang up out of his seat and threw the small, round table to the side, cracking the granite top and nearly shearing off Brandon's kneecap.

"Get out!! Get the fuck out of my store, you fucking piece of shit!"

Shawni wanted to get in one last piece of dialogue. "Senator, I'm sorry we didn't get around to discussing the topic we came here to talk about, but I'm always glad to..."

"...Get your fucking ass out of here!! Now!!

Shawni and Brandon walked quickly through the aisles and out of the front door.

They walked briskly across the parking lot to the sidewalk that headed past the east campus. Not a word was uttered.

Brandon could not hide the fact he was visibly shaken.

"I'm sorry you had to witness that," said Shawni. "I might have a cigarette or two in my bag if you want one."

Brandon was still speechless, staring at the sidewalk, his head slightly lowered.

"Normally, these discussions are more subdued," said Shawni as she fumbled in her purse for her own cigarette, "but this one got a little intense. I wanted you along, so you could get a read on what's currently in process."

"In process?" Brandon asked incredulously. "We are digitally shutting down this guy's life."

"Brandon, it's called politics. Bare-knuckled politics. And H-BIS plays the hardest of hardball. We have to because we are in an industry that saves lives, every second of every day. Our members have to have the kind of business environments that will allow them to excel. To keep saving lives. More lives. To improve quality of life. You think the healthcare industry could thrive or even survive if the scores of dumb fuck lawmakers out there who know nothing about medicine or science could get their idiotic bills passed? Bills that bleed taxes from companies and hamper new discoveries? Bills that dictate how machines are designed and made, and kick the engineers and biotechnologists who actually know how to do this stuff to the sidelines? Regulations that make health insurance impossible to manage? Rules that are passed only so some shithead lawmaker with an 8th grade education can beat his chest at his campaign speech at the Bumfuck County Fair? We've got to fight these assholes. Every hour of every day. My mother's cancer treatment that saved her life would not have been invented years ago in the small lab in central California if the state legislature had their way in demanding no animals, even rats, be used in testing. We've got to identify who's blocking the progress of medicine, and convince them to back off. We're not killing anyone, just influencing them in terms they will understand. Unfortunately, some have to experience a little adversity before they come to their senses."

"Well, it looks like he's not buying, no matter what we did to him," said Brandon, who was now calmed down.

"I'm pretty sure he'll come around. We're not done yet," said Shawni with a slight chuckle. "Come on, let's get some early lunch."

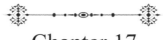

Chapter 17

Another crisp, clear night in Norwalk, another trip to the abandoned grain elevator far outside of town. Larry Eckoff, Ph.D, and Destiny Diggs pulled up outside of the old structure just as they had before. Except this time, there was a late model Jaguar SUV parked there, too.

"Whose is that?" Destiny asked.

"That car belongs to the only other person on earth who knows about this place and what's inside," said Eckoff. "The chairman emeritus of Landmark Nutra Science."

"You mean Harold McLandry?"

"Yes, I do mean Harold McLandry."

"What is he doing here?"

"You remember me telling you about my investment partner?"

"That's him?"

"Yes it is. He has total access to the facility, as he should."

"Are you sure I should be here?"

"Yes, you should. He'll be fine with it. You've seen the raw material production side of this project. Now you need to see how the final product is created–the little vials of the tincture you've been giving to our trial participants."

Destiny's eyes showed her nervousness and confusion.

"Why am I...."

"Calm down and let me explain. You're smart, you're reliable, you're great with people. You've been wonderful in helping me with this project. And now you need to know that the trial phase of this project is ending.

"But I was counting on...."

"Don't worry, you'll still get paid for the semester. No problem. But now, I'd like you to think about a new role I have in mind for you."

Eckoff cut the conversation short as he scanned his key card. The massive door slowly opened and the two entered the underground pavilion, red lights glowing over the circles of dirt and the growing, life-giving fungus.

"Hello Hal. Are you here?" Larry called out in the dark, damp air, the hissing of computer-controlled misters going off every couple of minutes.

A door along the side wall of the cavernous growing chamber opened. The lithe, tall frame of Harold McLandry walked through it, his mop of silver hair reflecting the red lighting.

"Hi Dr. Eckoff!" Larry shouted from a distance. McLandry always liked to call his Ph.D. colleagues doctor at least once during a given conversation. For him, it was a sign of respect for the highest degree of scholarship one could achieve in a given field. He never took that for granted."

"Looks like you brought some distinguished company with you," said McLandry.

"Yes indeed," Larry replied.

Destiny Diggs was feeling a bit woozy, suddenly being in the company of a business legend, long known throughout the state and the Midwest, and encountering him for the first time in this facility that looked like it belonged on another planet. The fact that he appeared to know who she was and that she would be here tonight made it all the more surreal.

"Destiny, meet Harold McLandry," said Larry, an extra note of pride in his voice. "Harold, this is Destiny Diggs."

The two shook hands. "Destiny, I am glad to meet you. Dr. Eckoff has told me all about the valuable work you have been doing on this project, and the especially wonderful way you have been taking care of our trial participants."

"I'm glad to…to…meet you, too, Mr. McLandry," Destiny said shakily. "I'm not quite sure what I'm doing here tonight but I'm still amazed at all this. It's like nothing I've ever seen."

"Don't worry about it, Destiny," said McLandry. It's perfectly natural to react that way. I was also a little overwhelmed when I saw this place in action for the first time. And I even saw the building plans."

"But how have you kept this under wraps for so long? I mean, someone had to know about this. Like, maybe the construction crews who built this?"

"Oh, they knew about it, alright. But we told them this was a growing facility for food-ingredient mushrooms. Which it is. But not the kind of ingredient anyone could imagine. So they forgot about it pretty quickly. And everyone who came within a quarter mile of here had to sign an NDA and keep their mouths shut. We also did the build-out at night to keep the trucks rolling in and out of here out of sight during the day. Told them we wanted to do it this way so we'd stay out of the way of farmers' grain trucks taking their corn and beans to coops during the day. And we paid a pretty penny for overtime labor. But it was worth it. Plus, we're in the middle of nowhere, so we don't have to submit zoning plans or anything. We can build what we want. And we did."

"That is just amazing…"

"…Well don't get too amazed just yet because the real whizzbang stuff happens on the other side of that wall," said McLandry.

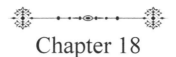

Chapter 18

The morning in Rose Park in Georgetown was sunny but cold. That was fine with Ron Holtzman. He was sure this call wouldn't take long. The burner phone he had just purchased had 30 minutes of time on it, and he would be surprised if that call lasted half that amount of time.

Holtzman pulled out a SIM card from his wallet, one that provided highly advanced encryption for all voice and data received on the burner phone. It would also generate random phone numbers for all calls, so whomever he called, or whomever tried to monitor his call, would not be looking at a real phone number.

He popped out the phone's factory SIM card and replaced it with his encryption card. He dialed the number belonging to Ursula that his boss, Turner Mansfield, had given him a week ago.

"Hello," said the young female voice on the other end.

"Hi. This is Ronald."

"Yes. I have updated data for you. I have identified a source in the Chicago, Illinois area, most likely in the south part of the city. I think this is most likely a physician, going by his or her postings. I will be texting you a transcript of their content. I assume you have appropriate encryption on your device."

"Yes, of course."

"Good. Anything else you want to ask about?"

"Yes, can you give me a good guess on where this doctor might be located?"

"My tracking tools have gone as far as Chicago; like I said, probably the southern section of the city. I'll leave it to you to make your guesses on who it might be or where they might be."

"Ok, we'll work with that. Thank you."

With that, they hung up. The text and attachment appeared seconds later. Holtzman would open the document at home. He race-walked to get there quickly.

…..

The door on the wall inside the fungus growing operation could have been an original door of the old grain elevator that soared above the vast subterranean chamber. It was kind of small, no signs or markings, just another red light above it, though this red light did blink every 15 seconds, so that it could be spotted among the phalanx of red lights hovering over the circular growing plots.

Destiny followed her hosts toward the door, walking along the concrete pathways that wove throughout the growing chamber.

Another key card and finger-print entrance pad opened the door, and they walked though.

A brightly lit laboratory greeted them. Sterile white throughout, machines measuring and processing who knows what lined all four walls.

"This is our quality control lab," said Eckoff. "Everything is pretty standard, stuff you'd find in any food or ingredient lab. Except it is very, very automated. Because you're looking at the only staff member for this operation. Me."

Destiny marveled at the sight of the lab in operation. It was much more complex and comprehensive than anything she worked in at Norwalk College. Endless digital displays, data graphics galore, air quality control units, they gave her a feeling of being in a compact, mini-NASA control room.

They talked for a while. After 10 minutes or so, Destiny was sensing the tour was wrapping up. Which was great, because Shay would be waiting for her to pick her up back in town.

"Just one more thing we need to show you, Destiny. If you would, please slip on this gown and shield mask. We all need to be a bit more protected when we enter the activation room."

Destiny was perplexed. There was more? She tied on the loose, sheer gown over her clothes along with Eckoff and McLandry. They affixed the clear, plastic shield masks to their heads and headed toward a vault-like door in the back wall of the QC lab.

After opening the air-sealed door, they passed into a 30' x 30' room. The wave of neon green-yellow washed over them.

Once Destiny was able to regain her vision and re-orient herself to the surroundings, she found herself staring at a large machine in the middle of the room. Eckoff approached the machine. "Let me give you a little demonstration," he said.

Eckoff grabbed a small tray of glass vials. He positioned the tray on a small conveyer that fed the tray into the round opening of the machine, kind of like a miniature MRI unit.

The tray slowly moved into the machine. Some muffled, pulsed bursts of mechanical noise emanated from inside. After 10 seconds, the tray moved on the conveyer out of the opposite end of the machine.

The once-dark glass vials on the tray glowed brightly, giving off a spectacular chartreuse glow. Eckoff took the tray and placed it on one of the shelves lining the walls, where countless other trays of vials were stored. The room was awash in the green-yellow glow.

"What am I seeing?" Destiny said slowly, staring straight ahead.

Eckoff knew she might be in mild shock, so he knew he could give her some comfort by getting immediately to the science. "Destiny, this is where the spores from the fungi we grow and pack into vials next door are fed through this gamma radiation pulse generator. The gamma rays impact the spores in a way that is invaluable in quelling the cell proliferation that is the root cause of cancer. The gamma-activated spores have an uncanny way of finding those out-of-control cells. Once found, the spores can signal immune T-cells and NK cells to come help in vanquishing those proliferating cells. Between the two platoons of spores and immune cells, that tumor or blood-cell abnormality or brain lesion can be eradicated fairly quickly, in weeks usually. The bioluminescence glow of the spores you see in this room wears off in several days, but the bioactivity of the irradiated cells lasts for years. Maybe decades. We don't want to give patients the glowing potion. That would freak them out. After the glow is gone, we mix a bit of alcohol in the spore vial to create a tincture that can be consumed. That's what you've been working with for the past four years. This is IH-3314."

"I'm just stunned," said Destiny. "I just can't believe what I'm seeing. How did you figure out the biology of all this? How did you set up this system?"

"Well, it all started as a hunch. My theory was that cancer and recurring cancer can be attacked in a different way. Why should cell proliferation just appear, and in many cases, appear again? There's got to be a solution. My graduate work was in hybrid wheat. You know that. But I grew interested in hybrid fungus, since I knew from

90

published research that certain fungi can impact immune performance. I worked for years on identifying the right combination of fungal strains that can be hybridized into genetic stacks that would have a superior impact on immune cell activation. The gamma irradiation gives those spores and the instructions they give to immune cells a lasting effect in the body with no major side effects. For how long, we don't yet know. But in our 1400 trial participants, we haven't had a recurrence yet."

"But gamma radiation is a sterilization tool," Destiny aptly pointed out.

"Yes, but we're not directing it on bacteria. We're dealing with spores, a whole different thing."

"Which brings me to the thing Mr. McLandry and I want to discuss with you," Eckoff said. "We have reached a point where we are ready to commercialize this process. Where we can produce thousands of doses a week. We may not need that many at first, but in the future, who knows? And there may be other applications for this bioscience that we haven't yet thought of. Other diseases, other health conditions, who knows? And with this grand plan in mind, we would like you, Destiny, to join us as our first official employee. We would like you to be the operations director. That means working with me on expanding production, getting regulatory approvals, working with outside contractors on legal, marketing, distribution, everything involved with making this into a business."

"Destiny," McLandry interjected, I know you came to Norwalk on a scholarship provided by Landmark Nutra Science, with the possibility of working for my company after you graduate this spring. Well, you could consider this to be that opportunity, only this will be an entirely new company, with Landmark as the original, major investor. We will keep funding the company as our footprint grows, hiring production staff, HR, brand management, IT, the whole ball of wax. And you'll be involved in all of it."

"But why me? You could hire anyone in the world, a Harvard MBA, a biochem Ph.D. from Berkeley."

"And we very well may, down the road. But for now, we want someone who we know well, someone who is highly familiar with what we've done to date, someone who we know is reliable, hardworking and trustworthy. We know that is you. We're starting small. We'll pay you a good salary, but nothing exorbitant. And as we grow, your experience and career will grow with us. That's how I like to run a business. With people I trust, who are motivated to grow with us for the long term. Needless to say, you can skip the internship!"

"I don't know what to say. I'm just overwhelmed with all of this."

"Well we have plenty of time for you to mull it over. You still have to finish this semester after all. But when you're ready, you let us know."

"Thank you. I will. Believe me I will."

Destiny rode home with Dr. Eckoff, asking him a million questions in his car. She was weighing the pros and cons of the opportunity in her mind. And she was coming up with very few cons. There was risk in joining a true startup company. Several of her fellow college students and friends from Waterloo had done the same thing. Some succeeded, others flamed out after two or three years. Working for a startup, especially in its absolute infancy, was risky. The only difference, as Eckoff had reminded her, is that this startup is backed by one of the most successful–and wealthiest– businessmen in the country. He knows a thing or two about building a company.

She also reminded herself she would continue working with one of the most brilliant scientific minds anyone could know. Maybe Eckoff wasn't a leading research luminary. In fact, he was, for all practical purposes, an invisible lone wolf. She had not realized just how brilliant he was until he revealed the entire medical fungi operation to her. It was dazzling. But not quite as dazzling as the unassailable results his research had produced. Time and time again.

"Dr. Eckoff, I have to say, I can't find any reason to pass up this opportunity. This is exciting and I want to transition to this new role as soon as possible," Destiny proclaimed.

"Destiny, that's wonderful. But are you sure? This is all still really new to you. We kind of walloped you with a lot of stuff back there at the facility."

"Yes, I'm sure, Dr. Eckoff."

"Ok, well, let's start slow. We'll put together a game plan over the next month. And your coursework and degree come first. That's the first priority for our 'business plan,'" he quipped.

"Sure. I understand."

"And one more thing," Eckoff said.

"What's that?"

"This is where you now start calling me Larry."

They both chuckled as they pulled off the gravel road and hit the county highway, cruising toward the twinkling night lights of Norwalk.

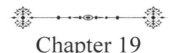

Chapter 19

R onald Holtzman entered the sunlit study of his Georgetown townhouse. He'd have all the time he needed to decrypt and review the document Ursula had sent to him. He connected his burner phone to his laptop, where he could access the phone's message and attachment and transfer them to his laptop file. The burner operating system would retain the files for 12 hours then automatically delete them. It was an extra precaution app he had loaded on his phone, even though the phone's cell calling number was temporary and untraceable, and would disappear when Holtzman destroyed the phone in a few hours.

The decryption only took 45 seconds. After the loading progress bar in the middle of the screen had reached 100%, a page and a half of text appeared on his screen.

Holtzman delved in.

Line after line of symptom descriptions. Observations. Patient descriptions. Journal-like dialog showing astonishment. Questioning results. Frustration and amazement.

How could anyone possibly know where to begin to find the author of this information. The Chicago area has more than 100 hospitals and medical centers and an infinite number of clinics. Even if you could isolate it to the south side, the numbers were still overwhelming.

And then...

"....Patient is the first cph patient to engage in this unconventional treatment plan and present with dramatically diminished symptoms, especially in such a short time frame..."

CPH. Holtzman had been to Chicago many times, collaborating with colleagues and member organizations such as The American Medical Association, headquartered in Chicago, the Illinois Public Health Association and the Public Health Institute of Metropolitan Chicago, among others. He knew the territory almost as well as he knew the world of Washington D.C. and its cut-throat lobbying culture.

CPH could only mean Chicago Public Health and its network of community free clinics. That narrowed the field instantly.

.....

The customer traffic at Wisconsin Senator Scott Woodson's organic food stores was starting to pick up again, although sales volumes were still sluggish and not at all close to volumes prior to the "hack" of Woodson's social media accounts. Woodson had hired a local digital marketing firm to try to contact Facebook and Google so they might intervene and stop this hacking campaign. But talking to a human at these companies was futile. Pleading his case via chat or direct messaging was time consuming, response time was lengthy, and when he did get a response, it was in "digital-eze" language which, to the best of the marketing firm's understanding, simply documented the pathways of the hack in which the sinister content was routed through countless servers and data centers, never to be isolated and shut down. Woodson had tried creating new accounts on Facebook, Yelp and Instagram, but the digital perpetrators were there instantly, as if they were actually waiting for him.

It was a hack of extraordinary technical savvy, and Woodson would not get relief anytime soon.

Woodson had purchased advertising time on local television and radio stations. He had prided himself on building his businesses through savvy social media strategies and simple word of mouth about the quality of his products and services. Paid broadcast advertising, in his mind, was way too expensive and not efficient enough for his business model.

However, a crisis necessitated emergency strategies to stanch the revenue bleeding, so he appeared on the air, cheerfully telling viewers and listeners his stores were open and ready to serve. He even had to offer some free products such as cans of organic cola and beer to provide some extra incentive for shoppers.

All in all, his financial base was shaky but operating, in dire need of returning to normal.

Woodson was helping out at all his stores, primarily because they needed the help as staff reductions had been necessary for staying in business, but also because he wanted his customer base to see him in action, so they would know he was on the job and working his butt off to keep things running.

This morning he was sacking orders at his south Madison store when his smart phone rang. He pulled it out of his back pocket. The display showed it was his long-time banker, Rick Oretano, at Madison State Bank.

"Yes Rick, it's Scott."

"Hi Scott. Say, we need to talk soon. At the bank. Your accounts here have been hacked. Payroll, business savings, money markets, checking. Your personal checking. They're gone."

"What do you mean, gone?"

"They're at zero. They've been drained. Somebody has netted out your accounts to a zero balance. We've got to figure something out. Fast."

Woodson's face instantly blanched. He felt dizzy. He had been struggling to get any sleep at all the last several weeks, was drinking a bit too much, and was overworked, to say the least.

"How the fuck can they do that?" pleaded Woodson. "You guys have security to prevent this kind of shit, don't you?"

"Yes we do, but this breach was highly advanced, something our security vendor had not seen. Ever. We're as perplexed as anyone. I just can't fathom how they, whoever it is, can pull off something like this. It's like ransomware, only worse. There's no message or demand for payment with a promise to restore the accounts. Nothing. It's goddamn baffling."

"Well don't you have FDIC insurance or whatever the fuck that is to back me up?"

"FDIC does not cover digital theft. It's for a run on the bank or bank insolvency. Not for the shit you're going through. It's just fucking crazy."

"Ok, well, I'll just transfer my accounts to another bank and that will stop all this. The hacker won't know where I went. I'll go to Timbuktu Savings Bank if I have to."

"Great, but you can't. You have no funds to transfer. You can't withdraw and redeposit zero dollars. There's nothing there, I'm telling you. We've got to figure out how you'll make payroll and keep your inventory payments ongoing. Hell, we have to find a way to pay your utilities. It ain't gonna be easy."

Woodson sat on the ledge of his storewide display window, staring at the ceiling. The shock was greater than he'd ever experienced. He could almost feel his conscious mind floating outside his body, like a near-death experience. Customers were staring at him as they walked by on the way to their cars.

"Scott," Oretano said loudly through the phone. "Scott, you still there?"

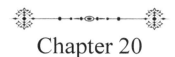

Chapter 20

"I've given Mr. Holtzman everything I've found to date, "said Ursula Halgren. She was sitting in the executive hangar lounge at Zurich Kloten Airport. The hangar and lounge were built, owned and used by one company, Microneutics. And for nearly every flight coming and going from the Microneutics hangar, there was usually just one passenger: Hans Mogen.

Mogen would, on rare occasions, allow a senior executive to fly with him, if the trip was important enough, such as a meeting to close a business acquisition or joint venture. But generally, Microneutics employees, including executive staff, had to make their own travel arrangements through commercial carriers. Besides, Mogen's jet, an Embraer Phenom 100 that could reach a speed of 450 mph and had its interior designed by BMW, a company Mogen considered almost as great as his own, had room for only two passengers. Originally designed for 4 to 5 passengers, Mogen had the interior revamped to accommodate him and one other in complete comfort. Several of the other jets in his fleet could hold up to 10 passengers for when he wanted to fly his family and friends somewhere.

Mogen sipped his orange juice as he awaited boarding, traveling to an industry confab in London, where he would give a keynote speech on modern cancer therapeutics.

"So tell me what you've found," said Mogen, a bit impatiently.

"A lot of dialogue from someone who I strongly believe is a physician somewhere in the south of Chicago, Illinois in the states."

"Ok, how do we find this doctor? And his patient?"

"I've taken it as far as I can. I provide data, not action plans. And I've taken a big risk tracking this private information. If EU data privacy regulators found out what I've been doing, we would be in big trouble. I'm sure Mr. Holtzman will figure out his next steps."

"I should emphasize to you that the bigger risk, to you, me and this company, is the possibility of this underground 'remedy' as I'll call it, coming above ground and into the global health market.

You've assured me that your tracking tools and encryption security are beyond anyone's reach. Am I to continue to believe that?" Mogen was becoming a bit agitated, as was his nature when he sensed he could not completely control methods, processes and, of course, monetary outcomes.

"Of course, but you should consider this: If I continue any further, and right now I don't have the digital assets–technologies if you will–to do that, we risk not only regulatory hell, but the prospect of Centrifuge becoming known to its users as not secure or trustworthy. The platform would lose credibility, users and eventually cease to exist. Right now, I believe I have demonstrated to the company the value of Centrifuge in product and pricing strategy. The company has profited well from the insights I've gathered. Do we want to jeopardize that?"

Mogen did not respond. Closure and niceties were not his bag. He figured Ursula was paid handsomely, so he didn't need to worry about social graces. He gave a slight nod, almost dismissive, swallowed the last of his juice, and headed to the waiting jet. He ascended the short stairway, which closed smoothly and quickly once he was seated. The small but powerful jet taxied a brief distance, turned left 90 degrees for takeoff, and roared down the runway, quickly pulling its wheels up and climbing sharply into the winter-blue Swiss sky.

.....

Chet Hunter rolled out of bed to the ringing of his phone. It was noon on a Saturday. He had been sleeping soundly since 3 a.m. Another corporate event in Crystal City, VA, had gone way too late. But that didn't matter. He had been hired to provide discrete security for the senior executives and their discrete escorts, who had taken over the top floor of a 5-star boutique hotel to "celebrate" the birthday of a Saudi royal family member who had made a significant investment in their neural implant device company. Such events happened more often than the average person could ever imagine. Sometimes they involved members of Congress or the Cabinet.

Hunter was good at his job. Reliable, skilled, inventive and committed. That meant he stayed on site for the duration of the event. Because of his reputation for performance and results, he had built a very solid client list. He had come far from the early days of starting his private security business, when he rented small studio apartments and the only assets he had to his name were a cell phone and a 17-year-old Lexus sedan, which looked much nicer than it ran. He had invested nearly everything he had saved in his new business, so he could front the cash needed for travel expenses, secure, encrypted equipment, a sufficient wardrobe, gym memberships to stay in fighting shape, and leases for SUVs for client transport.

He knew his craft, having served in defense intelligence posts and several years in the Secret Service on advance teams and guarding presidential families. To look at him, one would never know he was a highly skilled, experienced security professional. His 5" 8" frame supported 161 pounds of lean muscle, topped off with a head of curly, floppy brown hair and a diamond earring stud. He looked 21, not his actual age of 35.

Though Hunter could confidently and smoothly put potential adversaries twice his weight on the ground with one hook to the side of the head or a straight-on throat punch, there really wasn't much demand for that. Instead, he dealt mainly with logistics, threat assessments, site scouting, and any corporate data that could directly or indirectly lead to a vulnerability. As did many intelligence and Secret Service operatives, he had an undergraduate degree (history) from a reputable university (William & Mary), and an MBA from Johns Hopkins. But he did not want to end up on Wall Street or in a corporate management position. He wanted a career that would put him in the field away from a desk and laptop.

Today, he rolled out of bed in his Alexandria, VA, Cape Cod-style home to see the incoming call displayed as "Holtz," a nickname he had assigned on his phone contacts list to longtime client Ronald Holtzman.

"Are you up for a trip to the Windy City for a few days?" said the voice on the other end.

"Wherever you need me, my man. When?"

"How about now?"

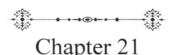

Chapter 21

The lobby in the main branch and headquarters of Madison State Bank was what one might call a modern northern plains look. Lots of rustic brown and deep maroon, polished cherry wood flooring and doors combined with minimalist office furnishings, a bit of dulled chrome trim and modern LED lighting fixtures.

Scott Woodson entered the bank, head slanted downward, walked past the lobby into a hallway off of the corner, and down to a stairway that led him to a second-floor executive suite. He walked briskly past the waiting room and into the office of senior vice president of business lending, Rick Oretano.

Oretano was on his phone, but quickly wrapped up the call when Woodson sat down at his small conference table.

"Scott, hi. Any coffee for you?" Oretano asked.

"Yes, please. The whole pot would be great."

"You got it. And I want to bring Jim into our meeting. He'll have some helpful thoughts to share."

Jim was James F. Everson, Madison State Bank president. Woodson had met Everson a couple times, at a charity golf outing and some forgettable holiday party for the Madison Chamber of Commerce.

Everson walked into the office, a tall, silver-haired, man of 60 or so, blue blazer, white collared shirt and dark gray slacks, every bit the stereotype of a patriarchal Midwestern banker. Sitting next to Scott Woodson, tattoo shop and organic food store owner, decked out in organic wool slacks, Timberland shoe-boots, and a mustard-yellow quarter zip sweater, made for quite a contrast. Everson's family had started the bank in the 1940s, as the Depression was coming to an end. The bank took risks in its early years, helping rebuild Madison's economy after the war by lending to many local entrepreneurs who wanted to get their foothold in the post-war economy. But starting in the 60s, the bank grew very slowly and carefully, extending credit only to local businesses and families with solid collateral and financial histories. The bank was not really interested in supporting start-ups. How

Woodson got his business lending account set up was kind of a mystery. With him being in the legislative leadership circles, especially his chairmanship of the senate finance committee, an exception was probably made, the loan covenants slightly relaxed.

Everson started right in, sparing no small talk. "Scott, we're glad you're meeting with us today because we have some serious developments to summarize for you and you have some decisions to make." Woodson wasn't surprised to hear this; he knew this would not be pleasant. But it still kind of shook him to hear it put that way.

"Your accounts here have been depleted now for 4 days. We apologize for this happening, but we have no solution in restoring your balances...."

"...Why can't you simply input new dollar figures into my accounts?" Woodson interrupted. "Just put $100,000 into my operating capital. Just type it in. Heck, whoever hacked my account just typed that in. Only it was a string of zeros. Your computer won't know the difference."

"Scott, our computers don't work that way. To return those balances to your account, we'd have to take those funds–and they are real funds, not just digits on a screen–out of other accounts. And of course, that would be fraudulent. Our clients would instantly know that, and state bank regulators would eventually know it. We'd be in huge, huge trouble."

"How about just giving me a new line of credit. Just a lifeline. You know my business has been stellar in making credit payments and managing cash."

"We'd do that in a heartbeat, except we did that already."

"What?"

Everson continued, "We set up three new test accounts in your name. Used $5000 from bank reserves to populate the accounts. Within 20 minutes each account was again zeroed out by the hacker. Until the financial software security industry makes some major advances, we can't combat this. Whomever is doing this is gunning for you, and you only. Do you have any clue why?"

Oretano then chimed in, "Scott, there are two choices that it's come down to. Either shut down the business right now to stanch your losses that continue to pile up every hour of every day, and hopefully save your credit history. Or sell the business, where you can gain at least some value from your years of invested equity, although, under the circumstances, you'll get a very meager valuation and price. In fact, you should probably do both. Close down now. That will gain you some time to find a buyer. We can help with that."

Woodson buried his head in his hands. He knew the scenario would be difficult but not this dire. His entire livelihood rested on what he would decide.

"How long do I have?" he asked as he looked up and regained eye contact with his financial overlords.

"We can go one more day. Maybe 36 hours. But that's the limit."

"Let me talk with my staff."

"Ok, but I'm not sure what more they could offer. This predicament is such it almost makes the decision for us," said Everson quietly.

Woodson, of course, knew who he had to talk to. And it wasn't his staff.

.....

"We may have found the trouble spot," Turner Mansfield said, talking on his mobile phone from one of three stone and brick patios outside his palatial country home on his Chevy Chase, Maryland estate.

"Good. Can you tell me where?" asked Hans Mogen, riding in his Land Rover SUV limo from Heathrow's business jet terminal on a rainy afternoon.

"I assume you already know it's in Chicago, on the south side. We are in the process of finding the exact location and person of interest. But I need to know, what are the plans going forward? We will hopefully find this physician, their patient, and even the scientist who's producing this material. But what then?"

"We'll arrange for some discussions to happen. And we'll assemble leverage points that can get this damn thing under control."

"What leverage points? And what does 'control' mean?"

"I have to confer with others on that, but it will all be discrete and harmless. Bottom line: I'm not going to allow some third-rate chemist to eviscerate my industry…and a good chunk of yours. And I do thank you for the work you're doing to help us. This is great information and I look forward to getting more results."

This was the most generous and complimentary Mogen had been in a long time. To anyone.

For Mansfield, the surcharge he would receive from Microneutics for this "special project" would be significant. He was happy to keep the investigation going.

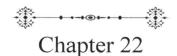

Chapter 22

Brandon Abrams finally had started working up a sweat. After 20 minutes of light machine weights with ample repetitions, he had now moved to the stair machine, set at a moderate pace. It felt good to work out for a half hour or so. Nothing too intense.

The university's student rec center allowed non-students and non-faculty to use the facilities on a paid day-pass basis. And it was a grand place. Weights, treadmills, yoga studios, smoothie bars for as far as the eye could see, all color coordinated in Badger red and white. And that was just the second level. The ground level showcased two Olympic-sized pools, a primo diving hall, and a rock-climbing wall that soared into the atrium's late-afternoon sky.

Brandon felt fortunate this rec center was only a couple blocks from his extended stay hotel, which featured a small room with four stationary bikes and two treadmills, with a low-def TV always tuned to CNN.

His phone rang as he hopped off the stair machine and wrapped a red and white striped towel around his neck. It was Scott Woodson.

"Hello Senator Woodson, this is Brandon Abrams," he said, not knowing if Woodson, who had exchanged phone numbers with him from their first meeting in the bar, would even remember his name.

"You can call off the dogs now. I'm throwing in the towel."

"I'm sorry, what are you talking about? What dogs?"

"Don't play coy with me, buddy. I know what you've been up to, completely eliminating my financial livelihood. Destroying my bank accounts."

"Senator, really, I'm not in a position to know how to respond to…"

"…Well you had better know how to respond because that partner of yours with her pretty face and fancy clothes won't return my calls. Ever. I don't know what tricks you guys play to get your way, but this was way, way over the top. You've destroyed a business, injured a long-established community bank, not to mention hurt dozens of my employees. You tell her I'm done with her and her shenanigans. She wants that bill stopped, I'll do it. Tomorrow."

"I'll pass that message along to her, but I'm really sorry if all this stuff is happening…"

"….IF??? What do you mean IF?! You guys have put a knife in my gut, waiting for me to bleed out. OK, you win. Tell her that. And watch my statehouse web page. I'll announce the end of this bill ASAP. Just stop what you're doing and restore my life."

Woodson hung up abruptly. Brandon walked slowly to the shower room, again stunned at what he was witnessing and what he was, undeniably, a part of.

…..

Chet Hunter spotted the sign. "Emma Robertson Public Health Clinic,' a block and a half from where he was standing in the bustling neighborhood of Bronzeville, a southside neighborhood in Chicago. Emma Robertson, now age 95, had for decades been a tireless social worker and public advocate for quality healthcare in the struggling parts of Chicago's south side. The years of cajoling and shaming city aldermen, the mayor, the Chicago Public Health board members who used their board seats for political and business leverage rather than the public purpose they were appointed to serve, had paid off eight years ago, when the clinic was finally built. The facility was modern but far from dazzling: a single-story brick structure that housed numerous observation rooms, 4 X–ray rooms, a large lobby with 5 admissions clerks and a functional urgent care clinic.

Chet had practiced his character and script to perfection before he began calling on all of the 13 free clinics on the south side three days ago.

Today would be his next to last shot as only one more location existed that he hadn't yet visited.

Dressed in khaki slacks, half-height Timberline boots and a tweed wool winter coat, he wanted to look respectable and presentable, not dapper, projecting the impression of a young man who could pay the sliding-scale clinic fee if needed, and not be completely dependent on public subsidies. His thick frame black glasses, shaved head and fake goatee seemed weird to him, completely unnatural. But to someone who did not know him, his appearance could pass for any grunger or hipster who lived in a major metro area.

Hunter entered the clinic's lobby and waiting room. He waited 15 minutes before an admissions clerk was freed up to see him.

"Hi there. How can I help you?" asked the clerk a bit dismissively.

"Hi. I'm here because I understand there is a doctor here who has been seeing patients that are using some alternative treatments for cancer. I was just wanting a brief discussion to see if I might qualify for that kind of thing. You know, something new that might work and not wipe out my bank account."

"I'll have to check with our medical director. I have no idea who that might be. In the meantime, do you have ID and an insurance card I can copy?"

"Got the ID, Social Security card. No insurance. That's why I'm here. But honestly, I do have the ability to pay some fees, if it comes to that." As he was talking, Hunter produced his counterfeit Illinois driver's license, belonging to a smart young chap named Randall Thorson.

"Alright Randy, let me call our medical director. By the way, any consultation with one of our health professionals is $45 dollars if you're not on Medicaid."

"Do you take cash?" asked "Randy."

"Of course we do."

And with that, the clerk called John Hixson, M.D., and asked if there was a doctor on staff who had been working with cancer patients taking alternative medicine.

"Well, yes, just one. I recall Dr. Hernandez had a patient who was undergoing some wild treatment that we knew nothing about. Wouldn't tell us what it was, how they got it or from whom. It's been a couple months. Haven't heard back from them since."

The clerk thanked Dr. Hixson and then called Dr. Luis Hernandez. Hernandez said he'd be glad to talk with Randy, but there wouldn't be much he could tell him.

The clerk then turned back to Randy Thorson.

"Dr. Hernandez said he'd be glad to talk with you, but there's not much he can share with you. He can see you in an hour or so."

"Great, I'll just wait here in the lobby. Thanks so much," the charming Randy Thorson replied. Chet Hunter then took his seat in the lobby, silently giddy that he may have struck gold.

Chapter 23

T he Wisconsin state government web page of Senator Scott Woodson was now updated with a "Message From Sen. Woodson To Constituents" headline at the top of the page.

Woodson knew this would create about 24 hours of chaos in the statehouse and in the senate chamber. But he had to post it.

He had already endured a near-shouting debate with several of his senate finance committee members. Those who were adamantly supporting SB-57–eight of the 15 committee members–had erupted in astonishment and anger when Woods announced in the morning committee meeting that he could not support the bill and would not introduce it to the full senate for a vote in this legislative session. The remaining seven members stayed silent, also surprised, but gleeful that this bill was dead. They could boast to their voters back home that they had heroically fought tooth, fang and nail against the bill and assured its demise before it even got out of committee.

Several members begged him to hold off and give them some time to edit the language or add amendments that could save it. Some had privately told him they would entertain the possibility of pushing for a new committee chair to replace him, or even throwing him off the committee altogether. But their efforts were for naught.

This afternoon, reporters from the Wisconsin State Journal, Milwaukee Journal Sentinel and several state government bloggers and TV pundits, would repeatedly ask hard questions on why he pulled an about face on this issue. And he had to answer them all – as best he could.

He would repeat, in his disciplined style, the main points of his Message to Constituents:

"As Senate Finance Committee Chair, today I'm announcing the withdrawal of our bill proposal, SB-57, from further action by the committee. This was a difficult decision as this bill would have raised significant new revenue for the State of Wisconsin to help fund many areas of state and local public services such as education and infrastructure. These services have been lacking in the past 20

years, and I truly thought SB-57 could help get our state back on track.

But as I talked with my district voters, and with the health and technology leaders around the state, I became convinced that SB-57 could do more harm than good. Wisconsin has built a wonderful, advanced health and technology business base, with cutting edge research and development spurring our state's growth and high quality of life. A new tax burden on these businesses would hamper such growth over the long term, creating bigger problems beyond year-to-year tax revenue totals. I became truly convinced that Wisconsin would forfeit a considerable segment of these companies and their outstanding sourcing of high-quality jobs and family income to other states, even other countries. I could not let that happen.

I know this will disappoint many Wisconsinites who were looking forward to the benefits of the new revenues to be generated by SB-57. I hope you will stick with me and my senate colleagues as we continue to look for new sources of revenue for our state and our critical public services.

As the posting appeared on the page, Woodson called Brandon.

Brandon Abrams answered.

"It's done," Woodson said sullenly. And he hung up.

.....

"How did this happen?" asked Rick Oretano as he looked at the computer monitor in his Madison State Bank office. "What changed?"

"Tell me what do you mean? What happened?" the senator answered, driving home from the capitol in his late model Jeep.

"Every one of your accounts at the bank has been restored. Some may even have a few more dollars in the account than before."

Woodson suddenly felt a massive weight lift from his chest and gut. But it wasn't as dramatic a feeling of relief as it might otherwise have been. The head of the state's teachers' union had stopped him in a capitol hallway an hour earlier and gave Woodson some quietly-stated hell for suddenly squashing a bill that educators and school boards were counting on to raise school district budgets. Road and bridge building lobbyists had also expressed major disappointment, in person and through emails. Even the lieutenant governor, not a

109

powerful woman in state politics, but a very popular one and someone who would likely run for governor next year, expressed her surprise. In total, lawmakers and leaders in his own party were seemingly aligning against him, and for good reason. Woodson was starting to be convinced that running for another term in the senate was probably futile. But he wouldn't make a decision for several months. The general public wouldn't give a shit about this legislative pirouette. If it makes the local news, the issue would be out of sight, out of mind in 12 hours. But the state government insiders and party leaders would remember for a long, long time.

"So tell me what the hell happened, Scott?" asked Oretano again.

"I'm at a total loss, Rick. I'm still trying to process all of this, especially who or what could have had it out for me so badly that they would do this. Sometimes I wonder if I was chosen as a random test subject for some wildly sinister new technology."

"The way they were hammering you and your entire asset base, I doubt it. My recommendation is that we change your account numbers right away. We'll also look at other steps with our IT team that we might take for extra security."

"I'm not only changing account numbers," said Woodson. "I'm changing my bank." He abruptly hung up. There was no way he would come remotely close to letting this happen again. If he could help it.

…..

"Looks like we won." Shawni Phillips was texting the boss as she was packing her suitcase ready to head to Dane County Regional Airport for a connecting flight to Milwaukee, then to D.C.

"Fantastic!" texted Ronald Holtzman. "How did the bill get defeated?"

"It never made it out of committee."

"Whoa! Now that's impressive!"

"Well, as charming as the Upper Midwest is, one month of winter is enough. I'm ready to get out of Badger country."

"We'll have a celebration dinner at your favorite Italian place waiting for you when you get back."

"Don't forget Brandon. He did a great job."

"Yes he did. Just make sure he likes Italian."

"He's a greenhorn. He'll like anything we tell him to like!"

110

As that conversation ended, Brandon texted to Shawni he was parked at the front entry, ready to head out.

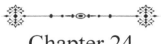

Chapter 24

Chet "Randall Thorson" Hunter heard his name called in the waiting room.

"Randy? Doctor Hernandez will meet with you now."

Randy got up and headed to the hallway door, thanked the nurse who summoned him and followed her through a labyrinth of halls until they arrived at a small, sterile-white office. Dr. Luis Hernandez was sitting on his exam stool, looking over some notes.

Thorson entered the room and Hernandez got up to greet him.

"Hello Mr. Thorson. I'm Dr. Hernandez. I understand you have questions about a cancer condition."

"Yes. And thanks for seeing me on such short notice."

"Certainly. And what kind of cancer are you dealing with?"

"Well, I haven't exactly been diagnosed. Not yet, anyway. But I feel like a mass may be growing in my abdomen and I understand you may have some information about alternative treatments, if I do indeed have a cancer condition."

"Well, that's a lot to unpack right off the bat. Let's back up a bit. Why do you think you might have an abdominal mass?"

"I just feel this lump from time to time. And some slight pain once in a while. That pain is getting more frequent."

"How frequent?"

"Oh, maybe twice a day now. It used to be about once a week."

"Do you mind if I do a quick manual check?"

"Sure. Go ahead."

Hernandez had Randy lift his shirt while he put on fresh latex gloves. He had Randy position himself on the exam table and lie down.

"How severe is the pain when it comes? Like 1 is no pain and 10 is agonizing pain."

"I don't know. I'd say maybe like a 5 or 6."

"Hernandez probed the front and back of Thorson's upper and lower torso. He was fairly impressed with his taut abdominal muscles and lean shoulders and lower back. As he applied pressure, he got no pain indicators from Thorson.

"What do you do for a living, if I might ask?" said Hernandez.

"Right now I'm between jobs but I'm hoping to get on at FedEx pretty soon. I'm in the background check phase, so who knows, I may be back here for a physical and drug test pretty soon," Thorson said jokingly.

"I've gotta tell ya, I'm not feeling anything. Which doesn't mean anything at this stage. What we really need is a CT scan to see if anything abnormal is happening in there. But before we can do that, we need to get you registered with the clinic. All that red tape stuff. But if you get on with FedEx, I'll bet you'll have benefits that will get you all the medical services you'd ever need."

"Yeah, I'm really hoping so, but I'm still kind of frightened that if it's cancer, my finances will be bled dry."

"Well, I think it's way too early to be worrying about any of that," said Hernandez as he returned to reading his notes. "It says here that the original reason you came here was to ask about alternative cancer treatments. How did you come to be interested in that?"

"Well I'd heard that you may have worked with someone who's had some big-time positive results with some kind of alternative treatment. Like a cure or something."

"How did you come to hear that?"

"You know, just word of mouth. Friends of friends of friends kind of thing."

"Well you haven't even been diagnosed with anything, so there's not really anything I can help you with right now. Unless you get that CT scan and we can see something there."

That right there gave Chet "Randall Thorson" Hunter the clear sign he had found the doctor Ron Holtzman needed. He had not denied the vague story that he might have engaged with a patient who was experiencing a miraculous remission.

"Yeah doctor, thanks for that. I'll have to think about it a while, see what happens. But can you give me the name of that patient taking the cancer treatment. I'd like to just talk with them."

Hernandez was getting uneasy with Thorson. Too many questions. Too vague about his problem, his life. If he was indeed having abdominal pain as he said, he should at least express some basic interest and even urgency about getting it diagnosed. Whether he paid the nearly zero billing rates of the free clinic or had it covered under his FedEx health plan, cost would not be an object. Thorson was too casual about all of this.

"I can't provide any details or any information at all about the patients we see. I'm sure you know that."

That was the capper for Thorson. Dr. Hernandez had seen such a patient. That's all Thorson needed. Just for the heck of it, he tried to push further.

"Yeah, but I'm just wanting to talk with them to see where they got their stuff."

"Sorry I can't help you pal. I've got to get to other patients right now. Let the folks know up front if you want us to check out your abdomen further. I think it'd be a good idea. And, no charge for this session."

"Not even the $45 the receptionist said I needed to pay?"

"Whoops. My bad. I guess I can't overrule clinic policy."

With that, Hernandez left and walked toward a new exam room for his next patient visit. That was a wasted 15 minutes, but at least there was very little cost involved, just some latex gloves and his public-clinic-salary time.

For Chet Hunter, it may have been the most valuable 15 minutes he'd experienced in a long time.

…..

Destiny Diggs looked through the notebooks full of pictures from rat lab testing of IH-3314. She was home on a later winter evening in Norwalk, a time of year when the sun was starting to stay up past 5:30 p.m., giving some hope for the spring that would be coming soon. When the high school basketball and wrestling tournaments were happening in Des Moines, that was a great sign that spring was not far off.

The pictures under the "Intervention" section of the notebook showed scores of rats in the "before" stage of their short lives. The stage before healthy rats were chemically induced with carcinogenic compounds that spurred rapid tumor growth showed rats that looked normal. The "after" pictures showed the same rats exhibiting horrible-looking growth in their abdomens and necks. The "outcome" section of the notebook showed that rats looking healthy again, having been given IH-3314 and experiencing the reduction and eradication of their tumors.

In another notebook, pictures of healthy rats dominated the front of the notebook. In the back half of the notebook, the same rats, two weeks after injection with IH-3314, looked just as healthy. In other words, the animal model experiments showed IH-3314 to be extremely effective in mitigating cancerous tumors in rats. But it was also safe, as healthy rats injected with the spore tincture appeared to have no serious adverse health effects.

Nearly two million Americans are diagnosed with cancer every year; around 18 million worldwide are diagnosed each year. And that's just the documented diagnoses. How many more cases in developing countries go undiagnosed?

Eighteen million doses of IH-3314 multiplied by $2000 per dose. That's $36 billion. Each year! And, in Destiny's mind, if testing among healthy people could show a preventative effect, where taking a dose of IH-3314 could greatly reduce or even clinically eliminate the risk of cancer, the financial profile for IH-3314 would be incalculable.

Destiny continued to ponder the enormity of it all, and how her future would be linked to Dr. Eckoff and his extraordinary science. As she watched Shay play with her Legos on the floor of their small apartment living room, she pictured her daughter, in the not too distant future, practicing her band instrument or doing her pilates in a not-so-small basement studio, plushy carpeted, huge floor to ceiling windows looking out on vast green and golden fields, elegantly lighted, with the furnishings and accouterments she could only dream of now.

Was she working for someone who was on the level of Einstein? Someone who had created something on the order of nuclear fission? Of Edison and mass electrification? Of Flemming and penicillin? The thought was staggering.

But before she could get totally lost in such dreams, Destiny had to start learning, implementing and managing the many operations and plans required to make this incredible science a reality. For openers, there were manufacturing plans to be drawn up and activated. Mass production of the IH-3314 tincture. Constant testing and quality control. Pricing strategies, labeling requirements. Marketing and distribution plans. Navigating the regulatory hell that was sure to emerge. Patent and trademark procurement. Legal and liability protection. The list was endless. And daunting.

But for now, everything had to be kept completely secret. And now Destiny completely understood why. If Dr. Eckoff's life's work grew to be widely yet prematurely known, the people, events, laws, regulations, politics, and elements of greed that could knock it off course or even ruin it were countless. Destiny, Eckoff, and McLandry. The Three Musketeers must stick together.

…..

"Dr. Luis Hernandez, employed at the Emma Robertson Public Health Clinic, south Chicago, IL, USA. I'm fairly certain this is our guy with the special patient," Chet Hunter texted in encrypted messaging to Ron Holtzman. Holtzman heard the ping on his phone, the special sound that alerted him to highly important messages.

"Thank you. We've got it for now. Will be in touch if more consulting services are needed."

Holtzman didn't like to be too literal in his texting, even if he was utilizing encrypted channels. One couldn't be too cautious when deploying unconventional strategies to influence the commercial global health complex.

After ending the texting with Chet Hunter, Holtzman immediately forwarded the thread, still encrypted, to Shawni Phillips. No introductory message was needed. She would know what to do.

…..

Shawni Phillips received the text alert ping as she and Brandon were deboarding the plane at Reagan National Airport in Washington. She could have taken the private jet that was at the disposal of all H-BIS senior executives, but she did not want to do anything to call attention to her or her work, especially on such sensitive matters that required unorthodox solutions. The more conventional and down to earth her actions and methods appeared, the better. Except, of course, for her "western Barbie chic" fashion.

She read the text, walking by the duty-free shops on her way to meet her Uber. Later, when she could break out her laptop at home, she would contact "Lonnie" for another assignment. Minimal language, basic data. That's all it would take. But there would be some unique instructions for this consultative engagement. Those unique, action-oriented opportunities were what made her job so rewarding.

Shawni arrived at her three-level condo in the Adams Morgan area of D.C. She thanked the Uber driver then strode up to the front door of her 19th century remodel, something she had painstakingly worked on for several years. Her home was next to a brightly painted, extremely narrow building housing a vinyl record shop that also sold some questionable CBD products in the back parlor. Shawni could afford to live almost anywhere in the National Capital area, but loved this neighborhood because of its bohemian vibe. She was not buttoned up D.C. She was not state dinners and embassy balls. She was singer/songwriter folk rock, love beads and rosemary-infused bread. And she was the wealthiest flower child in the tri-state area.

She dropped her large suitcase in her master suite, poured some bourbon over one ice cube, turned on the Tom Waits Spotify channel over her super high fidelity wi-fi speakers, and opened her laptop on her dining table.

After keying in her encrypted code for her Tor dark web browser account, she moved to a direct messaging channel connecting her to Lonnie.

"Need help with Dr. Luis Hernandez, physician at Emma Robertson Public Health Clinic, Chicago, Illinois, USA. Looking for any patient file(s) in the past year involving someone reporting significant cancer tumor reduction or even eradication. Patient using unknown alternative treatment."

After a two-hour nap and a couple hours watching Washington Wizards basketball on TV, her phone pinged with Lonnie's response: "Marypat Hammond. 2120 Jackson St., Chicago, IL."

Shawni immediately sent the response to Ron Holtzman, along with her comment: "I think we have a Bingo."

Chapter 25

Destiny, Eckoff and McLandry caucused in McLandry's office, rolling out preliminary blueprints of a new manufacturing facility. The architecture and engineering firms contracted to create the plans had been painstakingly vetted to make sure no legal, moral or ethical blemishes appeared on the profile of their key personnel. Even an unpaid parking ticket might raise eyebrows. All persons involved in the creation of plans had signed a highly restrictive non-disclosure agreement (NDA) which forbade them from talking about the proposed project to anyone outside of their project teams; no other employees at the firm, no vendors they might involve, no spouses, partners, kids, relatives. No one.

And even then, the Eckoff team had not fully explained the functional goals for the new business and facility. Same as when the current growing facility was built. For all anyone knew, this was just a new health food ingredient to be sold to energy bar and protein shake powder brands. "For added immune support" was the tagline.

The secrecy was necessary because risk of allowing any detail of this project to slip into outside hands was too great; Only Eckoff, McLandry and now Destiny understood the mission; to greatly reduce or even eliminate the suffering of cancer victims worldwide, and do so at a cost that would not financially ruin any patients and families.

The planned facility was to be built in either central Iowa, or Rahway, NJ. The New Jersey location would be a good one because it is in the heart of the U.S. pharmaceutical industry. Top talent from some of the biggest, most scientifically advanced companies in the medical field would be available there. And one could guess that a number of those scientists, production managers, engineers, distribution specialists and accountants would love to escape their corporate bureaucracies and join a true start up with limitless potential.

On the other hand, Iowa offered relatively cheap land and plenty of it. Iowa farms were being sold every day, converting into residential neighborhoods or commercial business parks. The research and business talent from nearby state universities was not insignificant, but not nearly on the scale of the east coast. Transportation and logistics gave Iowa the advantage, with the crossroads of Interstate 80 and Interstate 35 and thriving UPS and FedEx air operations all just a few miles down the road. Legal and patent/IP expertise was not an issue at all; that could all be done remotely from anywhere in the world.

The physical production of IH-3314 would be a bit tricky. For now, growing operations for the fungi spores could continue at the hidden rural location, with final processing and packaging taking place at a new facility. But as demand and production scaled up, a new grow site would need to be built. As would a research facility, scaled for a future in which various spore combinations and hybrids could be tested on other disease classes, creating tangible, real-world breakthroughs.

All of these plans and decisions were a bit overwhelming for Destiny. But the excitement seemed to cancel out that feeling.

"Seems like we could break ground soon. Maybe within the next six to 12 months?" said Harold McLandry.

"Sure seems like it to me," said Dr. Eckoff. "The question is when do we announce to the world that we're launching this business? And how do we do it in a way that won't have people stampeding the plant, demanding IH-3314 on the spot for their terminally ill child or wife?"

"We don't, at least not ourselves," said McLandry. "That's what large public relations firms are for. They know how to communicate on a global scale and in a way that will allow us to do business in a planned, orderly and profitable fashion."

"You mean put our dreams in the hands of scheming PR flacks who don't know a freaking thing about our science? No effing way!" said Eckoff.

"You're watching too much TV," said McLandry.

"I haven't watched TV since I watched reruns of Gilligan's Island when I was 9 years old. I've been kind of busy, ya know."

"Ok, Ok. I'm just saying there are professionals far more experienced than we are who know strategy, timing, message consistency, media management, all that stuff that we don't know.

Believe me, they can keep the public at bay while we have the time and space to do our work. We don't want to be getting calls from reporters or activist groups at 3 a.m. every night. Let them handle it. And besides, I'll bet I know your favorite character from Gilligan's Island."

"Yes, you got me. The Professor. Ok, I'm with you. But still, it's too early to start scouting PR firms. We can't let anyone have access to IH-3314 plans and data at this stage."

"Roger that, Larry," said McLandry.

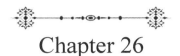

Chapter 26

Marypat Hammond exited the Chicago Bronzeville L-Train 35th St. station in the 6 pm darkness, as she had been doing for years, five days a week, reading material in hand along with some true crime podcasts loaded on her phone.

The old station, opened in 1892, was a staple in her life. The train was her lifeline to her job at a large consumer loan company in the South Loop in the city, not far from the Field Museum. There, she parsed data and analyzed loan activity. She was good at her job, knowing she would never have an employability issue for the rest of her career.

Today, the three-quarter mile walk from the station to her apartment would be a bit more joyful. The harsh Chicago winter was starting to recede, daylight was lasting longer, and she was, for all she knew, cancer free. Months had passed since her treatment, and she was feeling better than she had in years. Her once prominent tumor seemed to be a relic of the past. She was still sworn to secrecy with this treatment. Who knows? If Dr. Eckoff eventually discovered that another dose of the spore solution was needed at some point down the road, she wanted to make sure she would still be included in the trial, and not jettisoned because she violated the confidentiality agreement.

She entered the front door of her four-unit apartment house on a tree-lined street. She opened the main entry door, which tended to close very slowly due to its new pneumatic door closing arm.

Up two flights of stairs, she unlocked the two deadbolts of her apartment door, put her backpack on the kitchen table, turned on the floor lamp in her small living room and hung up her coat on the coat rack.

A sharp knock on her front door slightly startled her. But a couple of her neighbors knew her pretty well and she could rightly assume one of them was there to ask if her cable connection had gone down like theirs had, or if she could feed their fish while they were out of town for a couple days.

She opened the door to find a nice-looking young man standing in the doorway. Black skinny jeans, black hiking boots, black wool winter coat, tussled but stylish dark hair, and kind but penetrating eyes.

"Pardon me, I'm sorry to be so intrusive but you're Marypat, right?" the man asked softly, slightly embarrassed.

"Who are you?"

"I'm Randy. Randy Thorson. A patient of Dr. Hernandez. He said you have received a cancer treatment…something really new and amazing…that produced remarkable results but that he didn't have any more information on it, but that you might, if you would be willing to talk. I'm kind of in the same boat you are…or were. I'm desperate to find the same medical miracle you have, and…"

"Leave now!" Marypat said firmly and loudly. She knew Dr. Hernandez would never give her name out, let alone any clue as to where she lived.

"But I just wanted to get a simple…."

"I said leave now! NOW!" Marypat was now yelling and threatening to call 911.

She slammed her door shut. Before she could turn the first deadbolt lock, Chet Hunter turned the doorknob and slammed his body against the door, opening it, ripping part of the door frame loose and pushing Marypat onto the floor. She quickly got up. But Hunter was not waiting for her next command.

His leather-gloved fist squarely landed on her temple with enough force to knock her back on the ground, where the back of her head also forcefully hit the hardwood floor, rendering her dizzy and incapacitated but not unconscious.

Hunter got on the ground, wrapped his muscular legs around her torso, trapping her arms in his clench as well. He enveloped her neck in the crook of his arm, completely immobilizing her except for her skinny legs which would be completely useless against his dual grip and his highly conditioned body.

"OK, you need to listen to me," Hunter said quietly but menacingly. "I only want the name of the and location of the person who has been giving you this cancer medication, whatever the hell it is. Who is it? Where do they live? Where do they work?"

Marypat was struggling to speak. She mouthed some syllables, but the slight choking she was enduring made her words indistinguishable. Saliva drenched her mouth, and Hunter's coat sleeve.

Hunter eased up on his choke hold, but kept his legs wrapped about her arms and rib cage, so tight she was struggling to achieve any respirations.

"Tell me!" he said.

"I can't," Marypat said. "I can't."

Hunter reached inside his coat's chest pocket and pulled a small, hard-shell case. He opened it quickly, something he had practiced several times using one hand, and grabbed a syringe nestled in the foam lining of the case.

"Here's the deal. You're going to tell me now, or I have a syringe of saline with a nice, big air bubble in it, two inches from your neck. You tell me the name and location of your miracle worker, or this bubble gets injected and will kill you in seconds."

"Ok, ok!" Marypat said as she gagged and gasped. "Eckoff. At Norwalk College in Iowa."

"'Eckoff?' 'Eckoff' who? What's the whole name?"

"Larry Eckoff," said Marypat, still wheezing heavily.

Hunter loosened his arm around her neck, but still kept it in place.

"You said Larry Eckoff at Norwalk College in Iowa. You're telling me the truth now, right?"

"Yes, yes!" Marypat said in a weak, gargled scream.

Hunter tightened his grip again.

The hypodermic needle went cleanly and smoothly into the precise location at the base of the skull where the internal artery travels throughout the right side of the brain. The large bubble created a major embolism that would block critical blood flow to the brain, causing rapid cell death and loss of control of the major organs. Hunter had successfully used this method of killing one other time, in which his victim's obituary listed "natural causes" as the cause of death. Such a method greatly reduced any risk of an investigation into the death.

"I'm sorry, but this will be quick," whispered Hunter. And those were the last words Marypat Hammond heard in her life on earth. After several seconds of thrashing and moaning, her respirations ceased and her body went limp.

Outside in the streets of Bronzeville, the folks walking their dogs down the sidewalk, those walking to a nearby bistro for a week-night dinner out, food delivery guys heading to their next meal drop-off, did not notice the nondescript figure in black coat, gloves and a black stocking hat covering most of his face, leaving the small apartment fourplex, heading to a train station and eventually, O'Hare Airport, on the way back to Virginia.

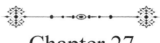

Chapter 27

The spring air in Boston was sunny and fresh, a bit chilly, but a welcome change after the gray, frozen winter in Washington D.C. Ron Holtzman had just landed at the private aircraft hangar at Logan Airport and was on his way to the Boston Convention Center. BIO-IT, the world's largest biotechnology professional conference, was having its annual convention this week, and Holtzman was in town to deliver a keynote address.

BIO-IT held its conference here every two or three years. And why not? The home of MIT, Harvard, Northeastern, Boston College, Boston University and Tufts was a gold mine of bio-tech innovators and researchers. San Francisco, nestled near UC Berkeley and Stanford in Silicon Valley, was also a regular choice for the conference site. But Holtzman's goal this week wasn't the speech he'd give. He'd done that a hundred times. It was to meet with the CEOs of many of the renowned pharma and biotech companies that would be in town. He would hole up in the presidential suite at the Four Seasons Boston, hosting cocktail and hors d'oeuvres get-togethers each night for small groups and individual CEOs, depending on their importance to H-BIS–meaning the size of their annual dues check.

Holtzman's driver dropped him off at the convention center, where Holtzman would check out the hall where he was giving his speech to get a feel for the space, acoustics, lights and audio system. He was on his way to the podium to work with the center staff on a sound check when his text message notification sounded on another burner phone he had purchased the day before. He stopped briefly and took a seat among the rows of empty chairs to read it, making sure no one who could have been in viewing distance was remotely close to him.

"Lawrence Eckoff, Ph.D., associate professor, Norwalk College, Norwalk, Iowa."

"Where the hell is Norwalk College? Where the hell is Norwalk, Iowa?" Holtzman whispered to himself.

"Mr. Holtzman, we're ready anytime you are," the event coordinator on the stage said over the microphone. Holtzman paused for a few seconds, still puzzling over the fact that the name he had been searching for during the past months was not a name he or any of his industry colleagues would recognize. No big-name research university or institute. No major metro hub. Just an unknown guy at a small college that was probably somewhere in the cornfields and pig farms of the Midwest.

"Mr. Holtzman?" the coordinator said again.

Holtzman looked up, slightly confused, but regained his senses quickly.

"Oh, yes," he said. "I'm sorry. I'm going to have to go. But everything seems good and I'm sure it will all be fine. Thank you."

And with that, Holtzman walked briskly past the endless rows of chairs and out the door of the hall. He stopped in a dark corner of the vast lobby to make a call to his executive assistant.

"Janie, can you do me a favor and cancel tonight's reception in my suite?"

"Sure. What's going on?"

"I'm just not feeling too great right now. Kinda just came on like a sledgehammer. And I sure as hell don't want to get anyone else sick."

"Sure, I understand."

"Tell them I'm truly sorry, that maybe we can reschedule if any of them will be at the bio-med meeting in Austin this summer."

"I'll get on it right now. You gonna be OK?" Holtzman's voice sounded a bit halting and slightly distressed, even for being sick.

"Yes, I'm going to stay in bed and try to lick this thing in a day or two. Maybe we can keep the rest of the schedule going this week."

"Get well soon! And have fun eating chicken soup in the presidential suite!"

"Yeah, yeah. Tell me about it. We'll see if they even have any on the menu. Thanks."

Holtzman hung up then immediately made another call.

"Hi Hans. This is Ron Holtzman. You have any plans tonight?" Holtzman should have known that a guy like Hans Mogen always has plans, scheduling his calendar in 15-minute increments.

"I'm meeting with some manufacturing folks tonight for dinner."

"Can you cancel it? Or end it early?"

"What's happening?"

126

"We need to talk. Urgently. It looks like we may have found Mr. Cancer Man."

"Good god, that's great news! Yes. I'll be there. Tell me where you're staying. Is 9:00 good?"

"Yes. Presidential suite at the Four Seasons. Give the concierge my name and they'll call me and get you to the right elevator. See you then."

.....

Brandon Abrams settled into the cheap, overstuffed couch in his 13th floor one-bedroom apartment. McLean, Virginia was a corporate town, where people worked for The Man in their faceless office parks during the day, then went home to their suburban neighborhoods or rural estates–if you were wealthy enough–at night. Except for Brandon. He would take the Metro to work and back, holed up in his apartment at night, but within walking distance of a couple bars and restaurants where his face was becoming increasingly familiar. He knew this was the early phase of his career where he was paying his dues, getting experience the hard way to prepare him for the next bigger opportunity. But what a price it exacted, implementing subterfuge and deception to accomplish a business and policy objective. Was this how the healthcare industry worked? Was he selling a piece of his soul to gain valuable, real-world experience? What would his business professors think? Would they be aghast if he told them his Wisconsin story, or would they say, "Welcome to the real world, son."

Shawni had told him on the plane flying back from Madison that a very nice bonus was in store for him because of the success of their "project." That would help ease the tension he felt working to bring a successful businessman and community leader to his knees. Brandon had spent the past several weeks monitoring state legislative calendars, and saw that several states had dropped bill proposals similar to Wisconsin's, for whatever reason. But he knew the reason. They did not want H-BIS bringing the big guns to their states and creating intense pressure to abandon any R&D tax proposals. Little did they know the big guns were actually a ghostly, phantom hacker located who knows where creating personal crises for individual lawmakers. Their ability to create financial ruin for anyone, anytime, shortened the time that H-BIS needed to expend resources to support or fight a bill from months or years to weeks. It was a marvel of efficiency and high-impact results, something he, as a business scholar, could certainly appreciate.

He was hoping this would be a one-off project, that he could get back to "normal" business practices. But partnering with Shawni Phillips would again prove that business in the world of H-BIS was anything but normal.

…..

The Boston Four Seasons Hotel sat in one of the most coveted pieces of real estate in Boston, indeed, in all of the Northeast: the leafy intersection of Boylston and Charles Streets, across from the Boston Common. The area surrounding the luxury hotel was the birthplace of the American Revolution. Tonight, it would be the quiet nexus of a global medical maelstrom.

Hans Mogen's chauffeured black SUV pulled up at the front entrance, where Mogen exited the vehicle and quickly walked inside. He hustled to the concierge desk, bypassing the registration kiosks, where he could quickly call Ron Holtzman's room. He then handed the phone to the concierge, who got the OK from Holtzman to escort Mogen to the express elevator to the presidential suite. Mogen arrived at the suite and was immediately greeted by Ron Holtzman with a Pappy Van Winkle neat bourbon in hand.

Mogen lay his coat over a dining room chair seatback and took a seat on the vast Italian leather U-shaped sofa next to the floor-to-ceiling black marble fireplace.

Holtzman sat across from him and got right to the point: "As I mentioned on the phone, we think we've got the guy who's producing the anti-tumor compound."

Mogen quickly interjected: "Which start-up is it? Any other drugs in their portfolio? What's their pipeline?"

"It's not a start-up, Hans. At least not that we can ascertain. It's an assistant professor at a small college in a really small town in Iowa."

"You are kidding me. Are you sure?"

"We are confident we have accurate information on this. His name is…well….I won't tell you his name. Doesn't matter at this point. For now I want to keep you at a healthy distance from any names. But we know he lives at the edge of this town in a little hole-in-the wall of a house. He has an office at the college but no lab that we can detect. We don't know how or where he is producing this therapeutic. Could be in his basement, could be halfway around the globe."

"How in the hell is he doing this? I understand the health social media platform we're involved with is blowing up now with people testifying about their amazing results. But no one–not one–of these people posting will say his name or where he is."

"I know. And I would guess that will change at some point as more people take this therapy and their family and friends witness the results."

"Well I don't want to wait for that point. I've got to get to him as soon as possible."

"What are you planning to do, Hans?"

"Simple. I'm going to approach him with a proposal that will transform his life and the lives of his future generations. He will go from being a small-time professor at a small-time college with a meager salary to being a very, very wealthy man. And it will happen much more quickly than if he tried to build his business himself. Assuming he even wants to build a business. He may be looking for a buyer right now. I want to be that buyer. I've done these kinds of transactions hundreds of times. He will become rich, more patients will gain access to his therapeutic invention, and our shareholders will prosper. It's what you Americans call a "win-win-win.""

"I've got to hand it to you, Hans. You're on top of the game."

"Information and timing. That's the crux of my business. The science is important, but markets don't wait for the science to fully form. Markets are made through data and speed and risk. But I like to think I take healthy risks. Before I leave, Ron, could you get your staff researcher who tracked down the professor on the phone. I'd like to ask a couple extra questions about his history, expertise, academic publishing, etc."

"Well, we got this information through other means. I don't have my staff assigned to this project."

"Well, whatever these other means are, I want to ask them a couple questions. That's doable, right?"

Holtzman hesitated.

"Right?" Mogen insisted firmly. Holtzman was now getting a bit leery, even nervous. Which was not something he had ever done in his business discussions, no matter how high-level and powerful his counterpart. Being that Hans Mogen was such a big part of his financial livelihood, Holtzman simply could not refuse to consider Hans Mogen's demand.

"Hans, I can get them on the phone. But they work clandestinely. I'm their only contact at H-BIS. If someone else is in on the discussion, they will end the call and probably end the relationship with me. So I have to ask you to listen only, and not say anything. I'll do the talking."

"I understand, Ronald. I have a similar resource in Europe that only I can talk to on such 'strategic' matters."

With that, Holtzman got his burner phone, which had 23 minutes of call time left on it, turned on the speaker function and dialed the number of Chet Hunter.

Hunter answered. "Yes?"

"Hi. Ron here. Say, can you circle back to your source and get us a couple extra data points on the professor. I'm trying to get a read on where they found his information, how they connected, and…"

"That won't be possible. Sorry."

"What are you talking about?" Holtzman was confused.

"I gave you the name and location of the target you were interested in. I've completed the project. That is all that matters. That's all I can and will do."

"Yes, and I appreciate that but this is just a simple follow up that won't even take five minutes…."

"It won't even take 30 seconds because I can't do it."

"Why?" Holtzman was now sounding both irritated and slightly fearful.

"Why? Why? Because my source is not operable anymore." Hunter was getting perturbed.

"What does that mean? What source?"

"You don't need to know the source. You don't want to know the source. And now it is not possible to know the source."

"Yes then. I understand. I don't need to know the source," Holtzman said in a conciliatory tone, trying to find his cool, diplomatic chops again. "But can you tell me their relationship to the professor?"

"Patient."

"And now they are not operable, as you say. Why?"

"The patient gave the information you needed. Under extreme physical duress. To simply walk away after that would have allowed the patient to run to that professor, whoever he is, and warn him that someone was taking extreme measures to get to him. Then, your prized target would likely fold up shop. Move it, maybe. Transfer it to someone else. Disappear. Go off the grid. Who knows."

Hunter was now sounding slightly proud of his horrific conquest and cool logic.

"It's called tying down any loose ends. It's what I've always done for you."

Mogen's face turned slightly white.

"I've got it. Tell me what comes next."

"You tell me. I've reached the completion point for this. And I've probably talked too long. Goodbye."

The phone went dead.

Holtzman and Mogen stared blankly at each other. Both were stunned. Mogen finished his whiskey in one $1000 gulp. Holtzman sat back on the couch, rubbing his temples.

"What the fuck was that?" asked Mogen with a pained look on his face.

"I wish I knew. No, actually, I don't know and I'm glad I don't," said Holtzman in a whisper.

"I think we both know, Ronald. In our quest to find the information we urgently sought, someone is no longer alive. A soul has surrendered its earthly life directly because of our actions."

A long silence ensued.

Hans Mogen was now subdued and calm. "Ronald, I honor this disturbing but necessary episode for two reasons; number one, it will help us in our mission to get this therapeutic into the hands of more cancer victims. And number two, it demonstrates the unyielding commitment your people have to achieving their objectives. These will both work to the advantage of us and of the world at large. Sometimes, unthinkable sacrifices are made so that the many can benefit."

Holtzman stared at the coffee table. He was not comforted. Mogen calmly collected his coat and exited without another word spoken.

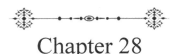

Chapter 28

Brandon Abrams pulled into the driveway of the updated, pre-Depression, classic midwestern farmhouse. One hundred years ago the house was surrounded by corn fields. Soybeans were just a southern specialty crop in American agriculture at that time.

Now the house was on Main Street in Norwalk, Iowa. A relic that had been beautifully restored, the three-story, white clapboard home with federal blue shutters and a wooden front porch as wide and long as three lanes at the bowling alley, had a soaring maple tree in the front yard and a large brick parking space in the back.

Brandon got out of his rental Nissan Versa and ascended the sturdy wood steps to the vast porch and the front door. He knocked firmly several times. The home's owner, a portly and gentle man of 60 or so, Jay Dittmer, answered. Dittmer had inherited the home years ago after his parents deeded it to him upon their retirement and move to Arizona. He had spent a good amount of time and money updating and repurposing several second-and third-floor rooms so he might generate some rental income to complement his day job running a small residential and commercial concrete company.

"You're Brandon?" Dittmer politely asked.

"Yes. Brandon Abrams. Thank you for letting me meet you here today." They shook hands.

"So you're looking to rent a room. "For how long?"

"I would like to go with a 6-month lease to start with."

"Sounds fine. I've got your online rental/credit app, so everything looks good there. Tell me, what kind of work are you doing?"

"I'm with a small medical and lab equipment company headquartered out east. We're looking to expand our sales territories to the Midwest so I'm here to scout the market, see if we can snag some new business."

"Why Norwalk?"

"Excuse me?"

"Why Norwalk instead of Des Moines? Usually, the renters I get here are new teachers fresh out of college trying to save some money for their first house. That or guys who just got divorced and had to give their house to their ex."

"Well, I'm a city boy. Grew up in New York. Went to college there. Still work in the city. I thought as long as I'm out here for a while, I want to see what this rural life is like. You know, a real farmhouse, Main Street, gravel roads, $2 beers at the bar, golf courses I can get to in five minutes without waiting a month for a tee time. That kind of stuff. Plus, it's an easy drive to the airport to pick up the boss when he flies in to check on me."

"Got it. Let's go upstairs and see the room. If you like it, we can get you all set up. And I will need one month's rent in advance plus a refundable security deposit, just in case your wild New York friends come to visit and trash the place! Just jokin'!"

"I can assure you that will not happen."

And with that Abrams and Dittmer disappeared upstairs to view the base camp of Brandon Abrams' new life…at least for a few weeks…in small-town Iowa.

…..

Brandon settled into his third-floor farmhouse apartment, though the term "boarding room" would have been more appropriate. It was clean and charming; original creaky wood floors, a small, four-burner stove and small fridge framing a two-seat dining table, small living room furnished with an overstuffed couch and a bed and bath suite that was all of 100 square feet. Thank god there was a window air conditioner for the approaching hot summer, but hopefully he would be moving back to D.C. before then.

Brandon sorted through the medical lab products literature he would be working with during the next few weeks. The brochures and spec sheets were somewhat crude, and deliberately so. Brandon had written and designed them himself. They were meant to look archaic so that the prospects he was calling on would not be real motivated to follow up with him or his fictitious company. His objective was to use the guise of medical lab gear salesman to get access to the office of someone named Dr. Lawrence Eckoff.

Ron Holtzman and Shawni Phillips had not told him much about the hows and whys of this trip. They just needed him to access

Eckoff's office–and lab if there was one–and report back his findings; scope, staff, and projects or research Eckoff might describe. Nothing too complicated, but the need for secrecy was kind of bewildering. Why not just present himself as who he was; a staff member of H-BIS interested in the professor's work. Little did he know H-BIS, with a homicide in Chicago that ultimately could be linked to the organization, could absolutely not risk any further connection to Larry Eckoff's world.

Brandon spent the evening researching other labs and medical centers he could call on in the coming days and weeks, from Des Moines to Omaha to Kansas City and points in between. He would act like he's selling something, and keep a record of his sales calls and locations, all in an effort to add legitimacy to his charade should anyone check up on him. If anyone tried to call the phone number on his business card, they would get a message saying the voicemail box was full and not accepting any new messages. Emails would get a polite "out of office response" with no date of when messages would be returned.

Holtzman had thought about sending Chet Hunter on this assignment, but didn't want to risk another violent episode in which Hunter might lose control and further endanger the entire H-BIS empire.

…..

Luis Hernandez, M.D., scanned the online death notices as he did every Monday morning. He had arranged a feed from the Chicago medical examiner's office, targeted to Bronzeville and surrounding neighborhoods. Hernandez and the staff of his public health clinic had a higher-than-average share of patients who were at greater risk of death, both from natural causes and from ODs, suicides or foul play. Hernandez was committed to following his patient outcomes and status, even if they had stopped coming to the clinic. He couldn't remember every patient he'd seen over the years, but in notable cases where had worked with a patient for many years, or had helped them overcome a particularly difficult health issue, he was always interested in how they fared, even years later. Some had expired not long after a treatment regimen. Some went on to live long, fulfilling lives. As a dedicated physician serving the underserved, he was intent on knowing some of these outcomes whenever possible.

As he moved through the listings while drinking his daily double-shot Americano, he felt a mental jolt that produced a small gasp and stopped his breathing for a second. The death notice for Marypat Hammond of Chicago, who died two weeks ago. Cause of death: cerebral aneurysm.

Hernandez was dumbfounded. He had examined her prior to her recent cancer treatment, including basic head and neck imaging, and had found nothing out of the ordinary. Except for her neck tumor, the rest of her physical health seemed fine. Had this aneurysm developed that quickly? Research showed brain aneurysms can take 30 years to grow to 10 millimeters in diameter.

Hernandez looked in Marypat's patient file. The only family contact listed was an aunt in Oregon.

Hernandez dialed her number, and, luck of all luck, someone answered.

"Hello, Ms. Hammond? Susan Hammond?"

"Yes. Who is this?"

"I'm Doctor Luis Hernandez. I practice at a clinic in Chicago. Marypat Hammond was a patient of mine. She is…was…your niece?"

Susan Hammond gave a long pause.

"Ms. Hammond, are you still there?"

"Yes." The sorrow in her voice was heavy. "Yes, I'm here. Marypat was my niece. One of my only living relatives."

"I'm so very sorry to be calling you at such a difficult time. But as the only family contact she listed on her patient file, I just wanted to double check to make sure you knew of her passing."

"Yes, I found out about a week ago. The Chicago police called me. They found her in her apartment and found my contact on her phone. It's so unfair. She was such a good person. Innocent, caring. She lived alone in that big city for most of her adult life, but made the most of it. A survivor. And she'd just had a cancer tumor disappear. Just like that. She was so excited to be able to get on with a new lease of life."

"Ms. Hammond, Marypat had discussed with me her experience with that tumor. It sounded miraculous. I never could really get any information on the treatment she had received, and who had been treating her. Could I ask if she had shared anything with you in that regard?"

"Yes she did, but she kept it really secret. She said the whole thing was really experimental, and that if anyone found out about it and they traced it back to her, she would be kicked out of the trial. So she didn't tell me much, only that her cancer had quickly gone into remission and the tumor was disappearing by the day. It was really too amazing to believe. But seeing is believing, I guess. She was due for a follow-up visit with that professor, but I guess..."

"What professor?" Hernandez asked, urgently. "Ms. Hammond I know that secrecy has been the priority on all of this, but if you know anything that you could share with me, I think that would be helpful for the good of this entire experiment."

"I don't know, it's so scary to think about breaking confidentiality and all that..."

"...Ms. Hammond, to be real about this, Marypat is not with us. And as terrible as that is, she obviously is not in danger of being removed from the trial. I don't know whether the professor who is running this research project may even know if Marypat is no longer alive, unless he reads the weekly death certificate reports from the south Chicago area, as I do. I'm sure he or she would want to know, especially if they were planning any follow-up exams or biopsies. Is there anything at all you can recall and tell me?"

After a long pause, Susan Hammond responded. "I guess you're right. What is there to lose at this stage? But she never gave me a name, just that there was this professor at a small college in Iowa–Norwalk, I think. Yeah, Norwalk, because I remember saying, 'Oh Norwalk, Connecticut.' But she said no, it's Norwalk, Iowa. She could drive there pretty easily. But that's really all I know."

"That's very helpful and I thank you for that."

"Oh yeah, and doctor? There's one more thing."

"Yes?"

"The police officer who called me said there may have been a scuffle, but wasn't sure. Not much to go on."

"You mean foul play is involved?"

"They're not sure. I told him Marypat didn't have an enemy in the world. She led a really solitary life, no real social circles that I knew of. I don't know how anyone who knew her–and that would be very few people–could harbor any ill will toward her. He said he'd keep me posted."

"Thank you, Susan."

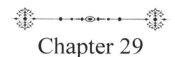

Chapter 29

Brandon Abrams pulled his car into the small parking lot of McLandry Hall. A sunny, early spring morning had him in good spirits as he thought this would be a quick appointment that could get him started on his way back to D.C. without spending weeks or months in Iowa as he had in Wisconsin. He loved hearing the robins and finches chirping from the newly leafed trees as he strode into McLandry's main lobby. There, he saw a directory on the wall, a collection of black and white name plates of faculty and office numbers.

This would be too easy. He noted the office number of Lawrence Eckoff, Ph.D, and walked to the end of the hall, around two small corners and found the door, which was halfway open, welcoming students and staff into Eckoff's cozy, earthy office.

Brandon knocked gently on the door. Destiny Diggs appeared, emerging from the tincture storage room. Brandon, expecting a nerdy professor with a bad haircut in a tweed coat with outdated glasses and vinyl loafers, was taken aback. For several seconds he caught himself staring at the long, lean figure in a white lab coat that contrasted with her smooth, deep black skin, hair in long, stylish braids, eyes and lips that flashed a sharp and sensual elegance, slender legs in skinny jeans that absolutely did not belong under a lab coat. Brandon had seen all kinds of young women during his college years in New York, even lusted after several. But he did not expect her, Not here in Iowa. Wasn't this the land of farmers' daughters in cut-off jean shorts and sleeveless flannel shirts tied off above the navel, Hee-Haw style?

"Hi, is this Dr. Eckoff's office?" Brandon said weakly.

"Yes, but he's not here this morning. His office hours are from 3 to 5 this afternoon." Destiny thought Brandon was a student or prospective transfer. Too young to be anyone else.

"Sure. Well, I'm Andrew Abramson. I'm making a few calls around the area to introduce myself and my company. We manufacture high-caliber lab equipment, specifically high-speed refrigerated centrifuges and advanced liquid chromatography machines. I thought maybe Dr. Eckoff might be interested in such equipment for any lab facilities he manages."

"Oh no, I don't think so," Destiny quickly responded with a slight chuckle. "I'm sorry. I didn't mean to think this is funny. It's just that we don't see salespeople come around here. Our department doesn't really have a lab. We just store a small inventory of supplies in the adjoining room back here." She pointed to the room where the tinctures were carefully labeled, organized and stored.

"Sure, I understand. Does Dr. Eckoff do any research, or is he strictly instructional faculty?"

"Oh he does some limited research involving human immunity, but nothing too heavy," Destiny said, articulating perhaps the biggest understatement of the century. "He spends a little time on it here and there, but he's really dedicated to teaching."

"Human immunity. That's important because immune system response, immunotherapy and all that, is really the new frontier in cancer and disease treatment. Lots of great work is happening in this field."

Of course he was right. So very right. Destiny got a bit tongue tied. "Well, yes it's really important and I've become…I just…I mean…I've learned so much about this topic from Dr. Eckoff. He's such a brilliant man and I know that…well…he's really going to add to the body of knowledge someday."

Destiny looked down, slightly embarrassed with her nervous answer. But she kind of liked this salesman. Polite, seemingly smart, someone who talked to her like an educated adult, not a dismissible black girl in a white state who didn't count for much. And he was youthfully attractive, short but fairly fit, maybe even athletic. It wasn't every day that a young, single, friendly, educated man roamed the streets of Norwalk. It would be great to give some more details to this guy about the world-changing work of Dr. Eckoff, but she knew that was completely out of the question. Maybe she had already said too much.

"Well can I leave you some literature and my card? If Dr. Eckoff ever starts a research program where he needs my wares, I'd love to help."

"Sure, I'll pass it along to him." Destiny took his card as their hands briefly brushed against each other. Brandon and Destiny both worked to maintain an expressionless face. But the touch was memorable for both.

Brandon Abrams–aka Andrew Abramson–gave a friendly goodbye and went on his way. Destiny watched from the office window as he walked to his car and backed out. She gave a tiny sigh and continued looking at the parking lot, wondering what else besides her promising professional career might be awaiting her throughout her life.

.....

It was a bright sunny day outside, but inside the underground bunker housing eight different mushroom species, the environment was dark, cool and moist, maintained at a precise temperature of 57 degrees f.

The latest crop of fungi was looking good. Within a few months, it would be ready to harvest, the spores captured, dried, and stored, ready for combining at precise ratios and eventually storing in the tincture solution. Larry Eckoff updated his notes on the growing progress, harvest estimation and inventory planning. By this time next year, the spores processing tincture production facility could be up and running. But he didn't want to let his dreams get too far ahead of reality. There was so much prep work to do in order to reach that stage.

Eckoff's phone vibrated. Destiny was calling.

"Dr. Eckoff, I just got a really strange and disturbing call."

"Tell me."

"It was from a doctor in Chicago. A doctor treating Marypat Hammond."

"And what about him?"

"Marypat is dead. He said Marypat died." Destiny's voice was distressed.

"What? How?"

"He said she died from a brain aneurysm. They found her dead in her apartment."

"My god. That's horrible." A pause ensued as Destiny and Eckoff silently coped with their shock. After the long silence, something dawned on both of them.

"I had been trying to get hold of her for the past few days," said Destiny, "to schedule her follow-up exam and labs, but couldn't get my messages returned."

"Yes, I guess that makes sense now. But how did that doctor in Chicago you talked to know to call you? Marypat had always fully complied with the confidentiality requirements."

"Don't have a clue. Unless she just flat out told him."

"Yeah, but he might have contacted us earlier if he knew about us. Not wait until her death. Do you still have his number on your phone?"

.....

Luis Hernandez saw the incoming call displaying Norwalk, Iowa on his screen. He did not want to miss the call. He was leading a group discussion with the clinic's physician assistant and nursing staff on updated methods of diagnosis and treatment of circulatory system disease, a common health condition among populations with poor diet and exercise habits.

Hernandez excused himself to take the call.

"This is Luis Hernandez."

"Dr. Hernandez, my name is Larry Eckoff. I'm on the biology faculty at Norwalk College in Iowa."

"Yes, I know of you. I had talked with your staff assistant yesterday."

"Yes, and we greatly appreciate your reaching out to us. The news of Marypat's death was shocking, to say the least."

"I can only imagine. And I offer my sympathies for your loss."

"Thank you, doctor. But I do have to ask, how did you know Marypat had been involved with our department?" She had been under a strict confidentiality agreement and I know she would not have wanted to violate that agreement."

"Dr. Eckoff, you need to know Marypat disclosed nothing to me, despite my best efforts to get information from her. Her tumor eradication was like nothing I had ever seen or even read about. To have a presenting tumor shrink like hers did, so quickly and without conventional oncology treatment regimens, it's nothing short of miraculous. In fact, she did not even want to come in so I could see her progress. She just told me about it over the phone. She wanted to be as absolutely secretive about it as possible, but did want me to know her great news."

"So she told you nothing about myself or Destiny or Norwalk College, but you were able to contact us."

"Yes. Well, I did not even find out about her passing until I read the county death notices several days ago. And I was as shocked as you. A young woman in good health, good weight, no prior circulatory system issues. I was starting to wonder if that aneurysm might be a side effect of the treatment, whatever it is, she was receiving from you." A brief silence ensued.

"I can't acknowledge or discuss any treatment...."

"...Dr. Eckoff I'll save you and me some time. I viewed Marypat's patient file when I discovered she had died. Her contact information only listed an aunt in California as an emergency contact. So I called her. She had said that Marypat told her about her miraculous results, but would not disclose what had happened to achieve that outcome. She did mention someone at Norwalk College, a professor she was working with. But that was it. So I reviewed your faculty roster, and read your CV. I figured with your research background in genetics and plant science, you might be a good starting point in finding this professor. And I guess I hit the jackpot. Certainly I wanted you to know about her death, in case no one had contacted you. We all know Marypat was pretty much a recluse. But beyond that, I want to know what you are doing. What is this treatment you've obviously developed? How many patients have you worked with? Is Marypat's case a fluke, or are there others out there going through the same remarkable experience? As a man of science, like you, I am extremely curious. And I can assure you I'll keep this all confidential."

"Dr. Hernandez, I don't know you, but you sound like a quality guy and I'm sure you would work to maintain confidentiality. But at this point, I'm taking no chances with my project."

"Dr. Eckoff, do you realize the potential of what you have created?"

"Without acknowledging I've created anything, I do understand the ramifications of a serious global disease that will seemingly be with us forever. I am hoping there is a highly efficacious treatment that will come along some day. That's all I will tell you."

"Certainly that's your prerogative. Let me ask one final question. If I have another patient sometime down the road that presents a similarly malignant tumor, can I refer them to your 'research project'?"

"Yes, Dr. Hernandez, you can. But I can't guarantee I'll accept them. I don't know where my work might end up, in the near term or long term."

"Fair enough."

The two were about to hang up when Hernandez thought of one more thing.

"Dr. Eckoff, quickly, one more item."

"Yes," said Eckoff, sounding slightly annoyed.

"Marypat's aunt also mentioned that the police were doing some additional investigation into Marypat's death, just because there was a small amount of evidence of a possible scuffle."

"I see. I can't imagine who would want to harm her, other than a random burglary. But the cause of death was an aneurysm, you say? That doesn't make much sense."

"I know. And speaking of confusing incidents, I'm just now recalling a young man who stopped by my clinic to ask about getting access to some miracle cancer treatment that he had heard about through a friend of a patient of mine."

Eckoff felt a slight interruption in his breathing.

Hernandez continued, "Of course I told him nothing. Hell, I couldn't. I didn't know anything and of course I am prohibited from even mentioning Marypat's name. Or that of any other patient."

"Yes, I appreciate that, Luis."

"But this guy was a little weird. He claimed he had cancer-like symptoms and wanted information on Marypat's treatment, yet he would not let me do any imaging or examine him beyond a cursory visual and palpation screen. I really didn't see anything wrong with him, but he wanted to get out of my office pretty quick. Like I said, it was weird."

The two ended the conversation. Eckoff would immediately call a meeting of the Musketeers.

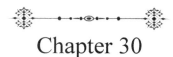

Chapter 30

"I just heard from Brandon in Iowa, said Shawni Phillips, who was taking some long-awaited vacation time in Aruba, but was never truly on vacation. Work dominated her life, and she was OK with that, even if it meant phone calls while on holiday, no matter where on the globe she was. "He had an introductory chat today with the professor's assistant at his office."

"Ah, great," said Ron Holtzman. He was on the fifth burner phone he'd bought in the past four months. "What did he find?"

"Well not a whole lot. She kept things really tight, didn't divulge much of anything, other than the professor is doing some leisurely research with 'immunity' as she put it. Brandon ran the cancer immunotherapy topic by her. Said she got a bit fidgety with her response, but did not dispel that topic. The professor's office is barebones, just some hippie bean bag furniture, a laptop or two and a small storage room where he keeps supplies. No lab. Nothing."

"Hmmm. Well, there's got to be something there. If he's the guy, that is. Tell Brandon to keep working on her."

.....

Harold McLandry, Larry Eckoff and Destiny Diggs were gathered in the basement of McLandry's sprawling farmhome at his rural estate. A basement it was anything but. It featured a lap pool, flanked by a 7-foot-high stone fireplace. And though McLandry was an extremely light drinker–a beer on July 4th and a little champagne on New Year's Eve–the dark cherry wood bar on the wall opposite the all-glass window wall that looked out on countless southern acres of rolling pastureland could rival that of any high-end drinking establishment in the country.

"Larry, you've called us in here, so it must be something pretty important," said McLandry as he sipped a diet soda. Destiny had brought her daughter Shay with her, who was gleefully splashing around in the pool. Eckoff had a bourbon, a tall one.

"I just wanted to make sure we all know what's going on so we remain cautious as things start picking up," said Eckoff, sounding a bit more serious than usual.

Eckoff continued," I got a call yesterday from a doctor in Chicago who had Marypat Hammond as one of his patients. Marypat died from an aneurysm several weeks ago. She was one of our trial participants and had experienced great results from IH-3314. Her doctor told me there may have been foul play involved, but nothing definitive has been discovered. He also told me about some strange dude who visited him in the clinic out of nowhere, before Marypat's death, and was asking about Marypat and her miracle treatment, as he put it. The doc wouldn't play that game, and got rid of the guy pretty quickly. But still, it's weird and I just want us all to be aware of anything strange we might see as we move forward."

"That is a bit disturbing, no doubt," said McLandry.

"Well as they say, if you see something, say something," said Eckoff, half-jokingly. "As we start getting people involved with plant site location, contracting plans, equipment procurement and all that stuff, it's to be expected that we'll have greater exposure. We just have to guard against divulging anything about our core science and commercialization plans. As far as anyone knows, this will be a health ingredient business, at least for now."

"So when do we go public?" asked Destiny. 'When do we announce our REAL product?"

"It's tricky," answered McLandry. We don't want to wait until everything's built and in place. We want advance orders, if you will, pre-release demand so that we can start cash-flowing this thing sooner rather than later. But we can't go to market too early. If there are delays or production snafus or quality control issues–which do occur, believe me–our business will suffer. Before we even get out of the gate. And I'm telling you, we need to hire a PR firm. And soon. Especially if we have some of this weird stuff starting to emerge. We have to get a strategic messaging partner we can rely on if things start getting messy. I'll be glad to pay their retainer for the first year until we can pay them from our revenue stream."

"Harold, I think you've talked me into it. But again, timing's the key."

"I agree. But that time is coming soon."

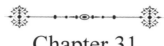

Chapter 31

Brandon pulled into the Norwalk city limits early Wednesday evening. He had been on the road in Missouri all day, calling on clinics, hospitals and research labs in St. Joseph, Kansas City and Shawnee. He had never made it past the receptionist in most cases. Two times he was able to talk with a lab assistant and make the pitch for his fictitious products. But the important thing is, any digital mapping records would show he had made the trip. Bought the gas. Ate in the restaurants. Even though he sold no product or made any follow-up appointments. He had no quotas. It was the best sales job anyone could have. The only sales goal he had was gaining the trust of a certain Destiny Diggs at Norwalk College. And he knew that if he came up with valuable information on Dr. Eckoff's "immunity project," another nice cash bonus awaited him.

Brandon headed to the town square, where he had decided to treat himself to a steak dinner at Charlie O's. This was the go-to restaurant in Norwalk. Great steaks and chops. At a third of the price you'd pay at a decent, but not great, Washington D.C. eatery. The cuts of meat came from local lockers or small food-service companies, which also sourced their meats locally or at least regionally. No frozen ribeyes delivered off a truck that was on the final leg of a 1,000-mile distribution chain.

Wednesday night was Kids Eat for $4.00 Night. So the place had a good crowd, but at 6:45 at night, a lot of the kid crowd was gone. Brandon settled into a small booth and perused the menu.

Suddenly, he heard a somewhat familiar voice that caused him to look up. An attractive young mom and her daughter walked in. He gazed at them as they walked by. Then, the woman backed up a few steps and locked eyes with him.

"I know you, don't I?" she said.

"You're Destiny, right?" said Brandon, not believing his good luck encountering his target.

"Yes, and you're, you're…"

"Bra….uh….Andrew. Andrew Abramson." Brandon became flush in the face. He could have killed himself right there for almost forgetting his cover name. But Destiny didn't notice. "And you're Destiny, right?"

Destiny was impressed he remembered her name. "Yes. Good memory!"

"Well it's great to see you again. You want to join me? I just got here myself. Haven't ordered yet."

Destiny thought about it for a couple seconds. A young black mother and daughter with a single white guy in the public square in small-town, church-laden Iowa? Yet, she had a good impression about this guy. And besides, it's someone to talk to besides her boss, her professors and fellow track teammates, who had their own free-wheeling worlds with no burdens of motherhood and a wicked work schedule.

"Sure. Why not!"

She and Shay, totally engrossed in her digital kids tablet, slid into the booth seat across from Brandon.

"Before you order, let me insist on taking care of the tab. My expense account will cover it, so you don't need to feel bad about harming my bank account."

"That is so nice of you. Are you sure?" Destiny was grateful for the chance to save some money.

"Sure. You're a business contact. That means you are a legit expense item. Bet you never heard yourself described that way!"

"Can't say I have," Destiny laughed.

"So expense items are allowed to order cocktails, too. Which I will be doing. And I invite you to do so as well. Wait, I'll bet you don't drink, and if so, I'm sorry for rushing that offer."

"I do drink. But only on Wednesday nights and only with cold centrifuge salespeople."

"That seals the deal!" Brandon suddenly felt incredibly fortunate to have this job.

He and Destiny talked for two hours, which to both of them, seemed like 30 minutes.

Destiny shared everything with him, her middle-class upbringing in Waterloo, her track career, college years, even the details of her pregnancy and how she has grown into motherhood.

Brandon described his somewhat privileged upbringing, the top tier schools he was fortunate to attend, college friends who migrated to Wall Street and tried to get him to come along with them, his aspirations for a health business career, his first impressions of the Midwest ("I spent a little time in Madison, Wisconsin recently"), and his somewhat isolated existence in the D.C. area when he's not on the road.

After dinner and a couple Midwest Margaritas (Cuervo and some pre-mix from Sam's Club), they headed out. Destiny said she hoped she'd see "Andrew" around again. He reciprocated, completely forgetting, for the moment, that Destiny Diggs was a strategic informational target who was key to his ultimate target: Her boss.

.....

Harold McLandry couldn't wait any longer. Larry Eckoff's project was scaling up, construction plans were being greenlighted, recruiting for senior management and technical specialists was about to start and he knew Eckoff and Destiny were overwhelmed with the day-to-day tasks of such a huge business operation.

He had received an agreement from both his partners to search for a PR firm to help in managing the brand development and communication strategies for this start-up.

Except he wasn't going to do a time-consuming search, in which business plans would have to be disseminated to multiple parties in order to get quality proposals, thereby increasing the risk of exposure and unwanted attention that could sink the project.

McLandry had one firm in mind; A small but powerful New York firm called Wiley Communications.

McLandry was familiar with the firm and its president, Liz Wiley. He had worked with her and her staff while serving on several boards of biotech and medtech companies. She worked efficiently and garnered great results: big press coverage in global consumer and business media; wise counsel in timing and positioning of new products; invaluable guidance in helping avert disaster when a business crisis occurred. He trusted her and her track record.

"Hello Liz? Hal McLandry here."

"Hal? My god how are you?!! It's been a while. In fact it's been too long. I can't believe you still have my number."

"I do and I'm glad you're still answering your phone instead of your staff taking your calls. You've gotten pretty famous over the years, you know."

"Oh I don't know about that. We just have great clients, right?! Speaking of which, when was the last time we were working together? It was on that Pfizer spin-off, wasn't it?"

"I think you're right. That was a fun one. And it made us both a nice bit of cash, didn't it?"

"You could say that, yes. And to what do I owe your wonderful call today?"

"Liz, I'm involved with a new company starting up right here in my little town. If you've never been to Norwalk, Iowa, I think you're going to want to get out here soon."

"You're right. Never been to Norwalk. Only been to Iowa once, and that was decades ago to help get that weasel Bill Clinton through the caucuses. I still laugh that he came in fourth, two spots behind 'uncommitted.'"

"Well, I know you'll have a completely different experience next time, that is if you want to take on this account. I'm pretty sure you won't regret it."

"Now you've got me intrigued. Anytime Hal McLandry has something big on his mind, I have to listen."

"Let me tell you about it...."

Chapter 32

The old Chrysler 300 pulled out of the parking lot of McLandry Hall on a warm spring night. Doing his best private eye impression, Brandon Abrams had watched Destiny Diggs and a person he assumed was Professor Eckoff get into the car. Having spent the day filling out expense reports and working remotely from his apartment on other projects for H-BIS headquarters, he wanted to get out from behind his small kitchen table and go somewhere. So he thought he might "stake out" McLandry Hall and see what happens.

Brandon put his cell phone down, with his sports betting screen still active, and started his car. He waited for Eckoff's car to get at least a quarter mile away as it moved toward Main Street. Brandon pulled out from the side street he was parked on and followed.

After 10 minutes of following the pair over what Brandon thought was a rat maze of country roads, his lights dimmed, he stopped on a gravel road while watching the Chrysler pull off the road and into a corn field.

"What the fuck?" thought Brandon. "Are these two doing something nasty in that car?" He should not have cared one way or another. This was strictly business. But he couldn't imagine this striking, intelligent young woman whom he enjoyed talking with and being with…at least in a small-town steakhouse…hooking up with a small-time college professor who was not that far from getting an AARP card.

Brandon stayed parked on the desolate gravel road and watched the distant headlights of Eckoff's car dart around the field he was obviously driving through until he came to a stop. The car had pulled up against a towering, decrepit-looking old structure. "What do they call these things?" Brandon wondered. "Elevators? Silos? Grain bins?" Whatever it was, it was the biggest he'd ever seen, and nearly obscured in the dark of night.

He watched as he heard the faint noise of car doors shutting, and then saw a bright white light emerge from the base of the old, giant grain storage structure. He saw two silhouetted figures move toward the light, which then turned to a deep red illumination washing across the nearby field. He then heard what sounded like a big metal door slam shut. And the light was vanquished.

He did not care if it was nearly 10:00 eastern time, he had to contact Shawni. Now.

…..

The private jet landed and taxied to the corporate aircraft hangar at the Des Moines Airport. Liz Wiley had just finished her morning Bloody Mary enroute from Teterboro executive airport in New Jersey. Her midtown Manhattan PR firm, Wiley Communications, was solidly profitable, with a small but highly experienced staff of 43, most of whom billed their time at the same rate as a high-pedigree New York litigation attorney. Wiley had a 14-way annual timeshare for a small, private business jet, but it was not available for today's trip. She could not afford to buy a jet on her own, even with business expense tax benefits. That's why Harold McLandry sent his jet to the east coast to pick her up and fly her to Iowa. The high-power PR business was lucrative and had made Liz Wiley wealthy. The agricultural science business, 50 years of it, had made Harold McLandry obscenely rich.

Wiley deplaned and McLandry was on the tarmac to greet her. Liz Wiley, age 52 going on 29, graying short pixie cut hair dyed deep auburn, adorned in a Dior olive pant suit and 4-inch heels to elevate her lithe 5" 7" frame, was nearly as tall as McLandry. Maybe that was one reason he liked her—from a business standpoint. She could look him in the eye as an equal, both physically and to a much smaller degree, financially. Both were happily married, fortunate to have spouses that understood and accepted their roles supporting high achievers who constantly wanted to conquer that next threshold, be it income, status, power, or influence.

"Hi Liz. Been way too long. So glad to see you." The senior statesman of the ag industry embraced the doyenne of the marketing world. "Let's saddle up and go. I've got a lot to show you."

The two got into McLandry's three-ton, five-passenger pick up, and headed to the rural county roads that led to the old elevator. Wiley had barely driven west of New Jersey in her lifetime, unless you count a rented limo in Los Angeles as open-road driving.

After a brief tour of the subterranean spore growing and production facility, they headed 15 miles northwest to another open field, this one not far off Interstate 80. There, behind a construction fence, they viewed immense earth scrapers and utility line trenchers preparing 22 acres for the construction of a research and production facility. A facility in which, so far, only three people on the planet knew its real destiny.

The final leg of Wiley's visit was a stop-in at Larry Eckoff's office on the Norwalk campus. As the two were driving back to Norwalk, Liz was sorting out all that she had seen.

"Hal, I'm really impressed with what you've shown me. But I'm even more curious. Right now. I've heard you talk a lot about immunity and immunogenicity and all that. But what are you really making? And at the end of the day, what does it do for people? If we're going to help you turn this into a global therapy that will endure for years, even decades or longer, we've got to know exactly what this does. In everyday terms and language that people will understand. You know what I mean?"

"Yes, Liz. I do. And I want to get this right. Make sure it's accurate so you know exactly what this is and what it isn't and what it means for the healthcare world. So I'm going to let Dr. Eckoff do the talking on this one."

"Well I hope he can speak in plain English. These wonky professors aren't the greatest business people, you know. They can fill up a chalkboard with technical proofs in two minutes. But they can't articulate a unique, understandable selling proposition to save their life."

"That's why I called you, Liz. You will help us get there. But I think you'll like Larry. He's got a practical, real-world side along with his brilliant scientific side."

They pulled up to McLandry Hall in the early afternoon, having stopped enroute at the local Dairy Barn for a cheeseburger and a soft-serve. Liz Wiley savored that lunchtime moment, knowing she would not likely ever be back in this town. In this state. It was a fun contrast to her typical beet salad with goat cheese and a Chardonnay.

They walked through the hallways of Hal's namesake building, and found Eckoff in his office, looking over student lab reports on his laptop he was starting to grade.

"Hello! Come in!" said Eckoff warmly.

Hal McLandry introduced each to the other, then they sat down on Eckoff's couch for a chat.

"So I asked Hal this question and he deferred to you, Dr. Eckoff," said Liz. "What exactly is the product you are creating here, and what does it do?"

"It is a fungal tincture, comprised of several different species of fungal spores, tested in varying combinations over a number of years."

"Fungal. You mean these are mushroom seeds, produced from different kinds of mushrooms?"

"Yes, you could say that. And they're combined in a basic tincture solution of ethyl alcohol."

"So it's mushroom vodka, so to say."

"Well, not quite." Eckoff was remaining calm and amiable during Wiley's interrogation. He had gone through doubts and questioning of his work for many years, and was proud of his ability to now answer such inquisitions without getting perturbed. "We put the spores through a gamma radiation unit to hyper-activate their bioactivity and, ultimately, their efficacy."

"I guess we missed that part at the growing facility."

"The facility?" Eckoff asked, now appearing somewhat flustered. "You went to our facility?"

"Yes. Were we not supposed to?"

McLandry intervened. "That was my doing, Larry. I'm sorry but I think Liz needs to see our operation to understand the scope of what we're doing here. We also went to the construction site. You need to know that as well."

Eckoff became slightly flush with exasperation. "Hal, I thought we were in the preliminary discussion phase in bringing on a PR firm. I didn't know we were in the show-and-tell phase. This is really...I don't know...just really kind of upsetting to me."

After an awkward pause, Eckoff continued. "Ms. Wiley, have you signed an NDA yet? I don't know if we've hired you yet or not, but it would at least ease my mind a bit if you had an NDA."

"Dr. Eckoff, I hardly know any more about what you and Hal are doing than those teams of construction workers building your new plant. Did you have them all sign an NDA?"

Eckoff pointed out that actually, yes, they all did sign an NDA.

"Well just to be clear, I haven't signed an NDA in my life. I expect people to trust me completely. I haven't succeeded in this business by talking out of school. I know I'm bound to confidentiality, and Hal would not have contacted me if he didn't have complete trust in my business ethics. I've worked for some of the biggest pharma and medtech companies in the world. And still do. Me signing an NDA means you don't trust me, and want the right to punish me. Not gonna happen. You don't have to worry about me."

Both Liz and Larry took a pause to collect themselves.

McLandry stepped in again. "Look, Larry, I have complete confidence in Liz. Just like we do with Destiny. And I have complete confidence that your discovery will be generating unbelievable business results sooner than we all can imagine. We all have a role to play to make that happen. In a pretty short time from now, NDAs won't be necessary for anyone. We'll be in the public domain, doing great things and changing the world."

"Speaking of great things and changing the world, I ask again," said Liz, "what does your discovery actually do?"

Eckoff, staring down at his green Converse tennis shoes, spoke softly, slightly above a whisper.

"Eradicates cancer. All cancer. In weeks. Is my mushroom vodka good enough for you now?"

Wiley's eyes locked onto McLandry's eyes. They stared at each other for seconds, until McLandry gave her a slight but assuring nod.

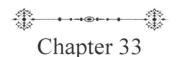

Chapter 33

"There's something really weird going on here," Brandon Abrams told Shawni Phillips, sitting in his apartment living room while the Monday Night Football game was on his small flat-panel TV. "The professor and his lab assistant drove to the middle of nowhere in Dirtfarm, Iowa, about 20 minutes from here, and disappeared into a below-ground level of some abandoned farm silo."

"How did you witness this? Did the good professor invite you to ride along?" quipped Shawni.

"I haven't even met him yet. But I tailed them out there. Him and his lab assistant, who I have met. Even had dinner with her the other night."

"You did what? You're now a private detective? And you've infiltrated your target? Man, you are going all James Bond on me. And I love it!"

"I don't know what the hell is out there, but I've got to think it's something pretty substantial because the professor has no lab at this college. Just an office. Whatever you're looking for, I'll bet it's there, under that ancient grain bin in that cornfield."

"Good work, Mr. Bond. If there's a way you can get inside there and see what's going on, that would be amazingly awesome. But don't risk your neck to do it."

"I'll see what I can do. But no guarantees."

"Sure, of course not. Like I said, be safe."

…..

Liz Wiley had not even taken off her coat inside the McLandry jet headed back to New Jersey when she pulled out her phone. She scrolled through her many contacts, most of them CEOs, publishers and editors at major media properties, or highly placed lawmakers and White House staff.

While the wheels were going up, she punched up the number of a long-time client. This client was special in that Wiley, on occasion, did more for him than simply provide counsel on communication strategy or crisis management. She also passed along industry information—non-public information which very few people had access to—that might interest him as a possible business opportunity. It could be inside information on a competitor, a recommendation for a potential senior executive to join the company's C-Suite team, or some dirt on a rival executive or government regulator that could help the company in an untold number of ways.

Today's call would be different. New territory for Liz and her client. But territory that could be of huge interest to him. Even a godsend.

"Hello, Hans? Can you hear me OK? I'm on a plane so it's a little noisy in here."

"Liz, yes I hear you. And so lovely to hear your voice. How are you?"

"I'm great Hans. Say, I'm just coming back from a visit with a new client. This client is in Iowa. A little town called Norwalk. But he's sitting on a startup business that I know has huge potential. I mean game-changing."

Hans Mogen excused himself from a dinner he was having with industry colleagues in a private, glass-walled dining room in Geneva overlooking the enormous Lake Geneva. He walked quickly to a small anteroom and remained standing.

"I'm all ears, as you say in the USA."

"Hans, this might be an early investment opportunity for you. One of the founders of this company is Hal McLandry, whom I'm guessing you might have heard of."

"Yes. I don't know him, but certainly know who he is. A great agri-science business leader."

"Well he and this professor that no one's ever heard of have created something here that is a bit mind-blowing. This professor has assembled a platform of truly astonishing science, but in terms of turning it into a business, he's in over his head on this. And Hal isn't getting any younger."

"This is all new to me. Tell me about what they're developing," said Mogen, pretending like he was completely unaware of the Norwalk professor and his potentially massive research outcomes.

155

Liz was about to provide important new details to him, and he wanted to appear eager but not too eager.

So Liz Wiley, after dramatically swearing an unwritten pledge of confidentiality, divulged the details of Dr. Lawrence Eckoff's proprietary, secretive work to the world's richest and most ruthless health care business titan. Afterall, Liz had thought, there may be a finder's fee in store if her "find" proved fruitful for Microneutics and Hans Mogen. And she was certain it would be so very fruitful.

Mogen missed the rest of his lunch, and sent the maître d to his table to apologize on his behalf.

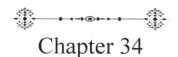

Chapter 34

Steve Robeson was watching his six flatscreen monitors in his office on the 15th floor in the offices of investment bank Richland Franks, or RF, as the Wall Street world referred to it. Robeson's RF office was on Spring Street in lower Manhattan bordering Hudson Yard. It was among a suite of offices of senior deal makers. The rainmakers. RF's two-level trading floor was located in the more traditional investment banking confines of the newly built Freedom Tower at One World Trade Center, rising from Ground Zero.

RF preferred to house its senior rainmakers in more inconspicuous dwellings to keep its hyper-driven trading business well distanced from its genteel, quiet investment banking business. It seemed like a healthy arrangement that had worked well over the 65 years Richland Franks had been in business.

And it was that kind of environment that attracted Hans Mogen as a client of RF. Robeson had advised Mogen on countless business initiatives over the past 20 years. Acquisitions (but no mergers; Mogen would never share leverage or wealth with any other company), bond sales, share buybacks, small, low-risk joint ventures and divestitures of Microneutics business units.

Robeson had a number of clients, but Mogen by himself had made Robeson a wealthy man.

This morning Robeson was scheduled to talk to Hans over a private Zoom channel. RF IT would record and archive the conversation in a special protected digital lockbox; no one in the firm of 7,000 bankers and staff would have access to it without documented permission of Robeson and the RF chief of information security.

Robeson switched one of his monitors from his Bloomberg markets screen to Zoom. Hans Mogen appeared.

"Hi Steve. Thanks for connecting on short notice."

"Not all, Hans. What's going on?"

"I've been made aware of a start-up in the…we'll call it 'alternative oncology' field…that I am very interested in. In fact, I'm beyond interested. I want to own it. And quickly."

"Ummm Hans, let's back up. You've never, ever had any interest in alternative health, let alone cancer treatments. In fact you've dismissed that industry at every turn."

"I realize that. But this is different. I'm getting reports from highly trusted cohorts that this research and the real-world, existing application of it is the real deal. A world-changer. Someone is going to invest heavily to get it. I want that to be me."

"Well tell me, what's the basic revenue and income stream right now?"

"There is none."

"What? Not even a basic financial statement? Are you joking?"

"Not at all Steve. I'm dead serious."

"So Hans, you are willing to move on a pure research play, one with no existing product, no market and no financial history whatsoever. How are they even funded right now? What's the headcount?"

"Right now, an angel investor has funded the research, the prototyping, and a new facility they are starting to build to achieve scale. And they have three people right now. That includes some consulting and oversight from the angel."

"Who is the angel?"

"Can't tell you, but trust me, I know them and they are legit. Highly successful over the long term in the ag-tech arena."

"Any business plan?"

"Don't know, but if they do have one, I'll probably blow it up and rewrite it myself."

"Jesus, Hans. I've never seen you this gung-ho on a business prospect."

"Well, I have multiple sources, working independently of each other, that have reported the same intelligence to me. I don't want to wait for other players to start sniffing this out. We've got to move fast."

"What do you want me to do? Make an offer out of the blue? And who is this guy…or gal?"

"I have all the contact information. I'll text it to you soon. No, strike that. I'll overnight it in a letter. I don't want anyone intercepting this in any possible way."

"Christ, Hans, I'm still trying to comprehend this. Where is this huge secret located?"

"Iowa. USA."

"You mean corn country??!!"

"Yes. I think that's what they grow there."

"Jesus H. Christ, I can believe this! And what does this miracle product do? Reduce chemo side effects? A home radiation kit?"

"You know that terrible brain tumor your late son had years ago? This Iowa outfit is eliminating the tumor. In weeks, not months or years. And they've done it over a thousand times."

Silence ensued.

"Steve, are you still there?"

"Yes."

"If you can get an audience with these Iowa folks, and we can come to an agreement, your fees will not just be based on the purchase price. You, not your firm, will have an equity stake for perpetuity. You will retire very early if you so choose."

Robeson ended the call and gazed numbly out his Lower Manhattan office window.

…..

Sitting on his back stoop in the early pink/orange dusk of an Iowa spring night, grill in full swing soon to offer up some sizzling butterfly chops along with a couple ears of perfectly charred sweet corn, Larry Eckoff looked down at his ringing phone. A 212 area code number shone brightly on the display. Normally, he would ignore it and let it go to voicemail. But he thought maybe this was that PR woman, Liz, calling to apologize for her brusque interrogation.

"Larry Eckoff," he answered. Steve Robeson was completely surprised. Usually he left three or four messages before a new business outreach gave a response of any kind. Years ago, when he was a green horn at a small bank that was a couple steps above a boiler room operation, the responses were usually "fuck off" or a quick hang up. After working his ass off to gain a foothold in the serious world of high cap bonds and equities, he had now arrived at a place where CFOs, private equity investors and fund managers would talk to him and even return his call the same day, knowing that RF was a firm with a good level of prestige in the global money centers.

The overnight package had arrived that morning, not by FedEx, but by one of Hans Mogen's business jets, flying direct from Zurich, handing the package to a private car service that would deliver it directly to Robeson, not a receptionist or mailroom worker. The package also had an embedded tracking chip; Microneutics security could see every centimeter the package covered in its transcontinental journey to Richland Franks, making sure it arrived safely and securely.

"Hi Dr. Eckoff. My name is Steve Robeson and I represent a major global investor who is highly interested in the research you are doing and would love to have a conversation with you in the near future if…."

"Now you listen to me," Eckoff said angrily, "I don't know who you are or how you found me or got my phone number, but I am not interested in anything you could possibly have to say to me. Not now, not ever! You need to go fuck yourself right now and never contact me again. Ever! You understand?"

"Dr. Eckoff, this could be a life-changing…."

"Didn't you hear me?! No! Never!"

And with that, Eckoff hung up, smoldering hotter than the meat on the grill.

Robeson got the message, loud and clear. He was experienced enough to know not to continue wasting his time on someone like Eckoff. Someone who, for whatever reason, refused to even entertain the possibility of reaping the highest possible rewards of a capital economy. But that didn't bother him. He had a second option. One that was highly likely to understand, in just a few words, what the name Richland Franks truly meant, and what kind of financial windfall Robeson would represent.

Chapter 35

"You can head on back now. We're done with this phase of the project." That was the text message to Brandon from Shawni Phillips. Three weeks in Iowa and that was all. Brandon was a bit startled by the message. He had planned on maybe several months of information gathering, not knowing exactly what H-BIS wanted with this Professor Eckoff.

Brandon hadn't even met Eckoff. Only got some observational information, mysterious as it was. Why the hell was Shawni suddenly satisfied that all was wrapped up?

"So what's the deal?" He texted back.

"We've got other info sources on Eckoff. So no need to waste your time."

"Ok, if you say so. I'll get out of here as soon as I finalize the rent status. May be a couple days since the owner is out of town."

"No sweat. And, if you can, get the name of the bank the professor uses. Same technique I used in Madison. Maybe do the same for that assistant you met."

Brandon suddenly felt his pulse race and his head get light. A repeat of the literal espionage and extortion they had pulled off in Madison? Brandon sat back down on his couch while the TV spewed The Price is Right in the background. He stared at the old ceiling fan slowly spinning overhead. He felt his life spinning as well, only faster. And he could not flip a switch to turn it off. Was he about to repeat the ethical transgression he had aided and abetted just a few months ago? The moral lapse that nearly had him vomiting from shame and confusion?

He thought he had overcome that emotional pain, but it was all coming back again. Could he stay with H-BIS any longer? If he left soon, he may likely sacrifice a quick career trajectory that could have him earning multiple times what he was getting now. His parents would certainly be proud of that eye-popping paycheck. But that paycheck would come at the cost of sacrificing the livelihood of not one but two people now. One of whom he was getting to know. And enjoying it.

In his estimation, more targets for financial espionage–and ruin– were likely in the coming years.

Brandon went to a kitchen drawer, pulled out the apartment rental agreement and looked it over. Maybe he might just stay a few more days to see what happens.

…..

Steve Robeson's fingers were hovering over his cell phone keypad, ready to dial up Harold McLandry, sole investor in the research project of Dr. Larry Eckoff. He was certain McLandry could be reasoned with and would not react like a rabid boar. But before he did, he had to call Hans Mogen, just so Mogen would not be surprised by Robeson's improvised outreach to a business luminary who no doubt knew who Mogen was. Mogen always demanded to know in advance every step being taken in a potential deal.

"Eckoff won't return my calls. I've been leaving messages on his voicemail twice a day for 20 days."

"Tell me more about your first conversation," said Mogen.

"Nothing much to tell you. He basically told me to fuck off and never contact him again And that's pretty close to a direct quote."

"Well, I'm sure he doesn't know who you are. To him, you're probably not much more than an annoying telemarketer."

"Thanks, Hans. You have such a delicate way of stating things."

"No offense to you, Steve. I'm just saying people talk to strangers over the phone much differently than they do if they know them, Or know of them."

"So you're going to give him a call, too?"

"Oh no. He wouldn't know my phone number. He would ignore me, too.

"Well how about I give Hal McLandry a call? I'm sure he knows our firm. He'll know how to have an adult discussion."

"Hold off on that. We don't want any end runs around Eckoff. That'll just piss him off even more. But not if I connect with Eckoff in person. That might render different results."

"You'd fly to American farm country to talk with this guy?"

"I'd fly to Pluto to meet with him if I thought he would give me 10 minutes to explain my thinking. And I think he will. I've dealt with reluctant geniuses before. They are extremely high and mighty, thinking that no one can be allowed to access their sacred science....until they see an offer letter containing several prominently displayed zeros in front of their face."

"Are you taking a tender offer with you, Hans? Are you serious?"

"Yes I am, Steve. And you're going to write it for me this afternoon. And please, don't save a copy to your corporate network."

"What dollar figure are you thinking?"

"It will start with a 3, and have 9 zeros behind it. For openers."

"You do need to get shareholder approval for an offer of that size, Hans," said Robeson, his head buzzing with disbelief.

"This offer will not come from Microneutics. It will come from the Hans Mogen family trust, domiciled in Zurich, Switzerland."

.....

In her office hidden away in the Zurich warehouse, Ursula Halgren booted up her laptop for another "brand management assignment." She would spend the next six hours scouring the web for information on a professor at a small college in Norwalk, Iowa.

She had done the same exercise a couple days earlier, with some unremarkable results. Copies of the professor's CV, listings of his published research, faculty news from the college PR departments, cross country team results in the local newspaper sports section, city and county property tax and assessor records. The usual stuff that illustrated the pursuits of pedestrian citizens leading pedestrian lives. She had reported the results to Hans Mogen, who was thankful but not surprised. But as usual, Ursula wanted to dig deeper, just out of curiosity, coupled with her uncommon digital skills.

She perused the popular dating sites in the U.S., the Match.com and Tinders of the world. Being that the professor was now almost 42, he might even be using the middle-age dating sites. Nothing came up on any of them.

Next step, facial recognition using Eckoff's Norwalk faculty page picture. Again, no hits on dating apps, dark web opioid and other street drug platforms.

Then, something registered. A clear search match. A photo of Eckoff on Grindr. Under the name he used on this site: Lare Bare. Larry and Lare. Plus the photo. No coincidence here.

163

Ursula went to work. She scoured other hook-up sites in the LGBTQ world. Skins, Humpers, DevilDawg, Jammerz, BottomsUp, HardOnes and others.

She dialed the number on her phone that would connect her to one of the most prominent business leaders in the world.

"Dr. Mogen, I have some new data on the professor in Iowa, "Ursula said. "I do not know if it will be useful to you or anyone else, but it's just another item of interest that can round out his profile."

"Yes. I'm listening."

"It appears Dr. Eckoff is a gay man." That was nothing notable to Ursula Halgren, a bi-sexual who identified as gender neutral. But Ursula thought that Hans Mogen, in his cloistered, power-business world dominated by proudly straight, white males, might find this useful. Especially the details of the professor's apparently wide search for intimacy.

And she was right.

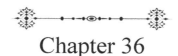

Chapter 36

The beautiful late May day at Norwalk College, the campus teeming with lilac bushes, begonias and mature green maples gracing the precisely manicured grounds, was the perfect setting for commencement ceremonies.

The vast portable stage was erected next to the antiquated but stately remodeled fieldhouse, just in case rain or wind might force the proceedings indoors.

Dr. Lawrence Eckoff, assistant professor of biology and biochemistry, would be on the stage in his doctoral black gown and colorful hood.

Eckoff always loved commencement exercises as he could watch his students walk across the stage and get the diploma that would be so key in determining their future. He would also attend the post-graduation reception under the large white tents in front of the student union, where food service caterers could quickly heat and serve hors d'oeuvres along with non-alcoholic cider in plastic flutes to students, parents and faculty.

The conferring of diplomas to Norwalk's 329 baccalaureate graduates went smoothly. The remarks by the guest commencement speaker, Mr. Harold McLandry, were predictable and forgettable. But when a small midwestern college had a global ag business leader and benefactor in its midst, one who contributed an entire new building to the college, you had to take advantage of it. Norwalk College usually had McLandry assume the commencement speaker role about every five years. That kept McLandry happy, which in turn kept the college happy.

Eckoff was thinking to himself how he might be able to stay involved with Norwalk, or at least with the faculty or commencement events, should the business he and the Musketeers were hatching take off and consume his daily life. The pure joy of learning, of research, whether incremental or world-changing in its impact, was something he fundamentally cherished. Today, he would celebrate that with the Norwalk academic community, the closest thing to family he had.

Eckoff was standing near a corner of the tent, talking to McLandry and a couple of accounting faculty about the early standings in Major League Baseball when a man in a superbly tailored blue blazer, crisp white shirt, open collar with no tie, khaki slacks made of obviously premium fabric, and navy leather buckled loafers, gingerly approached him.

Eckoff could not quite see his face, as the afternoon sun was invading that corner of the tent and made him squint as the man came closely toward him.

"Hello, Dr. Eckoff. I was wondering if I could have just a quick two-minute chat with you," said the dapperly dressed man.

Eckoff, still not recognizing the man, thought it might be a parent of one of his students. Maybe a student whose final grade in his class was less than exemplary.

McLandry saw the man also, but the blinding sun wasn't an issue from his position under the tent. McLandry instantly recognized the man and stared in slight amazement.

The two accounting instructors recognized the man as well, and quickly stepped aside, staring at him as well.

Eckoff and the man moved outside the tent to a small brick-paved patio and bench a few feet away, though all stayed standing. Eckoff still had to squint to keep the sunlight at bay.

"Dr. Eckoff, I'm Dr. Hans Mogen. I arrived here from Europe last night to try to get the opportunity to meet you in person."

Eckoff's defense shields instantly went up. He motioned to Hal McLandry, who was looking on from a distance, mouth slightly agape, to walk over and join him.

McLandry quickly strode to the group and introduced himself to Mogen. "Larry, this is Hans Mogen who heads the company Microneutics. You may have heard of it," McLandry said, trying to be a bit clever. It was like saying one "might" have heard of Microsoft or General Motors.

Eckoff still hadn't said anything yet. He was in total listening mode, not knowing what this guy wanted specifically. But he smelled something a bit foul.

"Mr. McLandry, I'm delighted you're here as well," said Mogen, "because I think you'll also be interested in what I have to say."

Eckoff put his glass of cider on the brick ledge and crossed his arms across his chest, his eyes never diverted from Mogen's face.

Mogen, undeterred, continued. "I think by now you may realize that word of your research has begun to circulate in certain circles. I believe I'm familiar with the basics of what you have developed. And it is nothing short of astounding. I think you and Mr. McLandry would benefit greatly–and I do mean greatly–from having a conversation at some point in the near future about how we could all work together to launch your business and optimize its vast potential. I know now is not the time or place for that discussion, but I'm willing to stay a few extra days here in Iowa if that would accommodate your schedule."

Eckoff and McLandry could not believe what they were hearing. McLandry was seriously imagining, for the first time, the healthy–maybe enormous–return on his significant investment in Eckoff he could quickly attain from a company like Microneutics.

Eckoff's disgust was growing by the second. Somehow, this guy had found out about him. And was throwing around words like "optimize" and "working together" to obscure the fact that he wanted to buy him out and take Eckoff's research away from him. At least McLandry would be on the same page as him, and dismiss Mogen out of hand.

"Dr. Mogen. You're a Ph.D. too?"

"Yes I am."

"Dr. Mogen I appreciate your traveling all this way to meet me and Hal….I mean Mr. McLandry. But unfortunately you wasted a lot of jet fuel. Hal and I are not partnering with anyone for anything. And I'm not sure how you came upon my name and my work, but I'm a bit doubtful that it was just by happenstance. You had to go to some work–maybe a lot of work–to locate me. That in itself makes me really not want to talk with you any further. About anything."

Mogen became irritated. He, a global business titan, had never been talked to that way. The disrespect by Eckoff was insulting. But he decided on the spot to not reciprocate and take a different route.

Mogen turned to McLandry, slightly flustered but still poised. Several onlookers inside the tent noticed the conversation suddenly getting a little intense.

"Mr. McLandry, I know you're a highly accomplished, respected businessman. You've been involved, as I have, in a number of business start-ups and restructurings, I'm sure. I know that Dr.

Eckoff has not, and is feeling a bit thrown off by all this, which of course is completely understandable. But do you agree that at least a conversation–no pressure, no urgency–might be worth having?"

McLandry, for the first time in his work with Eckoff, felt conflicted. He did not immediately answer but the look in his eyes, as Eckoff could see, was pained, as if to say, "Can't we just listen to the guy?"

Eckoff decided he would jump in before McLandry could gather his words.

"Dr. Mogen, don't try to pit my partner against me!" Eckoff was now talking louder, but not quite shouting. "You are here for one reason, and one reason only. To take what we're creating and turn it into an endless profit-making machine priced out of the reach of ordinary people, people who are desperate and will be financially destroyed if they have to rely on the monster you call Microneutics to save their lives. Go back to wherever in Europe you live. We're not discussing anything. End of story. Hard stop!"

Eckoff's voice penetrated the normal chit chat going on among the graduation-day crowd. The sound could not be ignored. Mogen could now see that Eckoff was every bit the pit bull that Steve Robeson had described. This would not be remotely easy. Not now. Mogen thought it was time to play his ace card. Maybe this would help quiet things down.

"Well, if we can't talk, at least not here or now, let me at least leave this with you."

Mogen pulled out a single piece of paper from his blazer breast pocket. He tried to hand it to Eckoff, but he refused to take it. Mogen then directed the document toward McLandry. McLandry reached out to accept it, but Eckoff reached across and hit Mogen's arm sharply, pushing it away from McLandry. Several people in the tent let out a gasp as they watched the commotion starting to build.

Mogen's lone security muscle man who had traveled with him, dressed in similar casual attire but tailored to the dimensions of a bodybuilder, stepped in and gently but firmly grabbed Eckoff by the shoulders and pulled him back from Mogen. Now the Norwalk parents, students and alums were all locked in on the confrontation. Two rotund campus security men came sprinting toward the scene, but ran out of breath before they could get close to Mogen.

Mogen and his muscle started walking away while Eckoff sat down on the brick bench to collect himself. Meanwhile, McLandry did nonchalantly walk to within arm's distance of the departing Mogen and quickly collected the single sheet of paper from his hand.

McLandry glanced at it and quickly put it in his jacket pocket while he looked upward toward the sun, trying to comprehend the enormity of what he had just read.

As the incident was winding down and a tamer atmosphere took over, another onlooker several feet away was still processing the bewildering scene she had witnessed.

"What have I gotten myself into?" thought Destiny, newly minted Norwalk College graduate, still donning her cap and gown.

.....

"How'd it go in Iowa?" Steve Robeson asked over the phone. Hans Mogen was comfortably nestled in his leather seat on board his corporate jet, which was flying over Pennsylvania at the moment, ready to approach the Atlantic coast, stop at the corporate aviation hangar in Bournemouth, England for refueling, then continue on to Zurich.

"I'm all but ready to tear up our proposal," said Mogen, sounding defeated.

"That bad?"

"This guy is a stubborn asshole who wouldn't know an opportunity of a lifetime–of two lifetimes–if it crawled up in his lap and sucked his cock."

"So is it dead?"

"Our only shot is if Harold McLandry can somehow convince the good professor to sit down at the table and go through the numbers. I'm not sure he is fully on board with Eckoff. I don't know what their partnership arrangement is, but if McLandry has majority control of their venture, I'd think he would have called me by now, just out of curiosity if nothing else. My phone number is on that offer sheet. I know he recognizes a great business proposal when he sees it."

"Well, maybe there will be a new leadership team down the road who will be willing to talk."

"I can't wait that long. I either have to own that research now, or make it go away."

"What?" said an astonished Robeson.

"If that professor's work continues to evolve without me owning it, Microneutics will be practically obsolete."

"You can't be serious."

"I'm deadly serious. Think about it. The professor's invention, whatever this fungal-based compound is, eliminates weeks and months–maybe years of chemotherapy for cancer patients. That means our chemo drugs. Our drugs that battle side effects of our chemo drugs. Our drugs that work in concert with other drugs. Our drugs that work on pre-cancerous tissue. Our diagnostic imaging chemicals. Our cancer recovery drugs. Our post-chemo drugs. Our pre-chemo drugs. That's 78 percent of our revenue; 78 percent of your paycheck, to put it simply."

"I guess when you put it like that...."

"That's just the beginning," Mogen interrupted. "Imagine the 71 cancer research centers in the States going out of business. And that's just one country. Imagine all of the hospital cancer wings shutting down. Imagine all of the pharma products–and companies like ours–going out of business. Imagine all of the university cancer research labs shutting down. And imagine all of the professional jobs, from Ph.D. researchers to oncologists, imaging specialists, infusion center staff, cancer PAs and nurses, drug manufacturing employees, The fucking National Cancer Institute, the CDC cancer division, medical textbook and journal publishers and editors. And that's just in the United States. You want that repeated in Europe and China and Japan?"

"I get it..."

"No, you don't get it. Cancer is the biggest business on the planet. I'm not going to let it wither away because some cocky, small-time professor thinks he can save humanity."

"But Hans, if somehow you would eventually own the professor's research, what would you do?"

"What do you think? It will never see the light of day. I will pay billions today to prevent the loss of trillions tomorrow. It just makes business sense. And healthy businesses mean healthy societies. That said, I might keep whatever small inventory he has in case I or my family need it one day."

The call ended as Hans Mogen's plane flew out of cell phone range. Mogen settled in for a short nap, knowing he would awaken in 30 minutes to begin planning the next stage of his engagement with Dr. Lawrence Eckoff.

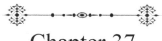

Chapter 37

Brandon Abrams would not be waiting for another chance encounter with Destiny Diggs. He was determined to find her and talk to her as soon as he could.

He knew from his latest stalking foray that she took her young daughter to the Jack Sprat daycare center. That happened to be within walking distance from his farmhouse apartment. He took a seat on a bench on the lawn of the Baptist Church next door, consumed in working on his phone with an ear bud inserted, pretending he was talking to someone.

After 45 minutes of his fake phone work, Destiny drove up to the daycare parking lot. Brandon got up and started walking toward the center, but not fast enough to intercept Destiny before she walked in the front door. Brandon loitered outside, hands in his pants pockets, looking around the area awkwardly so as to not have to look at anyone. Then he got his phone out and started in on a faux conversation again. After a few minutes, Destiny emerged from the daycare building, but without her daughter in tow.

Brandon was tempted to abandon the effort. Destiny was walking briskly to her car, as if on a mission. How dumb would it look to approach her so suddenly? Then he remembered why he was there in the first place. Not because he wanted to romance her (although that would have been a nice "side effect"), but because he wanted to help her avoid a major disruption in her personal, and even professional, life.

So he put the phone away and went for it.

"Hey Destiny!" he called out, maybe a bit too loudly as he thought the whole block could hear him.

Destiny had her hand on the car door handle when she swung around and saw that nice guy that she really liked talking to.

"Andrew! Hey! What are you doing here?"

Brandon again had to adjust his brain to hearing the name Andrew.

"Well, I was just wanting to talk to you about a few things…and…"

"…Great! I want to talk to you, too. I had a great time at dinner the other night."

"Cool. So did I. Really. But, well, where's your daughter?"

"Oh she's staying with a teammate of mine tonight. She loves watching Shay, and I told her I need a quiet night to myself. Stay up late, unwind a little, just like a teenager."

Destiny didn't hesitate as she continued on, "I'm grabbing a pizza and taking it back to my place. You wanna come along? This time you can be an item on my expense account!"

Brandon felt conflicted: a woman he was starting to have a schoolboy crush on was someone who was supposed to be a tool for H-BIS, working toward an objective he did not know about.

"You don't have to ask me twice," he said, suddenly feeling a little embarrassed for overcompensating for his inner conflict by using such an effusive cliche.

"Great. Hop in. You can ride with me."

…..

"You've got to figure out a way to shut this guy down," said Hans Mogen, talking on an encrypted Zoom chat with H-BIS Chairman Turner Mansfield. Mansfield was talking from his bed in his Chevy Chase estate. He was hooked up to a home dialysis machine, his laptop set up right next to it. He had shooed away his pretty, young home health nurse, who set up the laptop and the dialysis machine next to his bed.

Failing kidneys were among a series of health challenges Mansfield was facing. How long he might live was anyone's guess. The heavy smoking and drinking that had been a constant part of his 60-year career history–a life of schmoozing, persuading, entertaining and, sometimes, gently threatening members of Congress, prospective Society members, industry peers, and even a president from time to time–had no doubt contributed to his current health status, as they say in the industry.

Yet no matter his personal circumstances, Mansfield always made time for Hans Mogen. "Keeping Mogen Happy" could have been the mission statement for the H-BIS, displayed on a plaque in the office lobby. Scores of jobs, families, livelihoods and career depended on that.

"Hans, I'm sure you could buy him out with the spare change in your dresser drawer," said Mansfield, half joking.

"I've tried to approach him with such, and with more than spare change. Much more. But he won't even have a preliminary conversation. I've never seen anyone like him. Pig-headed. Rude. Insular. Whatever you want to call him. If I showed up again I think he might shoot me before I got out of the car."

"What can we do to help?"

"I'll let you figure that out. But we need some kind of leverage that convinces him to abandon his research, either by agreeing to be acquired or by shutting his project down altogether."

"Hans, you don't make life easy. Did you know that?"

"Let's see how easy life is when half of your membership goes out of business in the next five years, or sooner."

As always, Hans Mogen was being dramatic. But Mansfield knew this time he had a point.

Mansfield punched out of the Zoom call. His thoughts immediately turned to his longtime fixer.

Ron Holtzman should be at the office about now, Mansfield thought.

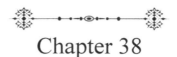

Chapter 38

The pizza was good. A couple diet sodas hit the spot as well. Brandon, aka Andrew, talked with Destiny for a couple more hours.

He compared her time in the 1600 meters in high school to his time as well. Yes, he told Destiny, he ran track, too. But as he discovered, she kicked his ass in her high school days. And no doubt would today.

She talked about her work with Dr. Eckoff, making sure to disclose nothing more than the basic phrasing she had used before; assisting with his work in his immunity research. It was extremely confidential, she emphasized. Of course Brandon knew that, in more ways than she realized.

Brandon got up to leave, but Destiny took his hand and beckoned him, with no words, to her overstuffed couch. Brandon's pulse suddenly went into overdrive.

The late afternoon sky had turned dark by now. No lights were on save for the small light over the kitchen table.

She stood about two inches taller than him, standing in front of the couch. She cupped Brandon's head in her hands and initiated a long, slow kiss. Brandon was trembling slightly from encountering the warm, long body pressing against him, taking in the scent of her young, rich skin and getting slightly lost in her full, warm, moist lips.

Brandon responded by wrapping his arms around her slim waist and pulling her midsection into his. The passionate kissing went on for minutes. Brandon wanted it to last all night. Destiny wanted to get closer, and pulled them both onto the couch.

Brandon unbuttoned her short-sleeve silk blouse without resistance and caressed her shoulders and taught stomach and bare back. He then managed to unclip her bra and slipped the shoulder straps off of her. Her smaller breasts and jet-black nipples, adorned by the long hair braids spilling over her slender shoulders was a sight Brandon never thought he would see in his lifetime.

Brandon had his shirt off by now. After more deep kissing and over-the-clothes petting, Brandon began to unbutton her skinny jeans. But Destiny lowered her hand and gently put a stop to it.

"I'm sorry. I can't,' she whispered amid her passionate breathing.

"Please," pleaded Brandon.

"I can't. Not now. I can't allow it after my last experience. I got pregnant, you know. I want to be completely sure before I go that far again."

"I understand," said Brandon. "I just want to enjoy you any way I can."

"Yes. Me too."

And they stayed half undressed the rest of the evening, tightly embracing their physical heat.

…..

Shawni Phillips tried calling again. This was her eighth time in one evening. Her calls were going directly to voicemail. Time was getting to be a factor, as her boss, Ronald Holtzman, was wanting some tangible action put in motion sooner rather than later. Why the urgency, Shawni wasn't sure. But if Holtzman was showing signs of getting impatient, there had to be a good reason.

Finally, on the 12th time, Brandon Abrams picked up.

"Where the hell you been, kid?"

"Oh man, sorry," Brandon said, seeing Shawni's call history and sounding somewhat tired and subdued. I've been out of commission for a bit. What's going on?"

"Just wanted to check back with you and see if you got those bank names yet."

Brandon looked at Destiny, sleeping next to him, sprawled out on the big sofa, looking angelic to him in the dark apartment, with only a little moonlight illuminating the room. The abrupt call for action— spurious action—during his most memorable romantic evening, caught him off guard and stoked his growing sense of anger and resentment.

"Um…yeah. I've got that stuff in my car. Can I get it to you tomorrow morning first thing?"

"Sure. Just want to make sure we get it ASAP. The powers that be are suddenly breathing down my neck."

"You've got it. I'll be back with you in the morning, first thing." The call ended, but not before rousing Destiny from her slumber.

"What was that?" Destiny asked groggily as she stretched and looked around the room. She was not used to having a date, let alone having him sleeping on the couch with her. She wanted to make sure, in her somewhat sleep-induced state, that Shay hadn't come home early and was watching her. But reality soon returned and she easily slumped back next to Brandon.

"Destiny, do you like me?"

"What kind of a question is that? You're here, on my couch, in my apartment, at 0 dark hundred, sleeping next to me with my shirt off. Could have had my pants off if I didn't put up a heroic defense! What do you think?" She giggled.

"Right, and obviously I like you too. I mean I really like you. And I care about what happens to you and your life."

"OK, this is getting a little heavy here. What's up with you?"

"If you like me, then I assume you trust me?"

"Well shouldn't I? Where's this going?"

"I've got to tell you some things that will probably end my job and maybe torch my career. But it's all for the good of you and Dr. Eckoff."

"Man, what's this all about? Now I'm, like, really concerned."

"I know, and I would be too, if I were you."

"That's real comforting."

"Please, try to hear me out. I'm not here in town as a lab equipment salesman. I'm here under false pretenses to get information on Dr. Eckoff. My business card, brochures, my so-called company, they are all phony. Bogus. They were all created to get me into your office and, someday soon, to Dr. Eckoff."

"You fucking with me? I'm hardly awake and I don't even know what I'm hearing."

"I was fucking with you over the past weeks, but not anymore. This shit has to stop."

"Why? Destiny said loudly, now fully awake. "Why? Who are you really? What the hell is going on?"

"I'm on the staff of the Healthcare Business and Innovation Society. It's called H-BIS for short. In Washington D.C. I'm a new employee, just months on the job actually, but they have me doing shit I don't want to do anymore. I didn't know this kind of deceptive work was going to be part of my job. A big part, it seems. So I want

176

to start working now to fix the damage I know I've done. I don't want this to go any further."

"So how do I know you're even telling the truth now? Is this another setup?"

"That is a totally valid question. You have every right to be suspicious. All I can do is ask you to see how things unfold in the next few days or weeks. That should demonstrate to you that, at least from this point on, I'm being honest with you."

"What?" What's going to unfold?" You don't know anything about what I do for Dr. Eckoff. I've told you nothing." Destiny got up from the couch and was now standing, towering over Brandon, who was still on the couch.

"You're right. I don't. I just know you, the beautiful, smart girl that I've been so lucky to meet."

"Hey, spare me the romance right now. What the fuck are you doing here?"

"First of all, you need to know H-BIS is powerful. Really powerful. They are the biggest influencer of the health care business in the United States. And I mean big. They have their tentacles in everything; drug companies, hospitals, research labs big and small, national and state legislation, consumer products. They have some level of involvement in everything from the Tylenol you buy at the store to Obamacare to MRI machines to the FDA to the medical cannabis industry.

"So what do they want with little old Norwalk College?"

"I don't know."

"What do you mean you don't know??!!"

"Look, I'm just a rookie punk. They don't tell me stuff I don't need to know. They want me to do some dirty work for them and not ask many questions."

Destiny looked completely puzzled.

"But I do know that whatever you and Dr. Eckoff are working on, it's of great importance to them. It has to be if they're paying me to live in Norwalk, Iowa with an unlimited expense account. So I know you can't tell me, but whatever you and Dr. Eckoff have going on, you need to be on high alert for some weird things that might start happening."

"This is just blowing my mind. I can't believe I'm hearing this. From you. In my apartment."

"Let me start by asking you to give me the name of your bank. And Dr. Eckoff's bank."

"Are you kidding me??!!"

"Destiny. Listen to me. Sometime soon, they are going to hack your bank account. They have some super-duper hacker somewhere—I don't know who they are, but they have scary skills—who can evade bank security software and make bank account balances just disappear. I saw them do it just a few months ago to a state lawmaker in Madison, Wisconsin who was on the verge of passing some tax legislation that H-BIS didn't want to see the light of day. They shut his businesses down in a matter of hours. Almost ruined him financially. He was begging them to back off, and they did. The legislation was halted. He got his money restored. It was the most disturbing thing I've ever witnessed. And the lawmaker had no idea who was directly fucking with his bank. Neither did the bank itself. But he knew H-BIS was behind it. They had him by the balls. There was nothing he could do except surrender."

"So what are they planning to do with me and Dr. Eckoff? Is that why you want my bank information?"

"I want to give it to them to make them think things are normal. Except you should move most of your money, not all of it, to another bank. Keep a small amount in your savings or checking or whatever you have. But get rid of the bulk of it. I'll give them the name of your original bank and they'll not be able to do much damage to you."

"Why would they mess with me? I just graduated from college."

"But you are close to Dr. Eckoff. And whatever you're working on, it's huge to them. Besides, if they don't get your bank info from me, they'll get it through some other means. It's just a matter of time. These people are determined. And they will leave no fingerprints, no trace of their involvement. None."

"I wonder if this has anything to do with the weird thing I saw during commencement weekend," said Destiny, whose outrage had now transitioned into serious contemplation and a grasp on the gravity of Brandon's confession.

"What was that?"

"Some guy was having words with Dr. Eckoff. And it got intense. And this guy had some bodyguard with him. That bodyguard had to step in and pull Dr. Eckoff back before things got physical. The whole crowd saw it. It was right outside the reception tent after commencement. Really weird. Even upsetting."

"What did this guy look like?"

"Middle aged but fit. Really well dressed. Definitely didn't look like a local. Might have even had a slight foreign accent of some sort."

"Destiny, I have no doubt this is related to what I'm working on. Someone at H-BIS or affiliated with H-BIS may be looking at your work as a real threat. A big threat. My boss just called me the other day and said I should come home. Said they have the info they need, and I don't need to stick around here anymore. Of course, I want to hold out as long as I can. But that absolutely means they know enough to do what they need to do, whatever that will be. It's a five-alarm fire now, Destiny."

"Jesus. What is going on?"

"Serious shit's going on. Again, can you give me your bank info? Dr. Eckoff's bank info. And, you need to tell the professor what's going on before the end of the day today. He needs to move his funds, but keep a little in the account. To avoid getting wiped out."

"He pays me for extra work I do sometimes out of his personal checking. I've got the name of his bank."

"You and Dr. Eckoff have to be extremely aware of your surroundings in everything you do. I just wish I knew more so I could help you better."

"What time is it?"

Brandon looked at phone. "Shit, it's after three in the morning."

"You should probably go. Before Shay gets back this morning."

Brandon got dressed. He and Destiny walked to the door. Brandon leaned over to kiss her. She moved her head to evade him.

"I think we'd better just be friends. I'm not sure if I'm grateful or mad at you. I've got to sort all this out."

"Destiny, one more thing, as long as I'm destroying myself in front of you."

"Yes?"

"My name is not Andrew."

"Why am I not surprised."

Chapter 39

Destiny was unsure if the notification would come. But it did. Through a phone call. 36 hours after Brandon had left her apartment.

"Hello, I'm calling for Destiny Diggs. This is Marie Mortino at Warren County State Bank."

"This is Destiny."

"Hello Destiny. I have information about your account here that I need to discuss with you in person. Would you be able to stop by the bank sometime today?"

"Yes. I'll be in around four this afternoon."

Destiny had been anticipating such an inquiry from the bank. But it still shocked her. Brandon was right. Some dark forces were at work in the pursuit of Dr. Eckoff's work. What else might be in motion? Was this bank "heist" of her account the first of who knows how many efforts that H-BIS would employ to somehow get her and Dr. Eckoff to abandon their work?

Fortunately, Brandon had warned her. A day earlier, Destiny had withdrawn $1150 from her $1200 checking account. She withdrew it in cash, put it in a drawer at home with plans to move it to another bank once the incident was well behind her. However long that would take.

She had told Dr. Eckoff about Brandon. The salesman who wasn't a salesman. She had passed along Brandon's warning. Eckoff was furious when he heard Destiny's story of Brandon confessing to the skullduggery that was under way.

Eckoff was torn between the outrage he was experiencing, knowing that some very big predators with unlimited resources were beginning to close in on him and Destiny, and a confused sense of gratitude that someone, someone on the inside, was at least trying to help him. At least for now. Was this Brandon guy just teasing them to gain his trust, only to turn on them when the predators were ready to strike?

Washington D.C., New York, Zurich. All targeting Norwalk, Iowa. Were other global centers of business and finance lined up to be a part of this predatory cabal?

For now, Eckoff would decide to heed Brandon's warning and advice. But that could change in a heartbeat. Eckoff would be just as skeptical dealing with Brandon as he was with Hans Mogen, maybe more so. Still, he had yet to meet him.

…..

Shawni was on the carpeted floor of her condo, lying on her back, lifting a couple of small arm weights. The notification alarm on her laptop sounded; a meager beeping pattern. Shawni got up and went to the dining room table, where she opened her laptop. Instantly, the encrypted chat screen came up.

"Lonnie. Everything go OK?"

"I'm not sure, Greta."

"What do you mean?"

"Well, these people are either dirt poor, or they don't keep any money in the bank. One had $53 in the account, the other, Eckoff, had $85. I shut them down, but I'm not sure it will make much of a difference in whatever you're trying to accomplish."

"No other accounts in the bank?" CDs? Savings?"

"Nothing. I would have seen them if they existed. These are small local banks. They don't deal with securities, money markets, bonds or anything. Not for their customers, anyway."

"Well, I'll have to see what else we might be able to do."

"Well good luck with that. I don't know why you're interested in these people and I can't imagine how they pertain to your organization."

"If you only knew."

"Right. And I don't want to know."

"Well, I may have another project for you."

…..

"Lonnie" was obsessed. Three days into a new project for Shawni "Greta" Phillips and he hadn't scored a single win. Not even close.

The Norwalk College data network was easy to access. Security codes were simple. Many passwords had not been changed for years;

181

when crossed-referenced with a list of stolen passwords in the region for user accounts that Lonnie bought every three months on the dark web, infiltration was not too hard.

But this Eckoff guy was different. Forget about accessing his data on the Norwalk server, it was like he didn't even exist. Like he was not on the faculty. Lonnie was at a loss. Hours of automated password variations, username variations and substitutes, email backdoor virus piggybacks, anything he could think of, nothing had produced results.

He would connect over encrypted chat with "Greta" (Shawni) and throw in the towel.

"Hi. I'm having no luck. None. This guy is a ghost. And I don't know where the ghost could be hiding."

"Are you serious? You can't penetrate this little college in Iowa?"

"Oh, I can penetrate it easily enough. But this guy. I don't know why. It's like he doesn't exist there. Are you sure you got the right guy?"

"Absolutely. We have been in his office and talked to his assistant. He most certainly is real and is at Norwalk College."

"Well the only thing I can conclude is that he does not use the Norwalk College network. Whatever he is doing, it's off the grid. Completely. I've not seen anything like this in a while, if ever."

"I see. So if you can't deliver anything on him, do we still have to pay you?"

"Are you kidding? Of course you'll pay me. And I did deliver something for you. The knowledge and insight that you're going to have to use other means to get whatever it is you need from this guy. That's just as valuable, in my book. He's a different kind of cat. You wouldn't have known otherwise unless I delved into this. But I'll give you 5% off, especially since crypto is so high right now."

"You're too generous," Shawni quipped.

"Glad to help. And one more piece of advice."

"Tell me."

"Just because this guy isn't connected online doesn't mean he doesn't have the data you're looking for. I'm sure he does. It's just that you'll have to find another way to get it. It's going back to the old days before the internet existed. Before networked computer systems existed. Before mainframes. He may have all his work stored somewhere on an external medium."

"You mean floppy drives?"

"Not quite that far back. But flash drives and such, possibly yes. SD cards, external hard drives. Those kinds of things."

"In other words, some physical, in-person activity is probably required."

"I'm not advising you on what to do. I'm just saying think old school. And think boots on the ground."

Shawni ended the chat. An immediate call to Holtzman had to happen.

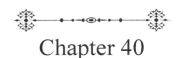

Chapter 40

"I don't trust Hal McLandry anymore."

Larry Eckoff was in his office with Destiny on a crisp, early June morning, The sun was barely squeaking through the slatted blinds covering the only window in his office. Normally the blinds would be pulled up to let in the full dose of sunshine. But Eckoff wasn't feeling very sunny of late. And he didn't discount the notion that someone could be looking in the window, trying to lip read their conversation.

"What's going on with you?" said Destiny, trying to sympathize but feeling a bit frustrated herself.

"You saw the conversation with Hans Mogen on commencement weekend. Hal was actually trying to talk me into listening to Mogen to cut a deal. So that Mogen could gain control of my project. My livelihood. Your future livelihood. Mogen wants to buy out your future."

"I know."

"And you know what else? He wants to buy out the chance for millions of people in the years to come—hell decades or even centuries–to conquer and maybe even wipe out–the most debilitating disease this world has ever known."

Eckoff continued, "I've even read speeches and papers where Mogen writes that cancer is nature's population control lever. That if we didn't have cancer, the earth would achieve overpopulation at a rate and level that would make the planet unsustainable. Of course his company can make cancer more comfortable and treatable for victims. He is a sick fuck. He NEEDS cancer for his company and the world medical industrial complex to grow and prosper. I cannot, for one second, fathom my life's work getting into his hands."

"Well I know that…"

"And your friend Andrew or whoever he is, is helping him try to do that."

"Not anymore, Dr. Eckoff. He's seen what's really happening. And he wants to help us make sure we don't get crushed by Mogen."

"Well, I don't know who to trust. But I've taken the capital spending account we've had in the Des Moines bank and transferred it to a digital account at that online bank FinGo. I've also got my checking and ATM card with them. It's got to make it harder for them to find our bank information again. I suggest you get your checking or savings account set up with them, too."

"I only have cash," said Destiny.

"Not a problem. Take your cash, get a cashier's check at your former bank, then get online at FinGo and find where you can send them your cashier's check. You might even be able to just send a photo of the check from your phone to your new account. We've got to start thinking about every way we can be invisible until we get the business established."

"I'll do it," said Destiny attentively.

"In the meantime, we've got to transfer our tincture inventory from our lab to the production facility."

"I was thinking about that, too."

"Yes. Your friend Brandon has seen this office. He knows this is where we probably store stuff. I hate to put everything in one location, but the elevator is a hundred times more secure than the office."

"I don't think you're giving Brandon enough credit for wanting to help us."

"You may be right. But for now, I'll err on the side of paranoia."

.....

"This guy doesn't exist. At least not in the digital universe. No email that we can find. No college computer network. No social media. No bank account with any significant funds. Nothing."

Shawni Phillips was delivering the frustrating news to Ronald Holtzman, who was in the middle of applying his amateur plumbing skills trying to stop a leak in a sink in the Holtzman family palatial primary bathroom.

"So what are you saying?" Are we out of luck with this guy?" Holtzman asked, t-shirt slightly damp from sweating while he had been hunched under the vanity counter.

"I don't know, but we might have to think about other 'non-digital' approaches, shall we say."

Holtzman stayed silent for a few seconds, thinking how the last time a non-digital approach was used ended tragically for an innocent victim.

Another burner phone call to Zurich, or wherever the hell Hans Mogen was on the planet today, would be his next step. This routine was starting to get old. But, as Mogen constantly reminded him and only three other people on the planet, the only hope for the future of Microneutics and the countless other companies–employers of millions of people worldwide, wealth generators for millions of big and small shareholders worldwide–was to contain and even disarm the small-town professor in America's rural heartland.

.....

"I think I might have an alternate route to achieve our goal," said Hans Mogen, who had been scheming possible scenarios ever since wheels up in Des Moines weeks ago. Mogen was in his office on a Saturday, eating a catered afternoon late lunch, preparing for the upcoming shareholders meeting next week. Of course his key senior staff were on the Zoom call, contributing their analyses of their business units that Mogen would add to his presentation screens. There were no real weekends if you reported to Hans Mogen.

At this moment, Mogen had taken a break from the prep session to walk over to the anteroom, door closed, and talk with Holtzman. For all his staff knew, Mogen's wife was on the phone needing Hans' card number for his invitation-only American Express black card, where one was expected to spend $250,000 a year to maintain card privileges, because hers had reached the limit, whatever that could possibly be.

Holtzman was hoping against hope that the alternative route would not involve him or H-BIS. At least not in any significant role. Holtzman was unaware of what exactly happened in Chicago, which is the way he wanted it. For anything else to involve H-BIS, there had to be a clean separation of duties that would not put the organization–or Holtzman's life as a free man–in the slightest jeopardy.

"The professor apparently has a business partner whom I am familiar with. And because he is a highly accomplished CEO, he knows how to size up an opportunity, especially for the long term. I think I'll reconnect with him. He took my proposal with him when I

186

was in Iowa, after the professor tried to take my arm off. He may be the key to turning this thing around for us. Maybe he even has majority ownership of their little enterprise, which could mean he can overrule the professor on major business decisions."

Holtzman was breathing much more easily now.

"That sounds like the best strategy, Hans. I'm in total support."

"Well don't get too comfortable yet. We may need a plan C or D or F."

Holtzman shook his head and fumbled with his pipe wrench. He gazed back at the pipe still dripping water on the towel he placed below it. Fuck it, he thought. I'm calling a plumber.

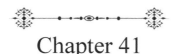

Chapter 41

Hal McLandry felt like celebrating a little. More than just a few sips of a weak rum and diet coke at dinner.

Tonight, a Grateful Dead tribute band, Dead Of The Night, was playing at an outdoor park next to the Norwalk Campus. It was a perfect summer night. And he had an offer letter in his home office for $3 billion from the biggest business magnate in the world. He was confident he could talk Larry Eckoff into accepting the offer, with some modified conditions. It would take days if not weeks or months. But McLandry was convinced that Eckoff could be convinced.

So tonight was for celebrating. He'd go to the concert and relive his youth for a few hours. Why not? He'd hang back on the periphery and not get into the thick of the crowd, maintain the veneer of the buttoned up retired business leader he was. His Lauren polo, long shorts and brand new Adidas white Stan Smiths were about as rock and roll as he ever got these days.

McLandry parked in a faculty parking lot. He had a permanent pass there, a small perk for being the biggest living benefactor to the college. He walked briskly to the park, where a couple thousand people, young and old, were getting juiced up for the band to come on stage. And to the roar of the crowd, they walked to their spots, did some brief tuning and final sound check. Then they broke into, what else, "Truckin."

McLandry grinned widely. This was going to be a fun night. A chance to be 20 years old again. On a college campus he loved. Under a warm starry sky. What could be better!

The show progressed to its third hour. The crowd was now more energized, free-spirited, with several young women waving their arms back and forth, sitting bare chested on male shoulders, the brew from the nearby beer tents taking hold. And McLandry was loving every minute of it. God forbid, he was even swaying his slender hips and torso to the music.

One of the Norwalk College deans had been standing by him. The crowd had grown a bit larger in the past three hours, slightly pushing up against McLandry. The dean seemed to be having just as good of time as McLandry, even though he was much too young to have known or seen "The Dead" in their heyday. He was costumed in his tie-dye t-shirt and sandals, with a bandana, doing his best to portray the Summer of Love that he had read about.

The dean grabbed a joint that was being passed around and took a toke. Then he passed it to McLandry. "C'mon Hal, let's cut loose a little."

What harm could come to me if I take one hit from something that half the college faculty and most of the students here probably partake in regularly? McLandry thought to himself. *Besides, it's legal in more than half the country, except for, of course, Iowa.*

McLandry took a puff. A big one. A deep, lengthy one. Of course, a couple coughs followed. But the dean was laughing as were a couple of his colleagues beside him. And McLandry started laughing as well.

"A little out of practice, eh Hal?" laughed the dean.

That made McLandry laugh even harder. He bent over to cough some more, not wanting to infringe upon his fellow partiers.

A slight sweat on his forehead was now spreading down his cheeks and to his upper chest. McLandry innately knew it was just the result of a warm summer night and the closely packed crowd.

His head started feeling quite dizzy, his eyesight blurry. Man, this stuff is pretty strong, he thought.

"You OK, Hal?" said the dean, looking a little worried but still giggling the cannabis giggle.

"Yeah, just gotta get used to this stuff."

Landry slowly stood back up, a little wobbly, then fell back to the ground, grabbing his chest, gasping for air. The dean got on his knees, grabbing McLandry's shoulders, repeatedly shouting, "Hal! Hal! Can you talk to me? What's going on? Someone call an ambulance! Now!!"

McLandry's face was now slightly blue, veins bulging, his only way to communicate was his slobbering, foaming saliva coming from his mouth and his terror-stricken eyes bulging.

The ambulance arrived in three minutes, having been parked close by as always for such community events. The horrified crowd looked on as the band stopped and decided to call it a night.

After a couple minutes of vital sign checks and an IV hookup, EMTs started performing CPR on McLandry's limp body, which was eventually loaded into the ambulance, the EMT still sitting on his chest, furiously repeating rapid compressions.

…..

Steve Robeson was about to make a phone call that could change his life. If his client, Hans Mogen, could gain control of Professor Eckoff's invention, Robeson would be awarded fees in perpetuity that would allow him to do damn near anything he wanted, buy anything he desired, live anywhere he wanted, and travel anywhere, anytime he wanted. It would be like winning a lottery, only without the publicity and therefore friends, family and strangers coming out of the woodwork demanding some portion of his money.

Just a conversation. That's all Steve Robeson was going to ask for. Getting Hal McLandry to sit down for a quiet discussion of the wealth he could realize from his investment in the research of Dr. Eckoff could trigger a turn of events that would satisfy his biggest client while greatly enriching himself.

Robeson dialed the general number of Landmark Nutra Science. He was confident the receptionist would either pass him along to McLandry's direct number in his office, or leave a message for him to return his call.

"Landmark Nutra Science. This is Haley. How may I direct your call?"

"This is Steve Robeson with Richland Franks & Company in New York. I'm calling for Mr. McLandry to follow up on a conversation he had with us during commencement weekend. Is he in today?"

"Sir, I am truly sorry to have to tell you that Mr. McLandry passed away last Thursday."

"What? You're saying he died?"

"Yes. I'm so sorry."

"From what?"

"I'm sorry?"

"How did he die?" Robeson was talking with a strained high pitch that he had never himself heard before.

"I'm sorry. We don't have further details that we can disclose. I hope you understand."

Robeson hung up without any further words and stared out from his window into the distance, watching children playing in a nearby park. Many more years of high-pressure investment banking work–of answering to hyper-demanding people like Hans Mogen–were suddenly a reality again. His thinning hairline would be completely gone by the time he could retire. Life suddenly seemed like drudgery again. Lucrative, but with a giant mortgage in Connecticut and private schools and college for four children, drudgery just the same.

A call to his client was now required.

....

The cause of death of Harold McLandry was atrial septal defect, a hole in the heart wall that had gone undetected for all of his 79 years. Smoking pot didn't cause the heart attack, but may have amplified the defect, leading to his demise.

Eckoff and Destiny took his death hard. McLandry was the financial backer of their budding enterprise. But he was also a great cheerleader for their work. And a genuinely nice man.

But with the strange goings on as of late–the mysterious death of a patient, a global business tycoon making a play for Eckoff's world-changing achievements, the untraceable meddling of H-BIS in his personal bank account–Eckoff knew he had to get his affairs in order to make sure his new business venture would carry on and achieve its full potential.

The first thing he had to do was formalize the transfer of shares from McLandry's estate. Their agreement, written as they formed their partnership, called for 75 percent of McLandry's shares in New World Molecular LLC, the name of their business venture, to be transferred to Lawrence Eckoff, Ph.D. upon the death of Harold McLandry. The remaining 25 percent would be transferred to McLandry's wife. This would allow her to share in the wealth created by New World Molecular in the years to come, assuming the company would grow profitably. But it would not give her any control over the company's business decisions.

McLandry's shares comprised 51 percent of New World Molecular's total equity. His majority ownership had not concerned Eckoff at the time of their partnership formation. Afterall, McLandry was providing the seed money and ongoing capital investment when the company had no meaningful revenue or income. But now Eckoff, having witnessed McLandry's recent apparent interest in Mogen's acquisition offer, was feeling relieved.

He had majority control of his nascent company.

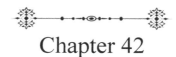

Chapter 42

"They want me to stay," said Brandon, talking with Destiny and now Larry Eckoff at an outdoor table outside Tank's Bar and Eatery just off the town square in Norwalk.

"What?" said Destiny trying not to sound excited.

"Yes. They want me to stay here a while longer. Apparently, the bank thing didn't work for them, fortunately, so I'm supposed to stick around and see what else I can find to leverage against you guys. I guess you'll have a front row seat to the dirty tricks the global healthcare colossus will try to use against you."

"This is too much. Why don't we just go to the cops or to the Des Moines office of the FBI?" asked Eckoff in his usual irritated voice.

"Because we have no evidence of any crime," said Brandon. "I keep trying to tell you, they leave no fingerprints on anything they do. ANYTHING. I've seen it firsthand. We're probably in the best possible position we could be in. I'll know what's coming down, and I can work a plan so that you can escape their traps, their threats, whatever they'll do next, without looking like you were tipped off. For now, that's the way we've got to play it."

"How do we know you're on the level with us?"

"Because, Dr. Eckoff, I've proven to you that I'm going to help you."

"Your help with the bank hack was appreciated. But maybe that was a decoy, to get you in our good graces. To get you closer to us."

"I hear you. I understand. Time will tell. Look, I'll walk away right now. Just pretend I'm stalking you, if you want. Never talking to you, never seeing you again. But right now, I'm your best protection. Your only protection, really."

Chapter 43

The "Lare Bare" handle that Dr. Lawrence Eckoff used on his various dating apps was a perfect way for Chet Hunter to investigate the professor and his personal peccadillos. He had no presence at all on conventional social media. None. But Lare Bare was a different story. It appeared the professor enjoyed engaging in chats with others on these sites, knowing he could remain as anonymous as he wanted to be. Hunter was especially interested in the fact that Des Moines hosted a Pride Week, and that Dr. Eckoff was asking around as to who would be going and where the parties would be.

Ronald Holtzman had passed along these sites to Hunter, by way of a source in Europe of which Hunter had no knowledge.

"I'm reluctant to get you involved in anything right now, knowing your recent history," Holtzman said to Hunter. But Hunter knew Holtzman would be back. It was a matter of time. Who else could Holtzman and H-BIS cultivate to do their heavy lifting? It would take years to identify, vet and orient a new operative to do the things Hunter did. But Hunter played along, feigning a bit of guilt and remorse.

"I know I went too far and I'm sorry. But you're still protected. And look where you are now. I think you'll win in the long run."

"You have to promise me, unconditionally, that you will not put us in the jeopardy you did last time. You will not go to those extreme measures."

"I promise," said Hunter. "But there is one thing."

"Good god, what?"

"My fee."

"What about it?"

"My billing amount for the Chicago project?"

"Yes."

"You will need to triple it."

…..

The funeral for Hal McLandry was held outdoors on the park grounds owned by Norwalk College, adjacent to where the esteemed community leader had fallen, joint still in hand, just two weeks earlier.

A trio of bagpipers played their Scottish dirges as McLandry's ornate, open wood casket lay across a brick parquet in front of a gently flowing fountain, surrounded by a semi-circle of tall arborvitae trees.

After an hour of eulogies, solo vocalists and more bagpipes, the large crowd gathered in the bright morning sunshine began dispersing.

Destiny and Eckoff stood alone as the crowd shuffled by. A solitary younger man, athletically built, neatly cropped hair, chiseled jaw and cheeks, in a black suit, made friendly eye contact with Eckoff from his position a few feet away. He gave a nod. Eckoff nodded back. He figured he should meet the young man, as maybe there was a shared history with Hal McLandry.

"Hi there. I'm Larry Eckoff. Did you know Hal?" They shook hands, with the young man giving Eckoff a warm, long shake.

"Well, I really didn't know him well, but I worked at one of his companies as a lab tech. Year ago. He was a great leader. He'd stop by and chat with our team when he was in our building. Great guy. Figured I should pay my respects."

"Yes, well we all loved him here. He did a lot of great things for this college…."

Then the young man reached into his pocket and took out his phone, as if a silent vibrate had gone off (it hadn't).

"Oh crap, something's blowing up at work. I'm sorry, but I've got to take this. Was so great meeting you."

"Sure, great meeting you," Eckoff said as the young man wandered off. Then Eckoff realized he hadn't really met him. But he sure could remember him.

Chet Hunter would repair to his hotel room, ready to create an online dating personality. He had always liked Paul Newman. "Hud" sounded like a cool name.

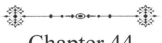

Chapter 44

"Think we can shame him into doing whatever it is you want him to?" Chet Hunter asked Ron Holtzman over the burner.

"Well, if possible, that's a lot better alternative than the last go round," answered Holtzman.

"What's the end game? What do you want this guy to do that will be satisfactory to you?"

"He agrees to sell his business, with the very generous terms he's already been given."

"And if he refuses? Or simply doesn't respond?"

"I can't answer that."

"I think you just did."

"Listen Chet, I am adamant! No physical stuff. Don't you even come close!"

"Calm down man. None of that's gonna happen. We'll be fine. You'll be fine. Now tell me who I can contact to get more info on what's happening with this operation. I don't need details, just the basics. Who on your side of the fence knows about what this professor's got going?"

Holtzman took his keys to unlock a bottom drawer on his desk, lifted a fake bottom shelf compartment and grabbed a simple legal pad that he leafed through to find the name Hans Mogen had passed along to him; someone named Liz Wiley.

.....

Chet Hunter felt kind of like an adult film star. He would need to assume an identity of a gay man, which may or may not be difficult for him. But since this was, as they say in the film world, "gay for pay," he looked at it as a challenge, one that could build his resume and skills capacity. Maybe even have fun with it. And, of course the pay would be stratospheric compared to the average gay film performer in the San Fernando Valley. And in Podunk Iowa, no less!

He had never been here before, but was pleasantly surprised. Yes, this was the land of giant tenderloins, pickup trucks, a revered state fair and high school wrestling mania.

But central Iowa also touted a great jazz club, lots of insurance and banking headquarters, and a choice of fairly good restaurants. And, an active Pride Week with many events and participants. And that is where he would connect with "Lare Bare" Eckoff.

"Hud" had spotted Eckoff at the Pride Parade that afternoon and followed him at a distance until he entered The Lucky Q to round out his night of partying. Luckily for Hud, he had met Eckoff days before at Harold McLandry's funeral. That helped greatly in quickly gaining his confidence after meeting him again and dancing together at the "The Q."

Hud had done some reconnaissance before flying to Iowa. On one of the many "social event sites" he had joined and perused, a party was scheduled for that night. Hud made all the online registration arrangements so that he and Lare Bare could gain admittance that night. This would be a perfect venue for using the highly advanced capabilities of his new smart watch. It had cost him a pretty penny, but he didn't worry about it for a second. He would add the cost to his invoice for H-BIS.

"I'm not sure about this," said Lare Bare to Hud as they were walking over to the party site, First Street Lofts.

"No worries. Everyone's anonymous. It's all to have a good time, then it's completely forgotten the next day."

"I know that, but there are a lot of people in the area that know me. Or know of me. Faculty, students, you know. What if I run into one of them?"

"Look at it this way. If someone recognizes you, you'll likely recognize them as well. They'll be just as shook. And they'll want to keep it on the down low, too. But I can pretty much tell you that won't happen. I really think you'll have nothing to worry about. People come from all over the state to these parties. Even out of state. Just enjoy yourself."

And the two approached the midnight window lights of First Street Lofts, with Hud's smart watch fully charged.

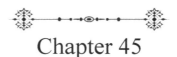

Chapter 45

The Norwalk mail carrier arrived at McLandry Hall around 10:30 on a sunny Wednesday morning. The yellow padded envelope, with a fictitious but important-sounding return address–Macro Bio-Analytics in Iowa City, Iowa–was addressed to Lawrence Eckoff, Ph.D. at Norwalk College.

The envelope was dropped off with the rest of the mail for the science faculty at the front reception desk, which was staffed on a quarter time basis by a senior biology student, Chelsea Stringer, who also served as a tutor and as a supply clerk for the offices and small labs in the building.

The mail would remain at the reception desk for several hours until Chelsea had the time to get to it and deliver it to the faculty offices. Sometimes the mail wouldn't get distributed until the next day. But everyone on the staff knew where to find it if they were expecting something that was time-sensitive.

The mailman proceeded to the center of campus, to the main administration building where he dropped off the day's mail. The full-time receptionist there took receipt of the mail, and had a clerical assistant promptly deliver it to individual offices, including the Office of the President of Norwalk College.

A similar padded yellow envelope was in the mail bundle delivered to Wendell Pershing, Norwalk's president for the past six years. It displayed a different return address–The Baxter Estate Trust of Johnston, Iowa–so as to appear to be a potential contributor to the college, which would no doubt get the attention of Pershing, who, like every college president, was on a non-stop mission to raise money and keep Norwalk operating in the black.

Pershing was in today, talking on his phone to an academic vice president candidate he was looking to hire. He leafed through his mail while talking with the candidate about salary requirements. The envelope from the Baxter Estate Trust did catch his eye, and he set it aside.

The conversation wrapped up and Pershing opened the envelope. Inside the bubble packed pouch was a thumb drive. A note accompanied the drive. In large type it simply said, "Your professor leads quite an exciting life outside of his work, as you'll see on this flash drive. His research must cease immediately, or this video will circulate widely in your community and beyond."

Pershing was alarmed and completely confused. He had never received a package like this, yet alone a threat about which he, so far, had no clue. He contemplated what it could possibly be, silently, for several minutes. Then he called his IT director, whose office was one floor above his.

"Hi John. Could you come to my office and bring an old laptop that no one uses. With no wi-fi interface. No Bluetooth. Nothing. I need to boot up something from an external drive. And I have no idea what's on it. Yes, you need to come now."

.....

The call came the next morning. "Dr. Eckoff? Wendell Pershing here. Have you seen the video yet?"

Eckoff stood up and looked around his office, not knowing why but feeling like he was supposed to look for something, like a VHS tape laying around his office or a video playing on a monitor somewhere, both scenarios completely ridiculous. But Eckoff was feeling a bit jumpy lately so nothing seemed too ridiculous to him.

"I'm not sure what you're talking about, Dr. Pershing."

"Did you get anything strange in the mail lately? Something in a padded yellow envelope?"

"What? What envelope?"

"Larry, you should come over to my office. As soon as you can. Can you be here in a half hour?"

"Umm, yeah. Sure. I'll be there. But Dr. Pershing, what is this about? What video?"

"Larry, just come on over and we'll discuss it. It's too...I don't know...bizarre...to talk about over the phone."

Eckoff hung up and began searching his small office frantically for any kind of envelope that might have been dropped off recently. With no success, he slowly ran down the hall to the front desk in the lobby. There, in the pile of mail still undelivered to the rest of the building, he saw the padded yellow envelope. He looked at the return address. It meant nothing to him.

He opened it on the spot and found the flash drive and a note, "You must cease your research immediately. Cease all post-research activity. Cease all business activity with the product you've created. We will know if you do or don't comply with this request. If you do not, this video will be distributed publicly and widely."

Eckoff raced back to his office and booted up his campus desktop. He inserted the thumb drive and waited for a file directly to come up. There was only one file, a video file named "Dr. Lawrence Eckoff 6-12-2022 Des Moines Iowa."

The three minutes of video had Eckoff shaking; images of him in a scrum of naked male bodies, faces obscured through video editing. Except for his. Anyone who knew him would recognize his face, even in a darkened room with minimal light. Whoever produced this video put some work into it. And it scared the holy hell out of Eckoff.

His mind was racing. Who did this? He had no doubt. Someone or some group connected to H–BIS and Hans Mogen. It had to be. How could he prove it? But even if he could, what difference would it make? Doing so would take forever.

Eckoff sat down to collect himself and keep from passing out. He grabbed a water from his small fridge and drank it slowly.

Who could possibly see the video if he did not succumb to the demands? His fellow faculty would probably be disappointed in him for a short while, but outraged at whomever was behind the recording. His students and runners, the community of young scholars and athletes he loved to teach and mentor. Having them see this would be devastating to them and to Eckoff. And Destiny. He couldn't imagine her reaction. It was too excruciating to comprehend. The church community in Norwalk, especially those affiliated with regional denominations that supported Norwalk College, would demand his head. Their instant reaction would be to scream that Eckoff and the college were "secretly grooming students to adopt the sinful homosexual lifestyle."

After a while, Eckoff got up and began his walk out of McLandry Hall toward the administration building. And what of the late Hal McLandry? Eckoff started speculating whether McLandry, if he were alive, would use this to demand that they sell to Mogen and Microneutics. Suddenly, everything that had seemed so promising and exciting within a community he knew and loved, suddenly seemed unfamiliar, ugly, threatening.

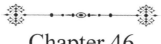

Chapter 46

"The video has been delivered to the professor and to the college president," said Chet Hunter from his Holiday Inn Express room outside of Norwalk.

"What are you talking about?" asked Ron Holtzman.

"The video. You know. One that will put the professor in a very, very bad light here in this bible belt."

"I don't know and I don't want to know. I am ending this call. Contact me when you've reached an end point."

. . . . .

"Dr. Eckoff, I have seen this video." Wendell Pershing was talking to Eckoff in his office, with his IT director, academic dean and outside legal counsel attending. "Should I assume you've seen it?"

"Yeah, I have," Eckoff said in a near whisper, head down looking at the floor.

"Can I ask you, honestly, is this a legitimate thing? Was this real? I could understand if it were one of those doctored deep-fakes."

"Yes, it was real. Not a fake. I am completely embarrassed, needless to say. And I apologize. I don't know what to say, other than this is an extortion attempt to stop my work. But I truly do not want this video to bring shame to alumni, donors, benefactors, local clergy, everyone associated with the college. I can't say how sorry I am that this happened."

"Larry, I can handle the locals. No one in my administration is going to condemn you–or anyone else employed by the college for that matter–for what you do in your private life," Pershing said. "But what is this research the scum who recorded this video referred to?"

"It's just a side project I've been working on for a while. Nothing all that significant, really."

"Well why would someone go to the extent they did to threaten you and this college?"

"I'm not sure why. Jealousy maybe? I don't know."

Max Wachtel, the college legal counsel, chimed in, "Well, I think there's more to it than jealousy. Tell me, did this 'side project' involve any people at Norwalk?"

"Just one. Destiny Diggs, who was paid part time to help out."

"And what about anyone outside of the college? Anyone else involved?" asked Wachtel.

"Yes, an investor."

"Who?"

"Hal McLandry."

The room of interrogators collectively gasped.

"Hal McLandry? Are you serious?" Wachtel continued.

"Yes. He liked the work I was doing and wanted to support me."

"I hate to ask, but anyone else other than McLandry? And, of course, Destiny? I need you to know, Dr. Eckoff, that you should be completely up front with us now, because we will look into this further, with or without your help. The more you help us, the quicker we can resolve this and hopefully avoid a lot of difficulty for this college and this community."

"I will then tell you that my work involved outside trial patients from around the country. They would come here and I would go to them, based on what was easiest for all involved."

"How many patients, would you estimate?"

"Approximately fourteen hundred over several years," Eckoff said softly.

"My God!" exclaimed Pershing. "You were testing something or some process on 1400 patients using Norwalk College facilities? And you made sure we knew nothing about this?"

"I needed to keep this completely confidential, because if anyone outside of myself, Destiny and the individual trial patients would get wind of this, my vision for the global impact…and I mean a significant impact…of my work would come crashing down. And it looks like efforts to make that crash happen have already started."

While the room went silent, Wendy Chu, dean of academic affairs, wandered over to the conference table credenza and grabbed a water. "I'm having a hard time believing what I'm hearing," she said. "Larry, what is this thing you've been working on with Hal McLandry and 1400 trial participants behind our backs?"

"It is a tincture, created through years of fungal hybridization and a radiation process, that has been shown to remediate malignant tumors. And I'm talking 95% positive outcomes. Generally within several weeks. With the likely projection that other cancerous forms besides malignant masses may also be eradicated. Leukemia, lymphoma, myeloma."

"A cure?" asked Chu, incredulously.

"I never use the word 'cure.' But if that's your preferred term, fine."

"Well, what materials were you using on campus? What equipment?" Pershing asked.

"I kept an inventory of the tincture in my office, along with some files and laptops. But they were my laptops, not the college's."

"And Destiny Diggs. Did she work on this project from inside your office?"

"Yes."

"And the trial patients," Pershing went on. "Did they see you in your office for this experimental treatment?"

"Many of them did, yes."

"Larry, any faculty scientific research carried on at this or any college must have the review and consent of the faculty's Oversight and Review Board. Human, plant, animal, cellular, chemistry, physics, anything that could potentially involve a hazard to humans or animals. You of all people know that."

"Yes, I do, Dr. Pershing."

"Then why the secrecy?" asked Chu? "I don't get it."

"I truly believe that if word got out about my research results, the project would turn into something extremely troubling that would destroy my ability to get this compound into the hands of people who desperately need it. I was–I am–committed to make this available to people in a way that is truly affordable and won't bankrupt common citizens of the world. If a pharmaceutical company gets a hold of this, they will turn it into a permanent economic windfall for them, and a hardship for everyone else. Tell me that a company such as Microneutics, which we're all familiar with, wouldn't want to possess my compound and own my research so they could charge–who knows–$1 million per dose? $5 million per dose?"

"I can't believe any reputable pharma company would try that kind of price gouging?" Chu said.

"Don't think so?" Eckoff retorted. "They just quietly offered me three billion, with a B, dollars during commencement weekend.

Without even having seen my research abstracts or knowing exactly how I make the stuff."

"Who did?" asked Wachtel, the attorney.

"Microneutics did. Hans Mogen was here in person with the offer letter. He and I got into a bit of a scuffle when I refused him on the spot. You may have heard about it."

"Hans Mogen came here to offer you three billion dollars in person?" Wachtel asked, astonished.

"Yes he did. And his weasley little investment guy was also trying to do the same thing for weeks before Hans finally flew here to try to make a deal himself. And I'm sure they won't be the last. That's why I need to see this to completion, gain the patent, protect my property, and set up this whole thing so that I can truly help people who need it. And control the price and distribution."

"Where do you make this stuff?"

"Hal McLandry funded the construction of a growing and processing facility in the country. I won't say where, but it's on some land he owns, very well disguised. But as you may know, we're building a new facility where we can soon ramp up production and start marketing and distributing this."

"Isn't this a pharmaceutical?" asked Chu. "A powerful one? How are you going to get FDA approval without years of clinical trials?"

"It isn't a pharmaceutical and it won't need the big, lengthy trials and approval. We're marketing this as an immune support supplement with no labeling mentioning any disease or medical health condition. But one in which its health benefits will be widely known and communicated as it spreads throughout the market. I've got 1400 successful outcomes already. I just give the word, and those people can ignore their NDA and start telling anyone and everyone about their quick recovery. I'm going to make this affordable and accessible, and not let the big pharma cancer bureaucrats and profiteers gain control of it."

"Ok," said Pershing, "we've got to talk about this in depth, and I don't know what we'll end up doing. But this is amazing and very troubling at the same time. We'll be in touch with you, Larry."

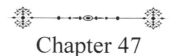

Chapter 47

"Do you always come out here at night?" asked Brandon.

"Always. Don't want anyone able to easily see us driving to the facility," said Destiny, riding in the passenger seat of Brandon's rental car.

"I don't think anyone could even see you in the daylight."

"Maybe not. But there are seed tractor/planters and harvester combines on these roads in the fall and spring. They go slow and farmers can see for miles in their elevated cockpits. We just don't want to risk it."

"Well I hope you're not feeling too bad about bringing me out here. I know you don't totally trust me, yet, but I think I'll prove you can."

"You're right. I'm not there yet on the trust thing. But at this point, I'm generally feeling we don't have much to lose. And if you're going to be our inside guy and watch out for us, you need to know what you're protecting. But I swear, if you turn out to be double crossing us, I will hunt you down and make you pay."

"I don't doubt it. But look, if I were still trying to work against you, I would have maintained my fake identity. You know who I really am. That has to count for something."

"Put it this way. I *think* I know who you really are."

Destiny had Brandon turn off of the second gravel road they had driven on to the third gravel road that went into the field and eventually to the old farm gate, locked with a heavy chain and digital padlock.

They drove to the entry point of the old elevator and got out of the car. Destiny activated and completed the two security keypads to open the main industrial doors to enter the growing room. The sea of red lights and circular growing pods gob smacked Brandon.

"What the holy fuck is this?"

Destiny proceeded to explain the scientific and mechanical details of the facility tucked under the old towering grain elevator.

"And in here is where we hyperactivate the spore load with gamma radiation. The next room over is where we combine the basic corn ethanol with the treated spores to make the final tincture. We have a pretty good supply of the tincture back at Dr. Eckoff's office that we'll need to move out here eventually. It's too risky keeping it on campus. Not secure enough with all the shit that's been going on."

Brandon continued looking around in amazement as they made their way toward the exit. The future of the world's most devastating chronic disease stood at a crossroads in this abandoned elevator in the middle of a corn field. He still couldn't grasp the enormity of it.

And neither could Chet Hunter, who was positioned outside the giant doors, hidden behind a nearby stand of young corn. He had followed his two targets, parked his car ahead of theirs about a quarter mile in a flat ditch. He had simply hopped the fence and followed Brandon and Destiny toward the elevator and watched them enter–and now exit–the glowing red cavern.

Hunter had no idea what he was seeing. He would get back to Ron Holtzman on that. But whatever it was, the next phase of his task would be more challenging than any he had faced.

.....

Eckoff arrived back at his office, completely dejected. Though the senior college administration had told him they could and would defend him if the lurid video were somehow publicly released, he wasn't comforted in the least. His name would be scorned in the local community, maybe throughout the state. Parents would be warned of sending their children to a college where "gay perversion and grooming" ran rampant. Church goers would hear fiery sermons blasting from the pulpit, using Eckoff as an example.

The thought of living with that was crushing. And if the faculty review board were to fire him for violating research oversight protocol, a distinct and even likely possibility in Eckoff's eyes, his work, no matter how life-changing for cancer victims worldwide, would be denounced and rebuffed by the scientific world.

In the event his work was somehow hijacked, which could happen in a dozen different ways, Eckoff knew he needed to protect his research and the long-term future of IH-3314.

Eckoff sat down at his computer and began typing.

After a day of deliberation, the letter from The Office of the President of Norwalk College, signed by Wendell Pershing with copies listed to Wendy Chu and Max Wachtel, was ready for personal delivery to Dr. Lawrence Eckoff.

The letter stated: *"Dear Dr. Eckoff: After much deliberation with faculty representing the Norwalk College administration and Oversight And Review Board, we have opted to allow you remain on the college faculty with the following conditions:*

•   *You will not be allowed to continue your research using any college resources. This includes lab equipment, office space, office equipment, lounge and public area spaces.*

•   *You must submit to the Office of the President with a copy to the Dean of Academic Affairs, a summary of your research, including abstract, methodology, outcomes, conclusions and any appropriate charts, appendices, footnotes and citations. This summary must be submitted prior to any public sales of products or services derived from your research and patient trials.*

•   *You will be on employee probation for a period of three years starting on the date of this letter. Probation, as outlined in our faculty and staff handbook, will involve quarterly reviews of any of your work outside of the classroom, as well as quarterly reviews of your classroom instruction. The reviews will be conducted by the Office of the Dean of Academic affairs.*

•   *Any new research you propose to perform must be approved by the college's Oversight And Review Board. Any violation of compliance with the Board protocols, no matter how minor, will result in immediate termination of your employment at Norwalk College.*

•   *Any violation of these conditions will result in immediate termination of your employment at Norwalk College.*

The terms stated in the letter were agreed upon and finalized after hours of heated discussion. Max Wachtel and several faculty and administrators aligned with him wanted immediate termination of Eckoff for putting the college at great risk. Wendy Chu thought Eckoff's research was fascinating, especially when one considered it was so revolutionary as to attract the personal attention–and enormous investment–of Hans Mogen. The director of institutional advancement argued that the college could rightly claim a percentage of any future earnings from Eckoff's work, which could put the college on a whole new financial footing. For decades or longer.

Wendell Pershing would have the final decision. He greatly valued both arguments, and opted to go with retaining Eckoff. The potential for revenue from IH-3314 could be addressed later. For now, he wanted Eckoff retained, knowing he would have to manage the fallout of the possible distribution of the video. But he was determined to do so.

The college cannot try to influence or monitor the private lives of its students and faculty. As disturbing as the video might be to many people, no laws were broken. At least none that the college knows of. We call on the community of Norwalk and the citizens of Iowa to support our decision to support Dr. Eckoff. He has been an invaluable contributor to the college through his scholarship, teaching and coaching.

These are the thought points that Pershing would use if confronted by any outside parties over the matter. Hopefully, such rationale would put any possible controversy to rest, and quickly, he thought.

He would have Wendy Chu deliver the letter personally and go over it with Eckoff.

…..

Chet Hunter, former star athlete in high school, baseball shortstop, basketball sharpshooter, track sprinter, would have fun this afternoon. He would visit the local sporting goods superstore and buy a baseball bat. Had to be wood, not metal. Maybe a 35 or 36, not too heavy but with enough mass to inflict some decent damage with a single swing.

While he was at it, two batting gloves seemed like a good idea, too, to secure a good grip on the bat and mask any fingerprints. And he threw in a couple energy drinks. Could be a late night or two in the offing.

Ron Holtzman might wonder what the hell these items were doing on his expense sheet, but that would be easy to explain. In fact, Hunter would just list them as office equipment. He would get no pushback from Holtzman. Simple.

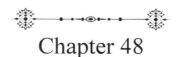

Chapter 48

D r. Luis Hernandez had never been visited by special agents from the FBI before. But there's always a first for everything.

Special agents Ford and Merrick had waited patiently in the lobby of Chicago's Emma Robertson Public Health Clinic, hoping Hernandez would be finishing up with patient exams soon so they could ask him some questions. They looked a bit out of place in their sleek pant suits and hard briefcase. But they were used to standing out in a room. A lot of FBI work was not sweeping in to capture bad guys. It was methodical online searching and key person scheduling and interviewing. And the blizzard of paperwork that would follow.

After 55 minutes, Hernandez was free for 30 minutes. The receptionist showed Ford and Merrick to his office.

"Dr. Hernandez, I'm special agent Ford here with special agent Merrick from the Chicago FBI office. We wanted to quickly show you a picture of someone to see if you might recognize him."

"Sure. I'll try."

Merrick pulled a laptop out of her briefcase, opened it and clicked open an image file with a photo of the face of a younger man, short cropped hair, fairly handsome. The photo was not labeled in any way, no text or artwork displayed. Merrick and Ford, however, both knew this was the official file photo of a former Secret Service agent who had served several years ago.

Hernandez looked at it carefully for 10 or 15 seconds, thinking that the photo might look familiar, but wasn't sure.

"Any idea whether you might have seen him before?" asked Ford.

Hernandez continued staring at the photo.

"Is there any way you guys could put some thick frame glasses on him? Maybe a goatee?"

"Yes we can," answered Ford.

Merrick accessed a clipart file where she could click on any of dozens of facial characteristic items–earrings, hair variations, make up elements–and took her cursor and moved a pair of thick frame glasses and a brown goatee to the face on the screen.

Hernandez instantly looked up with a serious look on his face. "I remember this guy. He was in here a few months ago. And he was strange. The whole discussion with him was strange."

"Can you tell us what you talked about?" asked Merrick.

"He wanted me to check him for a possible cancer tumor. Yet, he didn't have any symptoms, and he didn't want to permit me to take any blood or even do a simple X-ray. Then he left. Like really fast."

"Did he mention any other person when he talked to you? Anyone you may know or have known?"

"Jesus. Now this is hitting home for me. Yes, he did. Again, very strange. But I'm not at liberty to say who. HIPAA, you know."

"Dr. Hernandez, federal law enforcement can override HIPAA regulations if a suspected felony is involved. So please, save us all some time with court orders and all that if you would."

"Alright. He mentioned a former patient of mine, Marypat Hammond, who is now deceased. She died not long after she had communicated with me about some amazing remedy that had made a malignant tumor on her neck just disappear. It was the damndest thing I'd ever heard of. But Marypat would not tell me from where she got this miracle stuff or who provided it to her. She was scared of disclosing anything. And then she just stopped staying in touch."

"So what did this guy want from Marypat?"

"I don't know. I guess he wanted to find her to see if she could give him the information on this anti-tumor therapy. Like I said, he thought he might have a tumor as well, but never wanted to really get it checked out. Bizarre. Just bizarre."

The agents thanked Hernandez, packed their laptop and got up to leave.

"Wait you guys. I'm sorry, but I need to tell you I talked to her next of kin in California. She was listed on Marypat's patient file. She told me the college in Iowa that Marypat had been visiting for her treatment. I called the college and found who I think is the professor who might have been involved in her care. Marypat's aunt in California said there might have been foul play involved, but nothing definitive. Is that why you guys are here? Was she murdered?"

"We are looking into her death, Dr. Hernandez. That's all we can say. But can you remember the name of the professor and the college in Iowa?"

....

The late afternoon walk across the breezy, leafy campus was enjoyable for Wendy Chu. Especially knowing she would be delivering some good news to Dr. Lawrence Eckoff. The letter she was carrying would reassure Eckoff that the college would continue to employ him and he could have a future in academia. Some extra oversight would come with that support. But if Eckoff were committed to getting back in good standing with the college, those compliance requirements should be something he could live with, annoying as they may be.

Chu ran into Destiny in front of McLandry Hall, and gave her a cheerful hello. Destiny was on her way to Eckoff's office as well, which was no problem for Chu. She would just wait for a few minutes and then show up and ask Dr. Eckoff if she could have a few minutes. Chu was sure Destiny would graciously give them the privacy they would need.

They both entered the building, students and staff shuffling back and forth past the reception desk, vacated as usual. Chu took a seat in the lobby while Destiny ventured down to Eckoff's office.

The loud, desperate, sustained scream could be heard throughout the building. It was then repeated. And repeated again. For several seconds, Wendy Chu thought she was daydreaming, or maybe hearing the result of some student prank designed to surprise someone. But as the screams persisted, she got to her feet and ran toward the agonizing sound.

The screams were emanating from the west hallway toward the corner of the building. Several students and staff, with worried looks of urgency and confusion on their faces, also started gravitating toward the same area.

Chu closed in on Lawrence Eckoff's office. She slowed her pace and briskly walked through the office door. Chu instantly screamed herself, though it was more of a loud, sobbing wail.

The limp body of Lawrence Eckoff, Ph.D, was hanging by a plastic, yellow twine rope, suspended from a beam exposed from a removed ceiling tile. Destiny had wrapped her arms around his legs, desperately tugging, trying to pull him down. It was the only reaction she could muster in a time of such crisis and shock.

Chu quickly rifled through a desk drawer until she found some scissors. Others had gathered in the office by now. Wendy stood on a chair and cut the rope while the assembled crowd gently lifted Eckoff's body down and laid him on the rug. The rope marks, discolored face and obviously broken neck were signs that Eckoff was surely not alive. But one colleague started CPR immediately while another called for an ambulance.

Destiny was now sitting on a couch, crying hysterically. Chu, herself completely distraught, tried to comfort her. A white envelope, hand-addressed to the "Norwalk College Community," was sitting on an office desk chair. It was the last thing anyone was paying attention to right now.

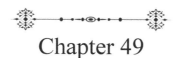

Chapter 49

"We have to get out there ASAP," a sobbing Destiny said to Brandon, the day after Eckoff's tragic suicide. "We have to get the remaining tincture inventory out of Dr. Eckoff's office storeroom and take it out to the elevator."

Brandon Abrams had heard the terrible news from Destiny, and had also been told about it by his landlord. News of this sort spread around town like wildfire. Brandon was shocked, however, he was starting to get accustomed to bad things happening to people he was involved with, all courtesy of his employer and its puppet master in Zurich. What was really disturbing to him now was the idea that H-BIS could have been connected to Eckoff's demise. Was it really a suicide? That Brandon could even ponder that question confirmed to him that he was right in quickly extricating himself from that organization, and soon. But for now, he had to play along. He knew that if he did not report Eckoff's death to Ron Holtzman soon, Shawni and Holtzman would wonder why they heard it from any other source. Afterall, he was their boots on the ground, a source closest to the target.

And his worries were validated: Someone known at Hud, who was tracking all news and social media regarding Dr. Lawrence Eckoff, made the first call to Ronald Holtzman.

.....

"Once again, I think you've achieved your goal, or at least most of your goal," said Chet Hunter, talking to Ron Holtzman from his hotel room.

"What are you talking about?" asked Holtzman, who was sincere since he only got news on such topics from his "operatives." Meaning Chet Hunter and Brandon.

"The good professor took his own life two days ago. I waited until I saw several local reports before I contacted you, just to make sure."

Holtzman was immediately worried, even though such an outcome was something Hans Mogen would welcome.

"Please don't tell me you had a hand in this. Please don't tell me he is inoperable in a way that you might be familiar with."

"You mean did I stage this? Are you fucking serious? This town is too fucking small and connected for me to take a leak without half the town knowing about it and knowing exactly if I did it standing up or sitting down."

"You can understand why I asked."

"All I understand is that the two principals involved in this research are now out of the picture. If I'm right, that's a good thing for you, isn't it?"

"I'll relay the unfortunate news."

"But I think one more step is needed, just for some added insurance."

The two talked for 20 more seconds. And after that, another burner phone was tossed into Ronald Holtzman's fireplace.

…..

A dozen boxes of the 2-ounce vials of tincture solution were loaded into Destiny and Brandon's cars. Destiny was determined to at least get the material to the country and in the secure confines to the elevator's underground facility. As always, the trips to the country would happen at night.

Destiny drove slowly, knowing that the death of Dr. Eckoff had her shook. Her mind was racing. Concentrating on the nighttime gravel roads was difficult.

What could have led to such a drastic, tragic act? And she was also punishing herself in her mind, daring to wonder, ever fleetingly, what her future would hold. How self-centered. How shallow, she thought.

She punished herself more, questioning whether somehow, in the slightest, she had something to do with his feeling that his life must end. They had accomplished so much together. Research that was on the cusp of changing lives worldwide. Business and financing plans that would practically guarantee a lifelong career making an enormous difference in the world, and would also make her financially secure beyond anything she could have imagined just months ago.

Little did she know that factors completely outside her day-to-day world combined to create the sense of total helplessness Eckoff felt.

And with Eckoff and Harold McLandry both gone, what would become of this venture they had so excitedly planned? There was no answer. Not for now. Her only goals were to get past her grief and to secure their work as best she could.

.....

Destiny and Brandon pulled up to the elevator in the dead of night, headlights still on while they began unloading the boxes of IH-3314. The door opened and stayed open while they would make several trips before everything was out of the car and in secure storage.

As Chet Hunter observed from his post some 20 yards away, obscured by June corn plants, he knew this could work well. He had followed Ms. Diggs out here once before. Someone who had talked to Ron Holtzman weeks ago, a woman named Wiley, had given Holtzman a basic rundown of the facility layout and what was growing inside. All at Hans Mogen's request.

Hunter had driven past the elevator earlier in the night and turned south on a gravel road a half mile west. He easily broke through a skimpy wire fence lining the field, heading back east. He accelerated through the mostly barren field lying fallow with short cover crops this summer to prepare for a change from corn to soybeans. Just 10 rows of corn remained toward the east edge of the field, a perfect cover to work from. His compact body could easily slip through the wide gaps in the electric fence just beyond the corn field. If he got a jolt or two, that would be easy to handle.

He waited for Brandon and Destiny to make their second trip inside, then ran, baseball bat and 5-gallon gas can in hand, and entered the red-light bathed production "cave." He was temporarily disoriented by the red wave of lights as he navigated toward a place on the edge of the cavernous room where he could remain hidden.

After 15 more minutes, Brandon and Destiny had their inventory transferred, securely tucked away in the quality assurance lab store room.

As they closed the facility's outer doors, Hunter began his rampage. First, he headed toward the QA lab, knowing an inventory of this mysterious product was kept there. The lab door was locked, of course. However, a few sharp swings of the bat to the lab window, executed by the former start shortstop, solved that. Hunter followed his simple instructions of getting a few samples of the tincture from the storeroom, as many as he could fit in the pockets of his black tactical pants, before he used his bat to smash the remaining batches vials, resulting in a floor covered in glass shards and clear liquid.

During his scouting of the exterior, Hunter had found what he needed: another door on the opposite side of the elevator. From all appearances, the door was not part of the original elevator built more than half a century ago. It was a recent addition, positioned 15 feet high with a metal stairway descending to the ground. That would be his escape exit, knowing the main entry doors were locked, but that the escape door had to remain unlocked from the inside in case an emergency situation arose in the facility. Which he planned on implementing.

Hunter found the emergency exit inside, a short, dimly lit stair climb from a hallway adjacent to the lab. With his exit plan now solidified, he proceeded to the red-light chamber and started pouring the gasoline throughout. His stash of sparklers, not flimsy matches, purchased with cash from one of several fireworks stores open year round in Iowa, would ensure a reliable flame to ignite the pools of gas. And the sparkler could be thrown from a distance, keeping Hunter from getting too close to the gas in order to ignite it. A mini flare. Except he had left his sparklers in his car. He had carried the bat, the gas, the lighter to light the sparklers, But had left the sparklers in the glove box, far away from the gas can in the trunk. No problem. He had plenty of time. Might even grab a quick smoke and enjoy the clean, rural, nighttime air.

.....

"We've got to go back and get that external drive from the lab," said Destiny, a half mile down the road from the elevator.

"What?" asked Brandon, sounding a little fatigued.

"That's the only real backup of the data we have. At least the only one I know about. The formulation ratios for the spore strains are on it, too. Production SOPs, patient records, everything. I just don't feel right leaving it there. Everything is on the laptop there, but that backup drive stays wired to the laptop at all times, backing up everything we input."

"What the hell? Have you ever heard of this thing called the cloud?" Brandon asked with a little snark.

"No cloud. Never. We've kept our work hack proof. We don't even use Bluetooth. I want to go back and get it, keep it where I can see it every day."

…..

Hunter searched around for something he could use to prop the escape door open so he could get back inside. After a couple minutes he found a firm, unopened cardboard box of new tincture vials. Perfect. He grabbed it out of the lab area and headed to the escape exit. He propped the door open. He headed down the stairs, walked around the vast, moonlit exterior of the elevator and headed toward his car parked in the field.

Just then, he heard the sound of the massive metal doors opening to the main entrance. Hunter froze, not knowing what to think. Then he saw a car parked in front.

Hunter ran back into the elevator, down the stairs and into the lab. He encountered something totally unplanned for in his detailed scheme; some young black girl and white guy inspecting the broken lab window, smelling the gasoline soaking the floor, looking and sounding shocked and confused. He ran through the hallway entry door to the lab, grabbed his bat still resting against a lab bench, and opened the main lab door to the growing chamber.

Destiny and Brandon saw him run right by them, too bewildered to react. Finally, Destiny yelled at him, "Who the fuck are you? Who are you? What the fuck is going on?"

Hunter ignored them and ran to the front-most pod nearest the entrance and grabbed his lighter.

He knelt to the ground, knowing he had to forget about the sparklers and just get the fucking thing lit. The first few clicks from the lighter gave off some small sparks. Small enough to make Hunter think he still needed a solid flame to emerge from the lighter, but enough to ignite the semi-dried stream of gasoline–and gas fumes–directly underneath him. The flame leapt violently from the ground, and instantly engulfed Hunter's right arm. He screamed, looking for a place not coated with gasoline where he could roll on the ground and vanquish the flame.

Destiny screamed again, "What are you doing?" She could do little but stand and stare, not understanding why she was seeing this take place in front of her eyes.

Brandon yelled at her as the flames started spreading. "Go get that drive. Now."

Brandon then approached Hunter, who was rolling on the ramp leading out to the entry. Brandon thought he could contain him, but Hunter reached up from his prone position and punched him in the face, stunning Brandon for several seconds as his nose began bleeding. Hunter ran to the entry, followed by Brandon, who was quickly met with a baseball bat smashing into his midsection. Brandon crumpled to the ground in the pea-gravel parking area, still yelling to Destiny, "Get the drive!"

Through the bashed-out lab window, Hunter saw her grab the small piece of storage hardware from a laptop. Destiny ran out of the lab, down the ramp and out of the elevator. Hunter instinctively knew that if she had come back for that item, it must be important. Certainly important to his client. He had heard multiple ribs crack when he had struck Brandon with the bat. He could not afford the risk of having another termination on his hands, so he punched Brandon hard in the side of his head, knocking him out.

Whoever this girl was, she would not escape with that drive. With a burned arm but a high threshold for pain and an otherwise fit physique, Hunter gave chase.

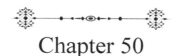

Chapter 50

The gravel road had not been refreshed with new gravel for years, so the road had relatively smooth tire paths to run on. Destiny, with the drive clutched in her left hand, was running down the road, knowing that a left turn on another road was coming in about three-quarters of a mile. Her breathing was steady and controlled. The biggest obstacle for her was to not let the adrenaline coursing through her body cause her to run at a faster pace than necessary, potentially bringing her to an earlier fatigue point.

She was grateful for the chilled, windless night air, filled with the oxygen her trained lungs needed to endure what would likely be a long run. She periodically looked over her shoulder to see Hunter pursuing her, nearly 200 yards behind her.

Chet Hunter was in pursuit, running at a similar pace. The wilderness boots he was wearing were laced tightly, maybe a little too tight. That could cause some high ankle pain if this turned into a marathon, yet would support his lower ankle as well. Either way, he was focused on getting that drive and its contents out of the hands of that girl running ahead of him. This should all be concluded in a couple minutes, he thought. Just hang in there and overtake her in the next half mile. His physical training during his Secret Service days gave him a solid familiarity with pain and endurance. A brisk nighttime run would be no obstacle.

.....

Destiny was in a steady stride now, putting a little distance between her and her pursuer. She was on the second gravel road. This one would eventually lead toward a paved county road, giving her an even better surface to run on. Destiny looked back to see Hunter still on her tail. More disturbing to her, she could see the elevator in the distance, flames leaping from the front entry area and smoke billowing from the top of the soaring structure. She knew in her mind the facility would be completely consumed. At some point the

219

sirens would start blaring as the fire trucks headed out of town, but only if a rare passerby, most likely in a pickup or ATV, saw the blaze and called it in.

Hunter was staying within striking distance but knew he was falling back. This girl was making this harder than he wanted.

The gravel road came to a T intersection with the paved county road. Destiny turned right onto the road, didn't pick up the pace but slightly smoothed out her stride on the solid surface.

Hunter was starting to struggle a bit. He was well into mile two and was breathing hard, at least harder than Destiny. The county road was far ahead of him, but he could see the girl had turned right on it.

.....

County road R-60 gave Destiny a ray of hope. It was a smooth paved surface and slightly hilly, which hopefully would give her an advantage over the guy chasing her, although she could still see him every time she looked back. Though she had not been able to shake him, another mile and she would reach Main Street which led to the middle of town. Maybe she might see someone she knows and could get to a safe spot. Her legs and breathing were holding up well for this long-distance course–a route needed to escape someone intent on destroying her in whatever way he could–but she was starting to feel a heaviness in her upper body and her stride was getting tight.

Hunter had been in this situation before, experiencing a high dose of pain that he had to work through in order to achieve an objective. He had chased people, been chased himself, pummeled in fight training, endured frigid and furnace-like temperatures for long periods of time. But he always fought through them to achieve the objective whatever it was. Now the objective was to get whatever this girl, who was obviously a distance runner, was carrying with her while working to evade him.

He comforted himself mentally by knowing that even if this girl was able to lose him tonight, he would find her eventually in this small town and capture his prize one way or another. Plus, in his dark attire in the dark of night, she likely did not see his face.

Destiny was on the paved county road now. One more look back and she might be confident that she had outrun him and could get back to her apartment safely. The look back was about a half second too long. A pothole, nearly impossible to see on the unlit road, grabbed Destiny's left foot and held onto it for a mere second, long enough for the downward pressure of her long, strong leg to force her ankle sideways and suffer a severe sprain.

Destiny instantly hit the ground, overtaken by a searing pain she had never experienced before. She writhed on the pavement hoping no car would be driving by anytime soon and run her over. But with the thought now out of her mind, she looked back again. She could not see the man who had been chasing her. She hoped against hope he had given up. She focused back on her ankle, which had some pretty significant swelling settling in. She rubbed it vigorously, hoping she could at least walk the rest of the way.

But after just a couple minutes, she could hear the distant rhythmic sound of boots slowly and steadily trotting on the pavement.

.....

Hunter saw the fallen Destiny Diggs sitting on the side of the road. She was obviously in some kind of distress, and that motivated him to pick up his plodding pace. His sides hurt, his breathing was tight, his legs were stiffening, but he felt a new wave of adrenaline, knowing he had made it this far and within reach of his prey.

Destiny saw her attacker coming into view. She forced herself on her feet, trying a fast walk, limping severely. After she got into a choppy rhythm, knowing she still had to push through the pain, she progressed to a slow, limping jog, each step feeling like burning a rod inserted into her ankle.

Main Street was a few yards ahead. Streetlights now appeared. But her pursuer was slowly gaining on her. She dragged herself, using mostly one leg onto Main Street. The town square was within sight. She walked for a few dozen yards to give her only good leg and ankle a brief reprieve. But she had to get back to a jog, at least. Now she could hear the man behind her yelling, nearly out of breath. "Just give me what you took from that laptop," Hunter was saying as loud as he could in a tortured, oxygen-deprived voice. Destiny could hear him, but ignored his plea.

.....

One great thing about Norwalk High School was that the athletes, musicians, theater students, gamers and science geeks could all hang out together. Many young people crossed over several such groups, creating a school that didn't have much cliquiness and segregation. Tonight in front of Franco's Pizza on the town square, as with most Saturday nights, a gathering of high school kids from all of these groups was hanging out on the sidewalk, laughing, having fun, doing a little play wrestling, trying some doo-wop singing, telling jokes, exchanging a little gossip, sneaking into an alley to take a quick toke.

Things really never got out of hand. Any patrons wanting to walk into Franco's for a meal would be met by the quick parting of the crowd as the high school brigade gladly opened a friendly path for customers to reach the front door. Friends would drive around the square, scooping the loop as they might say in years gone by, showing off their new wheels or their new girlfriends, yelling some friendly jabs back and forth. It was a scene of freedom, friends and youthful energy.

The young crowd in front of Franco's all turned at once as they heard screams coming from the woman practically hopping on one leg. Behind her was a man clad in tactical black gear, gaining on her and obviously in pursuit.

"He's trying to attack me!" She screamed as she turned the corner from Main Street onto the street and then sidewalk where the crowd was gathered 50 yards away from her. The kids recognized her as that college girl on the cross country team who ran the streets of Norwalk with her team every fall. "Help me! He's trying to hurt me!"

She ran toward the crowd, which was now moving toward her. She reached several girls, marching band members, who took her into their collective arms and helped sit her exhausted, injured body on the curb where she could catch some air.

Hunter kept moving toward her, undeterred by a bunch of high school kids. When it appeared that Hunter was locked in on physically confronting her, Football Star, the one who had harassed Destiny Diggs during her cross-country workout, stuck out his beefy arm and clotheslined Hunter, sharply hitting him in the throat with his straight arm and knocking him backwards onto the pavement. Three drumline boys and two female track sprinters descended upon Hunter and held him to the ground while someone called 911 to summon the police. Hunter tried to resist, but was physically depleted, unable to put up even a slight fight.

Destiny also pleaded with the kids to call in a rescue for an injured man most likely lying near a fire that had broken out at the McLandry Ag elevator south of county road R-60.

Meanwhile, fire truck sirens could be heard in the distance racing out of town toward an inferno in the middle of a cornfield.

.....

Norwalk Police placed Chet Hunter in a holding cell in the city jail. He was awaiting arraignment the following Wednesday for charges of assault with intent to do great bodily harm–the alleged victims being both Brandon Abrams and Destiny Diggs–when three U.S. Marshals arrived at his cell.

"Chet Hunter? You are Chet Mason Hunter of Alexandria, Virginia?"

"Yes," said Hunter.

"I'm U.S. Marshall Joe Hartman. I am here to place you under arrest for the murder of Marypat Hammond in Chicago, Illinois and transport you to Cook County Illinois where you will be formally charged."

Epilogue

Special Agents Ford and Merrick of the Chicago FBI office had taken DNA samples from minute particles of scraped skin found under the fingernails of Marypat Hammond. The crime scene in her apartment contained forensic elements that did not line up with someone dying from a brain aneurysm. Scuffed carpet, toppled end tables, and sounds of a struggle that were heard by some neighbors led Chicago PD detectives to execute a detailed investigation. Hunter's DNA matched the sample taken from him at the time he was hired and registered as a Secret Service officer assigned to the executive branch. A physical description provided by Dr. Luis Hernandez created additional suspicion, especially when matched with Hunter's plane ticket record of traveling from Reagan National Airport to O'Hare International Airport.

His whereabouts were unknown, however. When police documented his arrest, which was automatically entered on the National Crime Information Center database, the text alert received by Ford showed the person of interest was being held on an arrest warrant in Norwalk, Iowa.

.....

Hans Mogen was not immediately and directly implicated in the events that lead to the death of Marypat Hammond, the suicide of Dr. Lawrence Eckoff, the assault and battery of Brandon Abrams, and the destruction of the rural fungal spore production facility in Iowa. But he and Microneutics S.A. appeared in numerous new stories around the world in the following months, the subject of witness testimony and leaked investigation findings that linked the company with efforts to subdue and vanquish the work of the late Dr. Lawrence Eckoff in Norwalk, Iowa.

Regulatory pressure and intense protest and anger from shareholders and activist consumer groups forced Mogen to resign as chair and CEO of Microneutics, with no severance compensation paid to him. The Microneutics board also demanded the resignation of the company's entire senior leadership team to assure investors and the global healthcare industry that a house cleaning was taking place. Ursula Halgren considered starting an entirely new career outside of Europe, as her resume and LinkedIn profile, highlighting her position as a direct report to Hans Mogen, would eliminate her from consideration for any senior marketing position.

Ongoing legal and media investigations of his activities prior to the death of Eckoff and Marypat Hamond asserted that Mogen knew a murder had been committed and had implicitly approved the termination. This would eventually lead to charges of conspiracy to commit capital murder, punishable by life in prison after Mogen's extradition to Chicago, Illinois, USA.

Chet Hunter, facing first degree murder charges, agreed to testify against Ronald Holtzman as the supervisor and payor for Hunter's criminal deeds. Hunter had recorded the phone conversations he'd had with Holtzman, despite Holtzman's use of a burner phone, for insurance should any of H-BIS's nefarious plans be connected to Hunter.

Holtzman, himself facing significant prison time, had turned on Mogen, proving he was in Holtzman's suite in Boston the night that Marypat's murder was made known to them by Hunter.

Turner Mansfield had died in his home of natural causes. His H-BIS empire, now publicly vilified for its part in halting–and destroying–research that could have rid the world of its most vexing disease, filed a plan for dissolution with local authorities, facing the reality that member companies were quickly ending their involvement with the organization. Many member companies filed suit in D.C. court to claw back any dues they had paid during the period that H-BIS was helping Hans Mogen try to take down Professor Eckoff. The H-BIS headquarters building, sitting on its prime location in Washington, would be turned over to the American Cancer Society, which would sell it and direct the proceeds to its research budget.

The vials of the IH-3314 tincture found on Brandon Abrams were shipped to the FBI's massive laboratory in Quantico, Virginia. The lab analysis showed that the material in the vials, and in the entire inventory that Chet Hunter laid waste to with his baseball bat, was simple water. Nothing else.

…..

Destiny Diggs hobbled up to her apartment, Shay by her side, holding her hand on this rainy afternoon in Norwalk. Wearing a walking boot while her ankle healed, they headed inside and sat at the small kitchen table before Destiny would get some ice cream out of the freezer for both of them. Destiny sorted through the mail, separating bills from the junk as usual.

She came across a letter from an address she did not recognize; a law firm in Des Moines.

She opened it. The multipage document was titled "Lawrence D. Eckoff Trust." In the notarized document, several phrases were highlighted in yellow. One phrase read: "In the event of the death of Lawrence D. Eckoff, the shares of New World Molecular, LLC held by Lawrence D. Eckoff will transfer to the ownership of Harold C. McLandry of Norwalk, Iowa. In the event of Harold C. McLandry's death prior to that of Lawrence D. Eckoff, the Eckoff shares will transfer to the ownership of Destiny Ann Diggs of Norwalk, Iowa."

Since McLandry's shares had transferred to Eckoff, via the company's buy-sell agreement finalized shortly after incorporation, Destiny Diggs was the majority owner—save for the small amount of shares still owned by McLandry's widow—of the assets of the company, including the $500 million in cash holdings to be used in building the company's new facility and establishing the business as a long-term commercial entity. The transfer of shares and cash was dependent upon Destiny retaining a senior management team of at least, but not limited to, three experienced professionals: A chief financial officer, a chief operations officer and chief marketing officer. These personnel matters had to be concluded within the period of 12 months from receipt of the letter. Each senior officer hired by Destiny had to sign a legal affidavit acknowledging the founding mission of New World Molecular and any future subsidiary, joint venture or spin-off to "make their products available and affordable to all who seek their benefits." That affordability pledge was quantified as "pricing that can never exceed three percent of the national median household income in the country where the product is sold as defined each year by said country's primary governmental economic authority."

226

The letter was signed and witnessed by lawyers at a large law office in Des Moines. It was dated two days before Eckoff had ended his life, and postmarked the day after.

Destiny re-read the document several times as Shay ate her ice cream. "Mommy," Shay said, "when do I get my bedroom back?"

"Very soon, sweetheart," said Destiny. They walked to her small bedroom and opened the door, where 70 boxes each containing 400 vials of IH-3314 filled the pink and yellow-walled room, waiting to turn 28,000 cancer victims into cancer survivors. "Mommy is going to find another safe place to put these boxes."

She then dialed the number of a valued friend who was still in a hospital recovering from rib and head injuries suffered in rural Norwalk, Iowa. Brandon Abrams, washing down his latest dose of pain meds with a glass of water before starting his daily physical therapy regimen, answered his phone.

"Hi, Brandon."

"Destiny?"

"It's me, yep. Are you ready to help me build this company?"

About the Author

CRAIG S. MALTBY is a former corporate "suit" living in the Chicago area. He is a classic rock die-hard and plays a passable keyboard and bass. Craig is also a semi-lousy golfer and the only person over 50 in the U.S. who does not play pickleball. Yet. To pass time, he also worked as a COVID blood sample driver for a large pathology lab.

SUPPRESSION is his first novel.

Printed in the USA
CPSIA information can be obtained
at www.ICGtesting.com
LVHW051055040823
754028LV00002B/306